ADDIE SUMNER

BY
BRETT PERKINS

A
STOUT CITY
NOVEL

First Edition: November 2013

ISBN: 978-0615907635

Printed in the United States of America

Stout City
Stoutcity.com

To my mother,
Diane Martin Caldwell,
a whimsical adventurer,
a relentless giver
and a friend to everyone.

1

For two weeks, Addie Sumner had conducted her job hunt with optimism. Arising early, she would study the classified ads, circling the most realistic job openings and consulting her worn map of Stout City for directions. Each morning she walked out the door expecting to be hired.

But Stout City had other ideas, and today it was being especially mean. Seventh Avenue had been reduced to one lane after a bicyclist was hit by a florist's truck. Construction on the mammoth Imperial Building meant concrete trucks were double parking, then blocking traffic as they backed into place. The honking by motorists around Addie did nothing to hurry the lazy trucks. When she finally arrived at her first destination, Gompers Produce Distributors, she was frazzled and running late. She parked in the first empty area she came to and hustled inside the office.

The lobby was already crowded with job seekers. It had been this way since the stock market crash of 1929, which had sent America's economy into a tailspin. Jobs were scarce for even the most qualified men, and for a young woman not long removed from college, the prospects were even dimmer.

All the lobby seats were taken so she found a spot in the corner, standing next to a potted tree. When she'd first moved back to Stout City and began her job search, Addie would carefully evaluate the other seekers while they waited for interviews, hoping to find something in their appearance that signaled a clear advantage for her. But after a while, Addie had quit studying them as competition. She began to pity them, knowing they were hustling every day, just like her, only to lose another bit of their hope.

For forty minutes she watched intently as one applicant after another was summoned into a particular office and then spit out two minutes later minus their application form and minus their hopeful smile. When Addie's name was finally called, she marched into the office with all the erectness of gait that could be mustered. Everyone had a first impression trick. Some smiled extra big, others offered confident small talk. Addie strode into an interview like she was already employed.

As soon as she entered the office, though, she realized gimmicks were useless. For all of its life-altering importance, the inner sanctum to which Addie had finally been admitted was nothing more than a space separated from the warehouse by cheap plywood. The February cold was barely restrained by the "walls," and the intensely fresh smells of produce were not restrained at all. Addie, not a fan of onions, found that this particular scent seemed to reach out from the rest and surround her.

Seemingly oblivious to the cold and the smell was the bald man in charge of this operation. He sat in shirtsleeves, vigorously smoking while frowning at Addie's application as she sat across from him waiting politely.

"Ever work at a produce firm before?" he asked.

"No, sir."

"Mmmm hmmm," he mumbled, expecting that answer before even asking for it.

"Ever work in a warehouse of any kind?" he continued. "It can be tough work for a young girl like yourself."

"I don't mind hard work, but..."

"But what?"

"I understood this to be more of an office job. Not that it matters..."

"We'll call you tomorrow if we're interested, otherwise your application will be kept on file for sixty days and we will contact you if an opening occurs," he repeated for the twentieth time that morning. "Thanks for comin' in."

Addie was almost glad at being dismissed. The cold and the onion smell were miserable. She marched back out of the interview shack, avoiding eye contact with the mass of applicants who silently awaited their turn. Only when she arrived outside at her car did she dare glance back. Several of the job seekers stared back at her through the lobby's plate glass window, their faces blank with boredom. Her retreat provided the barest entertainment for those who still had a chance.

But the entertainment got better. The right front tire on her car was flat. Dead flat, and it was freezing cold. Apparently misery knew no limits today. With a heavy sigh of surrender, she began digging through the trunk of her Nash, where one by one she extracted the items needed for a tire change. Just before dropping to her knees to remove the offending tire, she peeked at the lobby one more time. A few more spectators had crowded around the window. *I hope you enjoy the smell of onions*, she taunted them in her mind.

As she worked on the dead tire she started thinking about her financial situation. Her savings were sufficient for a couple more weeks, maybe more if she didn't keep having unexpected expenses like new four dollar tires. Pretty soon she'd have to consider skipping a meal each day.

As she started to mount the spare, the ground beneath Addie's knees began to rumble. She heard the sound of an engine growing ever louder and nearer. She turned around in time to see a large truck come to a halt just feet away. Its huge grill loomed over her and she could feel the heat from its engine. A moment later, the idling truck's door swung open and two legs encased in leather work boots landed on the ground. A burly driver walked toward her. Though she was fully capable of changing a tire, it was gratifying to have a man respect her enough to offer his help, she thought.

"Hey lady, how long you gonna block this entrance?" the driver growled instead.

"I'm working as fast as I can," she responded, but the truck's engine was too loud for the driver to hear, and he didn't really care what the answer was anyhow. Addie glanced back at the lobby. Some of the spectators were smiling now, enjoying her predicament.

Addie tried to work faster but that only seemed to increase her clumsiness. She felt the truck driver glaring at her impatiently while his truck idled grumpily. Addie felt flushed with embarrassment, but she kept working, refusing to acknowledge the cold or his rude presence.

"You should tighten them nuts crisscross instead of in order," he finally offered, now standing directly behind her.

"This is how I was taught," she answered stubbornly without looking back.

"Either way, it ain't every day I get to watch a pretty gal in action."

"How about this for action?" Addie threatened as she stood up and gave the tire iron a little wave in his direction.

"Howdy now, you're a little tiger."

"Just wait in your truck, OK? The sooner you leave me alone the sooner I'll be out of your way."

The driver shrugged and returned to his cab. Resisting the urge to look back at her audience in the Gompers lobby, Addie finally finished the job, her hands black with grime. She threw the tools back into her car's trunk before calmly climbing behind the wheel. She tried to maintain a faint smile, as though this had been an amusing turn of events, but it was a thin attempt at dignity.

Only when she was a mile away did she pull over at a café and go inside to wash her hands. As she stood at the tiny sink, the urge to cry surfaced but she refused to surrender. It would come later, but it would be her choice, not the truck driver's, not the gawkers' and not the little men who refused her employment. With flared nostrils and a burning throat she battled, cursing the bit of moistness that made it to her eyes, but finally she quelled the storm.

Stepping outside of the café, emotionally tired, she thought the February chill felt so much colder. Her will to battle had passed and now she needed a diversion, an excuse to play hooky while her psyche regained its footing.

Being on this side of town, she decided to visit Newsome Street's art galleries. She had not been there since her teenage years. The majesty of art would lift her spirits, and being indoors might even restore feeling to her frozen toes.

Located in an older section of east Stout City, Newsome Street was the center of the city's art scene. Surrounding the galleries, which catered to wealthy buyers, were cheap eateries and cheaper housing which kept the artists alive long enough to create for the wealthy buyers. It was supply and demand commingling in a state of uneasy alliance, each side secretly envious of the other.

Since the economic crash, however, "class" balance on Newsome Street had tilted strongly toward the poor side. Even the street's middle-class art gallery owners were feeling the pinch. They stood pensively near their storefront windows these days, awaiting the next expensive car to pull to the curb. The sight of a recognized buyer emerging from a town car almost guaranteed that multiple gallery owners would happen to step out for fresh air at the same moment.

There were only a handful of owners who need not simper to the art-buying royalty. Their taste was so respected that regular patrons always made sure to drop in before looking anywhere else. One such gallery owner was Marry Yo, a woman of Chinese descent with a penchant for wearing purple. She had been a fixture on the street for more than three decades and was considered the unofficial historian of Newsome Street. Along the way she had discovered, hosted or sold many of Stout City's greatest works of art. Not surprisingly, buyers always stopped in to see what she had...when there were buyers. On cold mornings in 1932, even the pigeons stayed in bed.

Marry Yo's gallery was devoid of customers when Addie Sumner wandered inside, the sound of her heels echoing as she stepped along the plank floor. Taking her time, Addie moved from painting to painting, fascinated by what she saw. She'd already visited several other galleries and found their selections pleasant, but this gallery took the cake. Each painting seemed more intriguing than the last as she worked her way toward the back wall.

Marry Yo stood in the doorway of her office and watched, proud of the reactions playing out on the pretty face of her guest. She was also sizing up the young woman, trying to determine if she was a potential customer or just a looker. The visitor's naïve joy was one clue, indicating she wasn't an experienced buyer. The regulars acted like they were barely interested so that they could make discounted offers on pieces they secretly craved. Also, while the young woman was dressed nicely, her clothes were much too modest for a moneyed girl. Still, Marry had to admit, one never knew for sure. Penelope Kastin, daughter of the city's wealthiest automaker, often visited the gallery looking plainer than a spoonful of mashed potatoes.

"You like that one?" Marry asked after finally deciding to approach.

"Oh, yes. I can't believe how good this is."

"It's called *Storm on the Terrace*."

Enraptured, Addie only nodded and smiled. Had the thing been titled *Disembowelment*, her lovestruck expression would not have wavered.

"The artist's name is Rafael DeMontre," continued Marry. "He is cherished in Portugal, noted for his use of inclement weather. Study his works close enough and you can pick up that he is left-handed."

"How old is he?" Addie asked.

"DeMontre? I'm not sure, actually, but I'd guess early forties. Why?"

"I don't know," Addie admitted with a shrug. "Just curious where he is coming from."

Still unsure if her young guest was a potential buyer or just looking to warm her toes, Marry decided to push further.

"I'm Marry, by the way. This is my gallery."

"I'm Addie, and your gallery is breathtaking. I have never seen such a lovely collection of paintings. I mean, I've been to museums and they were really something, but I can't honestly say any of them were better than this."

"You are too kind, child," said Marry with an embarrassed laugh. "Which one is your favorite?"

Without hesitating, Addie pointed over Marry's shoulder to a painting just inside Marry's cluttered little office. The decisiveness made Marry's eyes widen with surprise. Even odder, Marry hadn't recalled seeing Addie look in that direction since entering.

"When did you notice that one?" Marry asked.

"When we first spoke. I saw it behind you. It was so gorgeous that I was saving my next look until I got up close."

"It's a print," Marry admitted. "The original is in a private collection."

"Who's the artist?"

"Armstrong Perzie. He actually lived in Stout City and achieved some fame around the turn of the century. We were sort of a team. I hadn't owned this gallery very long when I accidentally discovered him. A friendship developed and I became the exclusive seller for his works. It really established me, gave my reputation gravitas. No one was doing that sort of work at the time and his pieces were highly sought after. Still are."

"The colors are so...impossible," said Addie with reverence. "The way they work together is mesmerizing. What do they call that?"

"The name of the work or the name of the style?"

"Both."

"Well, he never cared to name his works so it's commonly known as *Number 11*. Altogether there are sixteen of his works known to exist. As for the style, it's jokingly referred to as abstract realism."

"I realize I'm an amateur, but it seems unusually beautiful," Addie gushed. "Why only sixteen paintings? Did he die?"

"That's the common belief, but the answer isn't that simple. Around 1904, at the height of his fame, he just stopped. I couldn't get hold of him. I don't know if he was painting and just not releasing or whether he simply quit. He was living pretty fast at the time; lots of champagne, lots of women. He seemed to be enjoying life to the fullest but then he just sort of disappeared. There was a rumor that he'd fled to Europe to avoid a jealous lover or some such thing. We never heard anything more and after many, many years figured he had died or joined a monastery because if he were still painting there is no way that such a unique talent could go unnoticed."

"Wow," breathed Addie. "That makes me so sad. Can you imagine if he walked in here today with *Number 17* under his arm?"

"I'd have it sold in less than hour, even in this dreadful economy. No exaggeration. I have three different clients who, every time they visit, remind me they are still craving his work. It's been three decades and the demand for his work has only grown. The commission alone would be enough for me to retire on."

"Can I look closer?" Addie asked.

By way of answer, Marry walked to her office, and Addie followed. They stood side by side and quietly stared at *Number 11*.

"How old was he when he painted this?" Addie finally asked.

"You and your age curiosity," Marry said with a laugh. "Let's see, he must have been about, um, thirty-eight years old when he did this one."

"And you were really close to him, huh?"

"I'm not sure anyone was close to him. Armstrong kept people at a distance. We had a friendship, and he shared things with me, but never the *real* stuff, know what I mean? I never even visited him at his place because he would never give out his address. He was afraid people would visit and trap him into being social. Still, as far as I know, he trusted me more than anyone he knew. I was his only connection to the traditional art world. Here, look at this."

From the bottom drawer of her desk, Marry extracted a leather-bound ledger. She opened it to the middle, squinted, and then flipped some pages. Finally she found what she sought and moved next to Addie so they could both admire the chosen page together.

"This is my first ledger. It's where I officially recorded our transactions," Marry explained. "Here is the date, and here is where the painting's title would normally go, but in his case it was just a sequential number. This column is the amount that each painting sold for and this column was my commission. Not bad, huh? And remember that a dollar was worth twice as much then."

"This is unbelievable. Thank you so much for sharing it with me."

"I'm glad to find someone so interested. He was an important person in my career, a creative visionary, and I'm just happy to see someone younger develop an appreciation for him. I don't have much opportunity to talk about him anymore."

"What's does this mean?" Addie asked while pointing to a name on the page. Marry smiled in remembrance.

"That was the name I paid him under the last two times. Armstrong was always a little different, like all artists, but near the end, when his fame was at its zenith, he got rather reckless. One of the things he did was to marry a dancer he had known for about two days. Her real name was Lily Gottlieb but she went by the stage name of Lily Gotem, and boy did she have 'em."

Marry illustrated this point by cupping her hands a foot in front of her own chest.

"I'm telling you," she continued, "the first time I saw her I thought she was smuggling a couple of large tortoises under her blouse."

The two women laughed self-consciously.

"I'm not saying she wasn't pretty, but Armstrong was apparently a lover of 'turtles,' because he made an impulse buy on that one. And predictably, the marriage lost its steam within a month. Lily was silly and lacked depth which was just the opposite of Armstrong. Apparently, two noteworthy lumps of fat aren't enough to carry a marriage. I guess we should be happy we'll never have to endure such confusion."

Addie wanted to protest. She was no Lily in the figure department but she had enough assets to remain in the game. Let Marry speak for herself.

"They both knew they'd made a mistake," continued Marry, "and they both knew a divorce was imminent, so Armstrong set up a separate bank account under the name Porter Armstrong, Porter being his middle name. That's why that's written there."

"So did they get divorced?"

"Eventually. Lily moved into the Townsend Hotel on 17th and Broadway. It's gone now but it was a beautiful place in its time, quite swanky. They began a war of words through telegrams, accusing each other of any number of infractions. He would stop by here and tell me all about it, completely amused by this disaster he had created in the name of turtles. Naturally, I thought the whole episode was ridiculous. Had I known this was the beginning of the end for our profitable friendship I'd have been more alarmed, but instead I laughed along with him. I guess it took about three months before attorneys were finally introduced to their battle, and that was that."

"You think the turmoil caused him to stop painting?" Addie asked.

"I've always wondered," admitted Marry. "After the divorce he continued to party and chase floozies, but the paintings stopped arriving. I'd ask him about it when he stopped in and he'd always tell me he was working on something, but I never saw another. Then he didn't visit at all. After that nobody saw him anymore. I sent a couple letters hoping he'd left a forwarding address but the first went unanswered and the second was returned, so I gave up."

"And what happened to Lily?"

"The last I heard she was married to one of those men who makes a mint shuffling money in a skyscraper. Mother Nature waved her wand over Lily and she's barely worked a day in her life, yet enjoys the best of everything."

"Amazing how a woman's looks carry so much importance, in directions good and bad," Addie mused aloud. "But I always wonder, is it because women are generally prettier or because men put so much emphasis on it, or because women put so much emphasis on men? Maybe it's all of that."

"And if the Lilys of the world take advantage of their advantage, how are we to ever change the game? Or maybe it's not the game I want to change, it's my looks I want to change and I don't want to admit it because I have no control."

The two women looked at each other solemnly, lost in their own attempts to solve a riddle that had forever bedeviled womankind.

"Can we at least agree on one thing?" Marry inquired.

"What's that?"

"We hate Lily."

They laughed the laugh of sisters.

2

Addie reached over and turned off her alarm clock. It was 7:03 in the morning and the room was cold. She pulled the covers up around her neck while debating whether to get up. The answer was never really in doubt but it was fun to pretend. So she closed her eyes and entered that glorious place between awake and asleep, where one has some control over their soft, warm dreams.

Then she remembered she was unemployed. It caused a jolt of fear to run down her spine. She began thinking about her bank account and rent and food and how she would die trying to live in her car during February. Fully awakened, Addie sat up, swung her legs over the side of the bed and slid her feet into slippers. She pulled on her heavy outdoor coat, unconcerned with the odd look as long as she was alone and getting warm faster.

In the kitchen, she sank two pieces of bread into her toaster before trudging to the front door and retrieving the morning paper. She returned just as the toast popped up. While it cooled she unfolded the newspaper and read the headlines. Then she opened a jar of peanut butter and spread its contents on the perfectly warm toast. It was the exact routine she had followed each morning for weeks.

Yet today something felt different as she sat down with breakfast and turned to the classified ads. Addie still needed a job but an idea had been germinating in her mind since her visit to Marry Yo's art gallery. What if Armstrong Perzie were still alive, and what if she could get a painting from him or convince him to create a new one? Based on what Marry said, there would be enough money involved for everyone to profit nicely. It was just a matter of whether Addie was willing to risk time and money on a scheme with no guarantee of success.

She frowned to herself at the use of the term "scheme." It sounded dirty and nefarious. She preferred "plan" or "activity." Still, was this plan really worthy of replacing a stable job or at least the hunt for one? Not by normal standards it wasn't. In other words, it was the kind of plan that her mother would dismiss with horror. But Addie wasn't her mother. And it was cold outside and job interviews were the worst. So, even though her eyes continued scanning the classified ads, her mind was wondering how one would go about finding a painter who didn't want to be found. *If he's even alive*, she conceded to herself. *But what if he is alive and what if he has dozens of paintings he is willing to part with for a song?* It could equal years of wages without bosses and morning commutes.

The more she thought about it the more the whole thing appealed to her. It seemed like a Nancy Drew type of adventure. The idea was so exciting, Addie declared to the walls that there would be no job hunt today. She needed to think, not to mention needing a break from employers' rejection.

With that dreaded task cleared from her mind, Addie got down to the serious business of considering her new option. She walked over to her favorite chair in the living room—briefly noting the small tear in the cushion that she kept meaning to sew—and sat down for some purposeful thought.

Its not like I'm making any commitment, she immediately assured herself. *If the hunt for Perzie didn't pay I'd just rejoin the rat race. Still, I will be using up valuable job search time, and my savings will only last so long, and there are gonna be expenses in searching for the painter, on top of that. Which brings up a good question: What would it take to find Perzie and where would I even start? What if he really is in Europe? Trying to find him on another continent would be overwhelming. Maybe this whole thing is too much. Maybe I've created some ridiculous dream adventure in order to escape the drudgery of finding a real job. And yet, the idea isn't completely unrealistic, and it could end up paying quite well. I wish I could talk to my mom about it but I already know what she would say. And then she would start hinting that I needed to move back home and tell me some story about a girl she read about who became a prostitute to pay her bills. All the joy of my idea would be forever crushed. Maybe I should call Lyla instead and see what she thinks, although I'm sure she'd say I was crazy, too. She'd tell me to get married like her, but not everyone can easily find a Ted like she did. Not that I would want to be married to Ted. Isn't it weird that he was wearing a bow tie the last two times I've seen him? I should ask Lyla what that's about but she'd probably get her feelings hurt thinking that I was making fun of her wonderful Ted who does no wrong. And she'd probably just be jealous if I started this adventure with Perzie. As long as I've known her she has always been a little competitive. But I guess I am too, if the truth be told. And it really would kill her if I traveled and met a famous painter and made a load of money. I mean, seriously, this would be a pretty fantastic thing, never to be forgotten. And it's not like I'm making any commitment.*

Addie's flow of thought was interrupted when she took notice of her little fern plant next to the kitchen window. It wasn't exactly dead but it wasn't exactly healthy looking either. She was never sure whether it wanted more sun or less sun, more water or less water. *Is it unhappy now because of the sunlight or is it still pouting from being over-watered last week?* There were so many elements involved in the plant's happiness, and she could never isolate the one element that was withholding vitality.

Her thoughts turned back to money, the thing which always hung over her head. It seemed to affect all decisions, and Addie struggled to find balance. It would make sense to have a roommate, for example, thereby splitting expenses, but Addie valued her quiet retreat where everything was based on her own wants. A roomie would be easy to find with the economy so rotten, but she knew how her luck ran. Within a week of sharing the rent, her new roommate would find a boyfriend—some creep, probably—and they would be necking on the couch every time Addie came home. Or eating her peanut butter. Or changing the radio station. Was it better to risk eviction from a lonely oasis or guarantee paid rent thanks to a cellmate?

It was the same type of quandary that made her Perzie idea so difficult. If all practical considerations were peeled away, she would pursue this scheme in an instant. But was she capable of ignoring practical considerations? Oddly, as she now thought about it, dismissing financial fear was not as difficult as ignoring her mother's voice in her head, the voice which always spoke of guilt and doubt.

Well, for starters, she just wouldn't discuss it with her mother...yet. And as far as money went, well, she would just pretend everything was going to be fine. Sometimes a girl just had to listen to her heart, and right now her heart was begging to embark on this adventure.

It was settled. Addie would give this crazy dream one week and if she had made no progress she would surrender. If, however, things were maybe, sorta, possibly beginning to work out, then she would cross that bridge when she got there.

The first thing to do was make a list. No, scratch that. The first thing to do was make some hot chocolate with extra marshmallows and celebrate a week with no job hunting. Then a warm nap. Then a list.

3

Addie made a list of the methods by which she might find Armstrong Perzie. The ideas included searching through archived newspapers at the library, contacting Atlantic passenger ship lines to determine whether he had traveled to Europe, contacting someone in London who might have some inside knowledge of the European art scene, and visiting Marry Yo for the names of Perzie's old painting buddies, then looking them up and pumping them for clues. All of the methods were grossly time consuming and offered small odds toward success, but every Nancy Drew has to start somewhere, she reasoned.

But then again, she couldn't afford to chase leads on unfounded rumors. It would be a complete waste of time, for example, if she combed Europe for answers when in reality he had never left America. It made more sense to start with legitimate information and work from there. Armstrong Perzie lived in Stout City in 1904. That was the last known fact and thus the jumping-off point for her search.

And it was while pondering this new direction that a brilliant idea occurred to Addie. The one thing that almost every citizen of Stout City needed was electricity, and to get electricity one needed an account. If she were to visit Stout City Gas & Electric and have them check their old records she could get his last address. They might even have a forwarding address for his last bill, but even if they didn't, Addie figured she could visit his last residence and perhaps get information from the landlord as to where Perzie had gone. It was still a long shot—

twenty-eight years makes for a cold trail—but at least it was based on fact.

***

The next afternoon, Addie arrived at SCG&E's main office and took her place in line. Nearly everyone in front of her was there to pay their bill or to vehemently dispute it, which made for some nice eavesdropping. She was so intent on her nosiness that when Addie finally reached the front of the line she realized she hadn't rehearsed her conversation. When the clerk asked how he could help, Addie had to pause before making her request.

"Um...I was wondering if I could get an address, please," she finally requested.

"I'm sure we can help you out," the clerk offered. "Do you need directions?"

He was a middle-aged man with slicked-back hair, wearing a suit that was slightly frayed at the cuffs and the buttonholes.

"No, no, it's an address for a friend—a friend of my uncle's if you want to be technical. They haven't seen each other for years and I was hoping to help them out—to reunite them."

"Truthfully, ma'am, we're not really supposed to give out information of that sort," he said with genuine sorrow on his face. "It's a matter of protectin' folks and it's just the rules, you understand. Company policy."

"Oh, I understand," Addie agreed, "but this friend of my uncle's—he moved a long time ago, like around 1904. So really, this is just a start in finding him. I wouldn't actually be tailing him or robbing him or whatever your company's concerns are."

The clerk eyes widened a bit and he gave a quick sidelong glance to make sure his nearest coworker wasn't listening. Then he leaned forward a few inches and lowered his voice.

"I really want to help you and it sounds like a good cause, but honestly, ma'am, if it ever got back that I had helped you and something was to happen to your uncle's friend, you can see how that would look."

"Nothing would happen, *if* I found him, and besides he lives in some other city now," she assured him in an equally lowered voice. "I just really need an address so I can help these elderly men rekindle a friendship. I could pay you a little money if that helped."

This time he looked to both sides and behind him before continuing.

"I could really get fired for accepting a bribe," he confided.

"I have no desire to get you fired," Addie cooed sweetly. "I only want you to get richer while I get my information. I'm sure your wife wouldn't be disappointed if you were able to buy a new, little something for her. Actually I'm sure she'd be quite grateful."

"How much are we talking?"

"Three bucks just for looking up an address. I saw a black enamel compact at Wedlord's Department Store the other day for $2.50. They'll engrave three initials at no charge. She'd adore it and you'd still have fifty cents for a couple nice cigars."

"Write the friend's name down on this paper," he continued while glancing around. "I'll meet you around the corner on my lunch hour—let's say about 12:10. Meet me in the butcher shop. I'll have the address ready and you have your part ready."

"Thank you so much," she said sweetly. "I will meet you in the butcher shop at twelve..."

"Next!" he called to the line behind Addie.

***

At 12:05 Addie was waiting in the butcher shop. She had arrived early just to be safe but had not considered the awkwardness of killing time in such a small shop. As the only customer, she was asked several times if she needed help and she had been forced to make excuses. First she was thinking, and then she was working on her shopping list. Finally, she actually had the butcher hold up a couple selections from the case before declaring that she needed to think some more. He shrugged and went back to slicing prosciutto.

When the electric company clerk finally arrived, he stopped at the door and waved her outside. They began walking up the street.

"Sorry, I needed to explain something," he said while looking straight ahead. "We can just walk for a minute."

"All right."

"So, I looked in the archives for a while," he began. "Tried different spellings, reversing the names, looking for initials, all the usual tricks, but found nothin'. It was a lot of work, let me tell ya."

"Sorry about that."

"Well, listen. I took a risk looking this up for you. I know you didn't get the answer you were hoping for but I still fulfilled my end of the deal, so..."

"Just a moment, let me think," she interrupted.

The clerk waited nervously, his eyes darting around like the feds were closing in on him.

"You checked every year from 1910 down to 1904?" Addie asked.

"I checked down to 1899 and up to 1912, just to be sure. Nothing."

Addie stared into the distance while the clerk fidgeted. An automobile two blocks over honked and he twitched.

"All right, here's your three dollars," Addie said while pulling them out of her suede handbag with the cute skirted design. "But I need you to check one last thing."

"You're joking, right?"

"One more peek in a file won't kill you. It's not like I'm going to mention this to your supervisor, right?"

His eyes narrowed in angry understanding of her threatening insinuation. He jammed the bills in his pants pocket.

"Just one more quick search, this time for the name Porter Armstrong," she instructed sweetly. "I'll wait in line after your lunch break and you can give me the answer when I get to the front. We'll act like I'm confirming that my account is paid up, OK?"

"Fine, but this has to be the last search. Three dollars isn't worth me losing my job."

Less than an hour later, Addie stood at the clerk's counter, questioning him with her eyes. For an answer, he slipped a paper across the counter to her with an address written in pencil.

"There was still no such name in the archives," he said softly. "On a final whim I checked the current file and found this name immediately."

"You mean he lives right here in Stout City? Right now?"

"Conceivably. Or the person who moved in afterwards left your friend's name on the account associated with the address. Or maybe he moved later than you thought. I have no way of confirming any of this, but now you have an address. Happy now?"

"Yes, thank you. And don't forget, black enamel compact at Wedlord's, the second floor. You'll thank me when you see me next."

"Please tell me there won't be a next," he begged in a whisper. "I'm not good at this cloak and dagger stuff."

Addie grinned and walked away. She felt like a wayward Nancy Drew, all grown up and not afraid to be a little naughty.

When she stepped outside she studied the scrap of paper again: 731 West Seventeenth Avenue. That was on the opposite side of the city from the Newsome Street area, the area where he'd lived when Marry knew him. Living amongst a different crowd might allow him to go undetected, Addie figured, especially using a fake name. Still, twenty-eight years was a long time not to run into a single former acquaintance.

Maybe this was just the first of many red herrings on her grand adventure.

She looked at her watch. It was 1:24 in the afternoon—as good a time as any to go find a stranger's door and knock on it.

4

Addie drove slowly along the narrow street, craning her neck as she looked for numbers on the buildings. She had lived in Stout City for most of her twenty-four years but had spent very little time in this worn section near downtown. It contained a mix of shops and apartments, none of them looking any too profitable.

And none of them seemed clearly marked for address, either. Addie squinted at a four-story row house as she rolled past it. There was a sign pointing to a pool hall in the basement. At street level was a dubious looking business "college," and beside it were steps leading upstairs. Painted on the face of each step was the name of a small business to be found at the top: an accountant, a medium, an answering service. The building seemed to have a little bit of everything except a number.

"Look out, sister," cried a bike messenger as Addie nearly ran him over. She jammed her foot on the brake pedal and gave the rider a sheepish smile, trying to convey an apology. The bicyclist only glared as he rode away. *No need to be so mean about it*, she thought.

Rather than kill someone, Addie decided to pull up to the curb where she could stop and get her bearings. She found a space, turned off the engine and rolled down her window. A cavalcade of noises came rushing in. Kids' laughter as they played games on the sidewalk. The honking of cars. An unseen trolley screeching somewhere nearby.

It was obviously a part of town where people survived. Everything looked neglected. Signs in the windows were faded and the style of lettering suggested something from twenty years ago. There were hard bits of gum on the sidewalk, shiny and black from years of heels. Even the sewn patches on the children's clothes were haphazard looking, reflecting tired effort, the hallmark of the poor.

Finally, after careful scanning, Addie discovered a street number in the window of Wilburn's Business College, just below its faded canopy. Even better, it wasn't far off from the number she was looking for. She decided to get out of the car and finish the search on foot.

A block and a half later, Addie entered the hallway of a particularly haggard looking apartment building. She climbed the stairs until she reached the fourth floor. A single lighting fixture barely provided light for the entire hall, forcing Addie to study each door up close until she reached the one she sought. Apartment 424.

She started to knock but paused. Once again she had forgotten to rehearse what she would say. What if this apartment was in Perzie's name but belonged to another person? Worse yet, what if somehow Perzie actually lived here?! Saying hello was one thing, but how would she bridge the gap from greeting him to owning a painting or two? What if he was angry at being discovered? Or blind? Or dead, sitting in his chair mummified?

Maybe this was the reason Addie never rehearsed her conversations. It only prompted her mind to imagine the worst. Pretty soon she would have herself believing a scenario so bad that she would run away without confirmation. It was a terrible habit, and one for which she chastised herself. She needed to be fearless like Nancy Drew. So what if he was angry? All he could do was yell a little bit. No harm done. It wasn't like he would pull out a gun and shoot her. Or would he?

This is absurd, she seethed. *I'm not tracking down Jack the Ripper. It's just an old painter. Or possibly some Hungarian immigrant who speaks poor English and has no idea why his electric account says Porter Armstrong. All right already, just knock on the door.*

And after a deep breath and some fussing with her hair, she did.

5

Addie knocked on the door and waited. She thought she heard a voice but couldn't be sure so she knocked again. This time the voice was unmistakable.

"Open the door!"

Not exactly the pleasant tone Addie was hoping for. She turned the doorknob and poked her head inside. It was dim, thanks to the blinds being drawn. The air was unbelievably stale and smelled like tobacco. And sitting in the middle of the room was a disheveled old man with an unruly beard. He was slumped deep into a leather club chair, his chin resting on his chest. All around him, at his feet and covering every inch of furniture, were empty liquor bottles. Addie entered slowly and stopped, surveying the prodigious collection of bottles while waiting for the old man to speak again, but he sat silently.

Addie moved closer, trying not to knock over any of the bottles. She finally got near enough to see that the old man's eyes weren't even open.

"Excuse me," Addie said softly. "I'm looking for Mr. Perzie."

"Armstrong Perzie?" the old man asked without opening his eyes.

"Um, yes, sir."

"Whaddya want to talk to that old jackass for?" he asked with a slight slur.

"Are you he?"

The old man raised his head and leaned it on the chair so he could get a better look at his visitor. His eyelids rose halfway, which was as far as they would go.

There was a long pause while he waited for Addie to come into focus, but he was too drunk.

"Does this involve a debt?" he finally asked.

"Not at all," she assured him with a delicate laugh. "Now, are you or aren't you Armstrong Perzie?"

"Mostly I'm thirsty. One of these is the one I need," the old man said with a tired wave of his hand, indicating the entire collection of bottles surrounding his chair.

Addie picked up the dark green bottle nearest her feet, shook it, heard some liquid move around and handed it over. The old man tipped it back and took a big swig but immediately spit it out, spraying bourbon all over the carpet.

"How 'bout a bottle that hadn't got cigarette stubs in it?" he asked with indignation.

Addie scrunched her face in disgust. She bent over, picked another one off the floor and held it up to her eyes, studying the contents. There appeared to be multiple stubs in that one, as well. The next few she examined weren't any better. The old man watched with an unsteady gaze, seemingly as curious about the outcome as his visitor.

"Hmmm, perhaps you have a fresh bottle somewhere else in the apartment?" Addie finally asked.

"Have you checked the kishen?" he asked with all the passion he could muster.

"The kitchen?"

"Yup. The kishen."

"Well, I guess I could look," Addie offered politely, "but don't you think maybe you should take a break? It's barely afternoon."

"I'm runnin' behind then," slurred the old man before laughing until he'd tired himself. Then it was time for a smoke.

Addie watched as her potential Perzie reached over to the end table next to him without looking. He fumbled for a tobacco pouch and some rolling papers, grasped them and pulled them onto his lap. Then, unsteadily, he dropped two pinches of tobacco toward the folded paper, with half the tobacco missing the mark and scattering in his lap. He rolled a clumsy cigarette, licked it closed, and after fishing for matches in the corner of his chair, struck a flame and lit his haphazard smoke. It took three attempts to blow out the match, but he finally succeeded and dropped the blackened stick into the nearest "empty" bottle.

Though slightly appalled, Addie's first instinct was to place an ashtray near him. A quick glance around the living room revealed no ashtrays, however. No doubt the ashes also went into the bottles. She shuddered remembering the big swig he had just taken a moment ago.

"I'll be right back," she said while walking away. "I'm going to check the kitchen."

The old man neither answered nor told her she was heading down the wrong hallway.

Addie ascertained her misstep the hard way, discovering an unkempt bedroom at the end of the hall, and next to it a bathroom straight out of her nightmares. Quickly retreating, she passed back through the living room and toward the opposite hall as the old man silently watched her journey, smoke curling up past his slitted eyes.

Addie found the kitchen and turned on the light, expecting to see unspeakable sights, but the kitchen was surprisingly clean. Upon further inspection, Addie found out why: the place barely contained anything. She looked through all the cupboards but tallied only some matchbooks, an eight-year-old phone book, two empty mousetraps (the mice likely having starved to death before they could be caught) and a big, fat, red candle. No booze and no food. *He has to eat something, and where does all his trash go?* she wondered. *Nobody can exist on liquor and cigarettes, can they?*

"Nothing new to drink," Addie reported upon reentering the living room.

"Did you check the kishen?" the old man slurred.

"That's where I just came from. I didn't find any food either."

"In the kishen?"

"Yes, in the kitchen," Addie repeated slowly. "You have nothing in this place."

"What day is today?"

"Um, Tuesday the eleventh."

The old man closed his eyes and Addie waited for additional comment that never came.

"Excuse me, sir."

The old man opened his eyes and stared at Addie. Then the slightest grin of recognition creased his face. It was the girl from fifteen seconds earlier.

"Tell you what," Addie began, "I'll run downstairs and get you some food if you'll just tell me your name."

"Armstrong Porter Perzie," he said, pleased with this turn of events. "Porter was my mother's maiden name. You married?"

"Nice to meet you, Mr. Perzie," she answered, ignoring his question. "My name is Addie Sumner."

"Andy?"

"No, Addie."

"Annie?"

"No. It's Addie. A-D-D-I-E.

"Is that German?"

"I'm not really sure. It's short for Addalyn."

"Evelyn?"

At this point Addie wasn't sure if the old man was hard of hearing or just drunk as a skunk. Either way, it was probably best to get off the merry-go-round.

"So, I'm going to get some food. I'll be back in a few minutes, OK?"

"OK. I'll wait here."

Addie was almost at the door when Perzie called out to her.

"Evelyn."

She took a deep breath for patience and turned around. Perzie waved her over. This necessitated another navigation of the bottles before she reached his chair.

"Go to the Greek joint 'round the corner," he instructed with a slur. "Ugly clown that runs the place will sell you a bottle."

He then offered a smile meant to reassure, but its sloppiness only confirmed how drunk he was.

When Addie returned fifteen minutes later she didn't bother knocking, figuring Perzie had settled back into his stupor. She was correct. Perzie's head was on his shoulder and he was quietly snoring in the corner of his chair.

For the first time since meeting Perzie, Addie took a moment to truly assess the old painter's condition. Upon closer examination, she noted that the front of his shirt was covered with pinhole-sized burn marks, the result of neglected cigarette ash. His nose was reddish and puffy from all the drinking, and there were bags under his eyes from a lack of good, sound sleep. The most obvious indictment was the sea of emptyish bottles. It was clear that Perzie had traded painting for alcoholism and he was no longer near the top of his game. As a matter of fact it was questionable whether he was in the game at all.

A lack of art in the place seemed to confirm this. Addie surveyed the room, but the walls were bare. Heck, there was barely any furniture. Had she missed any paintings in his bedroom? With a reluctant sense of duty she ventured back down the hall. She stopped at the doorway and looked inside, unwilling to enter his bedroom on principle, if not for health reasons. The bed was unmade as expected, and clothes hung from every object. Apparently, Perzie eschewed closets and drawers in favor of dropping his clothes on the surface closest to any given spot where he had undressed. She wondered when any of the clothes had last enjoyed soap. If this were the room of a prospective boyfriend, she'd have walked straight out the front door, but Addie was here on business and she took the time to scan for art. There was none here, either.

She stopped by the bathroom just long enough to glance at its walls, careful that her gaze never traveled low enough to inspect sink, tub and especially toilet. Other than some mildew and a couple cobwebs, these walls were just as bare as the rest of the apartment. If Armstrong Perzie was indeed capable of painting there was nothing in his home to prove it.

Addie returned to the living room and watched Perzie as he slept. She sighed. Was her plan dead before it ever really began? Granted, there was the possibility that Perzie could still paint if he wanted to, but based on the evidence, it was doubtful he could perform at his former level of brilliance.

After some pondering, Addie decided she would give this quest one more strong effort. She would return tomorrow morning, late enough for him to be awake but early enough for him to be...less drunk.

Addie carefully removed five "empty" bottles from the end table next to Perzie and set them on the floor. In the newly cleared space she placed the bag containing his Greek food and a bottle of ouzo. He could always enjoy a midnight snack if he awoke, she figured. After hesitating, however, she decided against leaving the ouzo and instead moved it to the kitchen where she hid it in a corner cabinet. It was important that Perzie was somewhat sober tomorrow, plus the new bottle could always be used as a bribe.

She walked quietly to the front door before stopping and whirling around, half expecting Perzie to have been faking sleep, but he was still snoring softly. *Could* Number 11 *really have been painted by this man?* she wondered before exiting and carefully shutting the door behind her.

She turned and took a few steps to the top of the staircase where she promptly dropped her purse. Addie winced as the purse tumbled down the stairs, leaving small possessions on each step. It finally came to a halt on the first landing, next to a door which opened almost immediately. An older woman with curlers in her hair surveyed the injured purse. Then her gaze followed the debris trail up the stairs to the offender. Addie gave her a sheepish smile of apology to which the woman in curlers frowned and shook her head as she retreated and shut her door.

You don't have to be so mean about it, thought Addie, as she bent down and began the retrieval process.

The next morning Addie tried to make sense of her initial visit with Armstrong Perzie. The whole thing seemed preposterous in the light of day. It was a far cry from her daydream of a charming man in a beret and a paint-stained smock, with a sparkle in his eye and stacks of paintings awaiting someone to appreciate them. The real Perzie was an inert drunk who didn't look capable of painting a wall.

There was just so much to overcome. She'd have to sober him up, nourish him, buy him art supplies and convince him to begin painting anew. And then she'd have to cross her fingers in hope that he was capable of painting anything of quality. And all of this would depend on his willingness to play along.

Fortunately, Addie was an optimist by nature. She believed all people had useful traits and a sense of goodness somewhere in their consciousness. Even pickpockets called Mom on Mother's Day. So, while Perzie seemed hopeless at first glance, Addie couldn't help but believe he was redeemable. Plus, she was just a bit stubborn. OK, more than just a bit. Even though her mother and friends had not heard of the Perzie plan, let alone discouraged it, Addie was already feeding off of the negative comments she just *knew* they would offer. She was determined to prove them wrong before they had a chance to be wrong. Yes sir, she would return to Perzie's place today and give it another shot.

After her breakfast of peanut butter toast and ice water, Addie began the soul-perplexing job of getting dressed. Choosing the day's outfit was difficult enough without having to decide what one wears to visit an old sot in his pigpen. In brassiere ("cotton mesh, cool and dainty") and slip ("Rayon in tea rose shade"), Addie stood before the long, oval mirror on her closet door. She didn't hate what looked back at her, but she didn't love it either. The shape had slowly changed over the last few years and she felt powerless over it. A little more breast was nice, but it seemed to work in tandem with a little more hip, which wasn't. And the kicker was that current fashion seemed to reward shapeless little things. Yet, in her experience it wasn't a lack of shape that made men look twice. All of which led her to wonder, once again, who was the arbiter of the right look. Was it the men, who as a gender valued a woman for her physical appeal above all other attributes? Or was it other women who saw beauty and shape as the primary factor in determining pecking order? And if it was women guiding this obsession, were their standards of attractiveness in concert with men or would there still be a pecking order on an island of women who didn't know men existed?

She frowned at her left brassiere strap, removed the little safety pin that cinched it to proper length, readjusted, and added the pin back. It had fit so well a couple years ago, but maybe it was time for a new one. She'd seen one at Wedlord's Department Store that had an elastic insert in the front which "lifted and rounded." That sounded like a good thing, but was that an instinctive opinion or a learned opinion, or was it even the right opinion? Then she laughed at herself. *Look at me debating about the part nobody will even see today. Or anytime soon*, she sighed.

Addie reached into her closet with closed eyes, determined to wear whatever her hands happened upon first. It was the green percale dress with white dots. She scrunched her face. *OK, any dress but that one,* she declared, abusing the rules of her own game. She reached in for another outfit and came out with the light blue dress made of flat silk crepe. She frowned again.

35

Normally I would, she promised herself, *but this one looks too nice for where I'm going.* With a gentle toss, it joined the green number, rejected on the bed. Had they been capable, the two dresses would have rolled their eyes at each other, veterans of this discarding process. Soon they were joined by two charcoal gray skirts, the older one too tight and the newer one too short. Not that it mattered since she still hadn't ironed any of the cotton blouses that went with them. She had to be in the right mood for ironing and that mood came around about once a season.

Finally, her hands emerged from the closet with a patterned sleeveless top paired with an ankle-length, knitted cotton skirt in coral pink. Satisfied with this choice, Addie returned the rejected clothing to the closet, selected shoes and a purse, dressed, brushed her hair one more time, and departed for downtown.

Two minutes later, however, she returned, having left her sunglasses on the dresser. And since she was back home anyway, how about a quick trip to the bathroom? The thought of using Perzie's facilities made her feel like she should go whether she really needed to or not.

She finished and stopped in front of the mirror one more time. Her dark brown hair was cut into a bob, with a part on the right sweeping over the tops of her ears into light curls at the middle of her neck. All of it seemed to be behaving today, which was unusual. Addie smiled with approval. She even admitted that her dark brown eyes were pretty and that a lot of women would like to have her lips. Tomorrow, that exact same face would trouble her for reasons unknown, but today she enjoyed a truce between reality and self-perception.

She departed once more, humming a happy tune.

Two minutes later she returned for the sunglasses left near the sink.

7

Upon returning to Perzie's apartment, Addie was pleased to find that one of the window blinds had been opened, allowing some sun into the living room. On the other hand, this allowed a clearer view of the room's shabby condition. The carpet was a tapestry of stains, burn marks and worn spots. The wallpaper, once white, was now yellowed and beginning to peel in a couple of places. Even the abundant dust seemed sadder than regular house dust. And there, sitting in his leather throne, surrounded by his kingdom of glass bottles, was Perzie, the king of booze. Only today he was sitting up straight, alert and smiling, as though yesterday had never happened.

Addie was relieved that her painter was capable of sobriety—even if he was wearing two different colored socks—but she figured there was a time limit on this condition. Already nestled in the chair next to his hip was a half-empty bottle of ouzo—the same bottle she had purchased and hidden the night before.

"How did you find that bottle?" Addie asked with fascination.

"There was a receipt in the bag with the food. The big Greek always writes one out thanks to a couple of disputes we had on account of my drunkenness and his cheapness, though I still don't trust what he writes. Anyhow, after I saw the receipt I just used my God-given ability to sniff out fresh nectar," he explained before giving Addie a wink and a soft chuckle. "You did a good job hiding it, too," he continued, "but why'd you buy it if you didn't want me to have it?"

"Mostly, I was hoping to catch you sober," she admitted.

"Well, it worked, 'cause I'm mostly sober, but workin' hard to fix that."

He laughed again. It was clear he was in the early stages of drinking where all of life is charming and full of whimsy.

"Actually, I'm surprised you remember me," Addie said.

"Yeah, I am, too," he admitted. "I recall the damnedest things when I'm really sauced. I don't remember our conversation, though. You wouldn't be a prostitute returning for some money I owe, would you?"

"What?! No, I am not," seethed Addie, her face flushing.

Perzie threw his head back against the chair and roared with laughter. He tried to stop laughing long enough for a drink but had to abandon the bottle at his lips to laugh some more. Finally, after sighing with satisfaction, he was able to knock off a giant gulp. A single rivulet escaped and seeped into the depths of his overgrown beard, never to be heard from again.

"I'm just playing with you, um...what's your name?"

"Addie."

"Pleasure to meet you, Addie. I'm Armstrong."

"Yes, well, we did converse a little last night," Addie added with a touch of sternness, trying to regain the upper hand. "You told me you were the painter," she lied, "and that I should come back and you'd tell me the whole story."

"I said that?"

"Mmmm hmmm."

"What exactly did you want to know?" Perzie asked.

"Well, for starters, what happened to you after 1904? After you painted *Number 16*."

"And what is your relation to art?" Perzie queried, suddenly suspicious of her knowledge.

"Um, no relation, really. We studied you a bit when I was in college," she lied some more. "Your paintings are stunning, and since we're both from Stout City it made me curious. So, I just sort of looked you up."

Perzie nodded thoughtfully before taking another swig of ouzo. He ran a sleeve across his lips before proceeding.

"Well, you're the first who's bothered to find me, although I haven't made it easy. I don't know which facts you're aware of but I'll give you the short version, in answer to your question."

He paused to reflect on the past thirty years. There was another hit from the bottle.

"Let's see, here," he finally began. "You obviously know about my day in the sun as a painter. I was never great with the form, actually. In that sense, I'm really not a great artist at all. My attempts at realism missed the mark, so I morphed my errors into something abstract, more as cover for my shortcomings than any desire to do abstract work. What set me apart at the time, and which I'm sure you discussed in your college class, was my use of color."

"Breathtaking," interjected Addie with reverence.

"Thank you. That's where I put most of my effort. I spent hours and hours experimenting with color. I introduced things into paint trying to create effects. Coffee, dust, egg yolk, you name it. Even tried crushed dragonfly wings, once."

"Ewwww." Addie frowned.

"Don't worry, the dragonfly was dead already. Anyhow, like I was saying, I was really more one-trick scientist than painter, but I will agree with you, the results could be breathtaking. And the thing is, I really enjoyed myself. Each little breakthrough was a thrill and when I could string together the right combination of breakthroughs onto poor form masquerading as purposeful abstract, magic really did happen. I could feel it in the very corners of my being."

Perzie paused, staring into the past, reliving that feeling of deep satisfaction. His right hand automatically raised the bottle to his lips. He drank without losing his thought. Addie was pleased to see him enjoying a happy memory but was dying to hear more. She waited a respectful amount of time before prompting him.

"So why did you stop? Painting, that is," she asked.

"Well, I guess I felt like a fraud. My pieces were selling for large sums of money, and I was enjoying my bit of fame, but it didn't feel right. Maybe I was listening too much to the art community. They're a bunch of jealous piranhas. If an artist enjoys any kind of success they will be sure to tear that artist apart. And to some extent maybe I deserved it. Like I said, my contribution was more science than art..."

"But who cares, if the finished product is gorgeous? Art is simply a unique expression," interjected Addie.

"Yes, you're correct. What I was doing was art, and I'm still proud of it, but at the time it felt like cheating, as though I was taking a shortcut. I felt like I had skipped a fundamental part. If I wanted to be taken seriously—if I wanted to take myself seriously—I needed more classical skill. So, still flush with money, I decided to take a break and head out west for a while. Didn't really have a plan, just thought I'd soak up the atmosphere, find a teacher and learn to be a real painter. There were some amazing naturalists working out in California and I wanted some of that skill."

"California?" interjected Addie. "So, you didn't go to Europe to escape a jealous lover?"

"I'm sure there were a couple husbands that wanted my hide," he admitted with a laugh. "I was a scoundrel, of sorts, at the time. Money will do that to you. Plus, as an artist, it was my duty to push the bounds of morality."

Perzie waited for Addie to protest but she had already written him off as a reprobate. His whimsical excuse for bad behavior had no effect on her. Not wanting to waste a good pause, however, Perzie tipped the bottle again. Addie noted that the remaining contents were dwindling.

"Anyhow, I got to California and bounced around while getting a feel for the place and, well, I guess I got distracted. The place had a different feel, less urgency. No one was in a hurry and soon, neither was I. It didn't help that there was no immediate taskmaster. A gallery owner who'd made good money off me here in Stout City telegrammed at first, but then I stopped leaving forwarding addresses. I just wandered in spurts, staying in hotels for a week here, and then a week or two there. I kept meaning to focus on my mission of becoming a true painter but deep down I'm really just lazy, if you want the truth. After a while, I just quit thinking about it. I had some money and no real duty to anyone, and that's a bad combination for a man like me."

He stopped for a drink, nearly finishing the bottle.

"So, that's my story," he declared abruptly. "I accidentally retired in California."

"That's it?" Addie wondered aloud. "You didn't do anything out there?"

Perzie tipped the bottle toward the ceiling, finishing it off with a flourish. He wiped his mouth and leaned forward, looking for an empty space on the carpet where he could place it. Finally he gave up and forced it between some other bottles. Remarkably none of them tipped over.

"Well, not that it matters much," he continued after leaning back, "but I did get married in California."

"Really?"

"Yep. She was actually from the East Coast, but we met in Cambria, which is a couple hundred miles north of Los Angeles. Her name was Julia. She was nine years younger than me. Below her eyes and on her upper cheeks she had the cutest freckles you ever saw. Anyhow, at the time we were both living in this little artists' colony within walking distance of the ocean. I was drinking and claiming to be waiting on inspiration, but she was trying everything—poetry, sculpting, making things using seashells, you name it. She was frantic with a need to create. There was just something about her that intrigued me. What she saw in me I have no idea, but we fell in love and got married. The minister that married us was a little wacky and I always wondered if the marriage was legit, but either way we were very happy together. She really was an amazing woman. Eventually, though...well, things happened. Julia went her way and I went mine. A few years later I returned to Stout City because it was my home and I just needed to be home. Of course, I had been totally forgotten by that time. No one knew I was back, nor did anyone care, nor did I inform them. I even chose a spot here, on the far side of town, and used a different name. So here I sit, considerably poorer but drunker than ever. The end."

Addie shook her head with a faint look of disbelief. She wasn't sure what she'd been expecting, but she'd figured it would be more substantial than that. To simply stop making beautiful works because of sheer laziness? It didn't make sense.

"So you never painted again after you reached California?" she asked, trying not to sound incredulous. "*Number 16* was it?"

"I never said that was my last."

"There are more?!"

"One more, to be exact," he said with a bemused smile. "I painted it when I got back, using some of the old tricks from before. But I felt bad—the colors weren't even based off new experiments and my blending was rusty— so I never did anything with it. Didn't even sign it. I guess I also thought the galleries would laugh at my work, like some outdated fad. Here's an old man thinking he is still in vogue, when really he is now just a joke, trying to sell stuff that was popular when people still drove horse and buggy."

Addie wanted to console him but bit her tongue. If Perzie didn't see value in his work it played right into her plan for making money. If she wanted a chance at *Number 17*, though, she needed to play it smart.

"This last painting," she began, trying to sound very calm, "where is it? I'd love to see another example of your genius."

"I'll tell you what," said Perzie. "I need something to eat and a couple new bottles. Let's get out of here and I'll tell you about that last painting over lunch."

"All right," agreed Addie. "And speaking of food, I didn't see any in your kitchen last night. How do you survive?"

"I go out once a day and try to eat up then. Sometimes I bring a little food home for later."

"Where does the trash go? I didn't see any of that in the kitchen, either."

"A neighbor kid comes by once a week. Little Jewish fella who lives upstairs. I pay him a nickel and he gathers trash and takes it to the trash chute in the hall. His mom won't let him touch liquor bottles though, so I'm holding out for a kid that will. Or even better, a pretty young woman," he added with a devilish smile. "How tall are you without the heels?"

"About five nine, last I measured."

"That's too tall for me," Perzie declared as he stood up, showing himself to be only slightly taller. "But you'll still make a good lunch companion."

He put on a sorry looking coat, grabbed a walking stick and held the door open for Addie before shutting it behind them without bothering to lock it.

***

Perzie and Addie walked to the Bonus Café around the corner from Perzie's apartment building. Once inside, they passed through an unmarked door next to the ladies' room, which led them down some steps into the basement. Here was a converted speakeasy.

"Everyone calls it the Bonus Basement," explained Perzie as they took a seat in the second booth. "The fella that owns it pays a little rent and buys all his food at a premium from upstairs. Nothing about either place is quality but it's nearby and cheap."

"And it sells bottles on the side," Addie added knowingly.

"Its like you've known me forever," Perzie beamed.

He ordered a couple ham sandwiches and two double whiskeys for them. Addie smiled politely but as soon as the waitress walked away, she leaned into the table to share words with Perzie on the other side.

"I don't really drink liquor much," she confided.

"Glad to hear it," he declared. "The stuff will kill you. Look at me; I'm only 43 years old."

They both laughed.

"Just polish off this one drink," he promised, "and I'll tell you about that last painting you are so interested in."

Addie could see that Perzie was having a little fun but now she had to calculate her role in this game. One drink wouldn't kill her, but her thinking needed to be sharp when Perzie revealed the availability and price of *Number 17*. Still, all things considered, one drink seemed safe enough.

"All right," she agreed, "I'll have the drink with you, which, by the way, should prove how enamored I am with your paintings." *Maybe flattery will convince him I'm worthy of ownership*, she thought. *Who knows, maybe he'll just give it to me. He doesn't seem too enthralled with possessions.*

When the drinks arrived, Perzie held up his glass for a toast. Addie followed suit.

"To my only remaining fan," he saluted.

"To *Number 17*," she added.

They clinked glasses and Perzie proceeded to down his in one fantastic guzzle.

"Down the hatch, Addie," he implored. "In honor of old *Number 17*."

After a nervous smile and a deep breath, Addie squinched her eyes shut and slowly but steadily downed her glassful. She sat her glass down, red-faced and desperately fighting the urge to cough, much to the amusement of Armstrong Perzie. As she battled to maintain her composure, Perzie motioned to the waitress for two more.

"Sorry about that whiskey," Perzie said to Addie. "It's not the softest stuff in the world, but I appreciate you keeping an old man company."

Addie nodded with watery eyes, still working on regaining her voice.

"As for *Number 17*—which, for your information, I painted in, oh, about 1921—it is no longer in my possession," he announced, studying Addie's reaction.

"That makes sense," she answered with all the coolness she could muster. The whiskey had gone straight to her bloodstream and she was already floating a tad.

"I gave it to my daughter as a wedding gift," he informed Addie.

"I didn't even know you had a daughter."

"Her name is Irene," he said.

Rats! This daughter surely knows the value of the painting, figured Addie, *and even if she doesn't, it undoubtedly holds sentimental value*. Still, ever the optimist, Addie wasn't ready to surrender just yet.

"What a fortunate woman," Addie admitted. "I'd still love to see the painting, though. Does Irene live in California with her mom?"

Perzie was smiling silently and looking beyond her. He was watching two fresh whiskey doubles moving towards them on the waitress's tray. He enjoyed the troubled look that came over Addie's face as they were set on the table.

"Actually, Irene isn't that far away," he offered with his impish grin. "Drink up and I'll tell you which city."

"Oh, no, I can't," Addie argued while shaking her head. "Another one and I might be asking for trouble."

She wasn't kidding. This type of thing was something she never did. Sure, she'd had liquor before, but it was watered down and nursed, not raw and guzzled.

But deep inside Addie wondered whether she could handle this challenge, whether she could handle a little loss of control. Maybe a second drink was what this adventure called for. Let's see Nancy Drew pull this one off.

Perzie raised his glass for a toast.

"To dragonfly wings," he saluted.

"To my poor liver," Addie reluctantly toasted.

They clinked glasses and downed their doubles. As the force of the alcohol slammed her nervous system, Addie shook her head like a dog drying himself. Perzie laughed. He drank this much for breakfast.

"All right, here's the kicker," confided Perzie, "Irene lives right near Stout City. Didn't anticipate that one did you? She actually visits me about once a year."

"Wow, how 'bout that?" said Addie. Her optimism was paying off. If she could just get a last name or an address while her brain was reasonably intact, it might just work out.

Thirty minutes later Addie had an address but she had paid a heavy price. There'd been three more rounds, and their effect on Addie had multiplied too fast for her usually cautious reckoning to keep pace. Perzie, who had been drunk for over a decade, didn't realize just how powerful his tolerance was, and thus he couldn't fully grasp how unprepared Addie was for this game. When he got up and left for the bathroom—without the slightest trace of a stagger—he unknowingly left behind a girl losing her grip on stability.

When Perzie returned she was gone.

Addie slowly awoke, noting first that her head hurt and second that it was nearing evening. What really caught her attention, though, were the surroundings. She was in a strange bedroom.

The last thing she remembered was being in the speakeasy with Perzie, but this wasn't Perzie's room. It was too clean. Well, "clean" might be an exaggeration as it needed a good dusting and there were books and newspapers scattered about. But more importantly, and certainly more troubling, it was definitely a man's bedroom. There were neckties visible and a couple of men's hats hanging on a hook. Plus there was nothing pretty about the room. It was strictly for business.

And what a man considered bedroom business concerned Addie. She quickly studied her clothes, relieved to find that everything was in its place. Her shoes were missing, though. She looked over the edge of the bed and saw them neatly arranged. That had to be a good sign, right?

Addie sat up and swung her legs over the side where they dangled as she grimaced at the sudden pain rushing to her brain. Why had she gone along with Perzie's crazy drinking game? It was obvious after the first whiskey that she was no prize drinker. After some thought, Addie admitted she had done it partly because she hadn't wanted to look like some delicate woman. She'd also done it in the name of greed as she tried to track down that darn painting. Well, she'd asked for an adventure and she was getting one. Now it was time to find out the awful truth of her current situation.

Addie slid off the bed and put on her shoes before looking into the dresser mirror. Her hair was a mess but not so messy that she'd use the strange hairbrush lying nearby. The eyeliner under her eyes wasn't looking any too fresh either, but at this point she was already low on pride. With a shrug she reluctantly began the process of discovering whose house she was occupying. As she reached the bedroom door it occurred to her that maybe she'd gotten so plastered that she'd broken into a stranger's home, like a fallen Goldilocks.

Addie slowly opened the door, praying it wouldn't squeak, which it didn't. She stuck her head out and craned her neck in both directions, but all she saw was a darkened hall. With quiet steps, she exited and moved toward the lighted living room where she again peeked around the corner.

There, sitting at the kitchen table, was a man, all alone, reading the newspaper. He was almost facing her but the paper covered most of his face. Addie tried to breathe quietly as her heart raced. Finally, the man lowered the paper to change pages and she got a good look at him.

"Zep?!" she called out

He looked up and beamed.

"Hello, Addie. How you feelin'?"

"Like a fool," she admitted. "A fool with a nasty headache."

"Sit down," said Zep as he rose. "I'll get you some water. That's the biggest contributor to a hangover, the dehydration. And some food wouldn't hurt. I'll whip you up a fried egg sandwich."

A look of disgust came over her face.

"I'm not ready for heavy food," she pleaded. "Maybe a piece of toast?"

"Coming right up," he said. Addie sat down at the kitchen table and watched as Zep retrieved a loaf of bread from the breadbox. She dreaded asking the big question but knew it was inevitable.

"So, how exactly did I end up here?" Addie asked sheepishly.

"I carried you," Zep answered without turning around.

"Oh lord," she groaned. "You mean like a sack of potatoes?"

"Yep. I started by carrying you in my arms, but that got heavy fast, so I threw you over my shoulder and carted you off like I was a caveman."

"I'm not sure which is more embarrassing, being toted in public or being called too heavy," said Addie.

"Actually, I'd think being cross-eyed drunk in the middle of the day would be the worst part."

"You know that one well," said Addie with a smirk.

"Touché."

Zep pressed the lever on the side of the toaster, making the bread disappear. He turned back around.

"So how did you find me?" Addie asked. "And where are we, anyway?"

"We're at my place, but finding you was pure luck. Wife of a friend asked me to look for him—Phil is his name—and she mentioned a couple joints he frequented. The Bonus Basement was the first one I walked to since it's only three blocks from here ..."

"What?! Are you serious, Zep? You carried me three blocks in the daylight?"

"What did you think happened, that I smuggled you through dark alleys on a magic carpet?"

"I figured you had driven. At least then I'd have been out of view."

"Sorry, I wasn't expecting a drunken damsel. And by the way, it was no picnic for me either. The whole way here I kept expecting some old woman to call the cops on me for kidnapping. You might want to thank me, actually. I could have left you there."

"Thank you," she said sweetly. "And thank you for taking my shoes off when you put me down."

"I considered taking your sweater off...in case you got sick," he added with a mischievous grin.

Addie glanced down at her sweater, re-inspecting the buttons. Knowing he'd gotten her, Zep's grin turned into a full-fledged smile, but Addie knew how to erase that smart aleck expression.

"How is Mabel, by the way?" she asked with fake innocence.

It worked. Zep's smile melted, and he turned and gingerly pulled the toast from the toaster.

"Nothing has changed since you last saw me," he admitted. "She is still in South Carolina at her mother's. We still talk, but...I don't know. She's still waitin' for proof that I'm marriage material, and I don't blame her. I guess we're both waitin' on me. So, that's the story."

"You, uh, started drinking again?"

"Some. Not as much as I used to."

"That would be nearly impossible."

"What about you?" he asked, trying to change the subject. "You ever forgiven me for getting you tangled up in the mayor thing?"

"There is nothing to forgive. I was just as excited about it as you were, and I really don't have too many regrets. It was just bad timing, really."

They were silent, remembering that period when their lives had first intersected. Zep and his brother had purchased a tiny, debt-ridden women's college with the idea of shaking it up. Mostly their plan was to add boys to the enrollment—boys who could play football. Every college in America, regardless of size, was raking in football riches during the late 1920s and the Decker brothers thought they had cooked up a shortcut to gridiron gold. It had never really panned out, though, especially with the depression hitting them. But along the way Zep had been forced to run a school, and one of his crazy publicity stunts was to get a female student elected mayor of Elberton, the school's rural hometown located thirty miles north of Stout City. Addie was that girl, and she actually won the election, but the depression derailed her, too. Economic strife devoured any agenda she might have pursued, and when her two years were up she was only too glad to leave Elberton and return to her hometown of Stout City.

"So what have you been doing since you left Ponder Grove?" Addie asked, referring to the college.

"Well, I tried to get my old dispatch position at the freight company but with jobs being so scarce these days all they could give me was work as a relief driver. I cover for anyone who calls in sick, or if things get too busy, neither of which happens often enough."

"That's better than I've been doing," returned Addie. "Apparently listing 'mayor' on your application means you are dishonest or unqualified for real work."

Zep laughed. He'd always seen something special in Addie. It's why he chose her for the mayor gimmick. She was popular with all the students, and her understanding of personalities bordered on remarkable for her age. Zep figured if she accidentally got elected, she'd do a legitimate job, and she did. He had been proud of her in a paternal sort of way even though he was only eight years older. To find her drunk in a speakeasy was stunning, to say the least.

"I guess that scene in the basement was what happens after a bad morning of job hunting," he quipped.

"Very funny. No, that's what happens when one agrees to have lunch with a drunken old artist."

"Ah, so you are quitting the job hunt and trying to land a man instead?" Zep inquired with a laugh. "Because if you are, you might want to aim a little higher than a drunken old artist."

"You are just full of wit these days, aren't you, Zep? I think I enjoyed you more when you were busy pretending to be a college administrator."

Zep chuckled again. He enjoyed laughing at himself, and appreciated a woman who could help. Mabel was good at that, but she didn't always enjoy the role. She really loved him and wished there was less to tease and more to be proud about.

"All right," said Zep, trying to be serious. "Tell me about this artist—who, by the way, was nowhere to be found when you were mumbling with your head on the table."

Addie told Zep the whole story of her plan for profiting off Armstrong Perzie, the genius of yesteryear. She noted the interest on his face as she talked and it dawned on her that Zep could be very useful. Having already attempted his college scheme, Zep had proven himself a willing participant in creative shenanigans, and she could use such a partner.

"Listen, Zep, I think I have a way for you to help with Perzie."

"Please don't make me haul your drunken body every day. I really think you've put on a couple pounds."

"First of all, you have never carried me before, so that is a total guess on your part. And it's a mean one, at that. Secondly, and worst of all, it's true. I've gained twelve pounds since the summer before my junior year."

"Well, the twelve pounds have been distributed well," he said with the genuine intention of fixing his mean comment. Addie was flattered, embarrassed and cautious.

"Well, I'd rather look like Mabel," she conceded. "She doesn't look like she's ever had to worry about a few pounds."

"No, Addie, I didn't mean to say..."

"I know, you idiot," she agreed softly. "Now, do you want to hear my idea or not?"

"Please."

"OK. Here's the situation: I need to visit this daughter of his and see if I can somehow talk her into selling her painting. It won't be easy, seeing as she got it as a wedding gift from Dad. Maybe I'll tell her I'm from a museum or that it's my final wish to own it before dying—no, that's terrible, isn't it?"

"A little terrible. But you've already been hauled through the streets today, so your reputation isn't exactly sterling."

"I'm ignoring that. As a matter of fact this whole episode today is stricken from my memory so don't bother with it anymore. Now back to business. While I'm visiting the daughter, you could visit Perzie. As a former...um, heavy drinker, you know better than anyone how to quit drinking, so maybe you can slow him down enough to be...productive. Getting him to paint again could be much more lucrative than finding one painting, assuming the alcohol hasn't killed whatever skill he has left."

"Or he could inspire me to pick up my drunken ways where I left them."

"Oh, I hadn't thought of that. I'm sorry, Zep."

"Nah, don't worry about it," he said gently. "Besides, I need a little excitement, if it's worth it, of course."

"You mean if you get paid?"

"It's not for me. It's for my landlady. She's obsessed with me paying rent occasionally."

"All right," said Addie. "I'll cut you in for 30 percent of whatever I get."

"And what do I get for saving you today?"

"A feeling of pride for doing something selfless and wonderful. Feels strange, huh?"

"I should have left you in the speakeasy."

They grinned at each other.

"We have a deal?" Addie asked as she extended her hand.

"Deal," agreed Zep.

They shook hands and planned their next move in the Armstrong Perzie escapade.

A few blocks away, Perzie slept unaware of his growing relevance—and equally unaware of the tzatziki sauce on his beard.

9

Maple Hills was technically a small town outside of Stout City, but over the years it had been swallowed up by the metropolis and was now considered just another suburb. It sat on the opposite side of the city from Addie's apartment, so she decided to take the trolley for her visit with Perzie's daughter, Irene. It was going to be a full day and Addie didn't feel much like fooling with traffic. It was also a nice day, still quite cold but sunny, perfect for sitting back and watching her city.

She timed it so that she would arrive at Irene's house just after ten o'clock in the morning. That was late enough for husbands to be at work but early enough that a housewife might still be at home. And if Irene was also gone to a job, so be it. Either way, Addie still felt it best to arrive unannounced for a couple of reasons.

Perzie had hinted that his relationship with Irene was strained and thus she may have outright rejected Addie's request for a visit. Also, Addie feared a phone call or letter would have looked too formal, too important. It might alert Irene to the idea that Addie had something in mind, putting her on guard if the subject of selling *Number 17* should come to fruition. There was risk in this strategy but Addie felt strongly that a surprise visit was the best course.

She disembarked at Vine Avenue, the second trolley stop into Maple Hills. From there it was a five-minute walk over to Fern Street where Irene lived. The neighborhood was a little on the unkempt side, with untrimmed trees, picket fences missing boards and front yards of patchy grass and dirt. The place had been nice at one time, but that time was long gone.

When she arrived at Irene's house and knocked on the door, Addie couldn't help but note the same sickening, excited feeling she'd had when facing Perzie's door the first time. *What if I walk in and Irene is sitting drunk in a chair surrounded by empty bottles*, she thought with a laugh.

Instead, her knock on the door stirred up a beehive of activity. Multiple voices could be heard hollering as to who would open the door, and they had to holler because a dog was barking like it was possessed. Having set in motion the calamity, Addie could only stand there, mildly dreading what awaited her on the other side.

When the door finally swung open, Addie was confronted with a small girl, about four years old. Her face had food stains and her curly, blonde hair was unbrushed. She giggled as she battled a dog that wanted to get around her and jump on the visitor.

"You better come inside before Fritter goes away," the little girl instructed while hanging on to Fritter's collar.

Addie stepped inside and closed the door behind her while the girl wrestled Fritter toward the living room, her arm around his neck like a cowgirl in a calf-roping contest. There were toys and dolls scattered everywhere. This was certainly a surprise visit, all right.

Addie waited politely near the door, expecting an adult to emerge, but nothing happened, so she called out.

"Hello?"

"We're in the kitchen," a female voice called back.

Addie followed the sound around a corner. There she found a woman sitting in front of a high chair, feeding a tiny spoonful of goop to a squirming, messy, little Buddha.

"Sorry," said the woman, "we were just in the middle of eating."

"You've definitely got your hands full," sympathized Addie.

As if on cue, Fritter came galloping through the kitchen, his paws struggling to keep traction on the linoleum. The little girl soon followed in hot pursuit, giggling at her predicament.

"Please take him outside, Madeline," Mom pleaded as her daughter ran past.

"I am," she protested, "but he won't behave."

"I didn't mean to intrude on your busy morning," Addie lied, "but I was in the neighborhood and wanted to stop by and say hello. I'm a friend of your father."

Mom turned to Addie with a look of curiosity, ignoring the baby who now craned its neck toward the hovering spoonful just out of reach.

"Do you mean Armstrong, my stepfather?"

"Um, yes, although I didn't realize there was a...'step' part to it."

This seemed to please Mom. She grinned slightly and returned to feeding the baby.

"Did he send you?" she asked.

"Oh no. He'd just mentioned where you lived and I made a mental note to drop in if I was ever nearby. I'm Addie, by the way."

"Nice to meet you, Addie. I'm Irene as you probably figured out."

Madeline's voice rang out from another part of the house.

"Mom, I put him outside!"

"Thank you, dear," she responded with a pleasant holler.

"But now he looks sad!" Madeline continued.

"He'll be fine. Now have Olga play with you."

Irene rolled her eyes at Addie, who returned an understanding smile.

"I know it seems crazy around here," Irene admitted, "but this is normal. The only thing that's crazy is that it makes me happy."

"That's not so crazy," said Addie in support, but feeling dubious about it.

There were times when Addie dreamed of a child or two. She could think of nothing more meaningful, in theory. In reality she wondered how she would handle the chaos and emotional investment. Standing there now, watching Irene operate, made Addie a little jealous *and* a little queasy. But maybe Irene was meant for this. Maybe her temperament was such that she could embrace the madness and the tears and the silliness. Addie had heard from many women that you couldn't really appreciate the beautiful depth of being a parent until it happened. Maternal love trumped all else with the first swell of the belly. But maybe they were brainwashing themselves into justifying their choice or perhaps their hormones had hijacked their good sense.

"Let me finish feeding Hugh and then I'll put him down for his nap. After that we can talk."

"Listen, I can come back if this is just adding more work for you," offered Addie.

"No, please stay. Like I said, this is normal and I'd love to meet you. I'm not sure I've ever spent time with a friend of Armstrong."

"OK," agreed Addie, "but why don't I just wait in the living room so you don't feel rushed?"

"That's kind of you. I'll be there shortly," said Irene as she used her little spoon to herd food from Hugh's face to his mouth.

Addie wandered slowly toward the living room, carefully scanning the walls for a glimpse of *Number 17*. There was nothing resembling Perzie's abstract realism, however, just some standard prints, the type found in a department store. There was absolutely nothing unique about the home's decorations or furnishings. Addie figured it was a combination of finances and utilitarian purpose. The place was a hatchery. It wasn't meant to be a showroom. Then again, her own apartment was done in postmodern flea market, so who was she to judge?

She stepped over some Lincoln Logs and took a seat on the sofa's only empty cushion. The other cushions were occupied by a threesome of stuffed inhabitants, namely a doll, a bear (wearing clip-on earrings) and a monkey.

A few moments later Madeline entered the room. Without hesitation she hopped onto the couch, directly beside Addie.

"Who are you?" asked Madeline.

"I'm here to talk to your mother."

"Are you her friend?"

"I hope to be her friend."

"I'm four," she declared while holding up five fingers.

"No, you're not," corrected a voice from behind the opposing armchair. "You're three until August."

Addie leaned over onto the armrest of the couch where she spied the bare knee of a child poking out from behind the chair.

"When is August?" Madeline asked Addie.

"It's several months yet, but you should enjoy being three. Three is a good age."

Madeline took the advice without any reaction. She grabbed the monkey and set it in her lap, wrapping her arms around it.

"She always wants to be old like me so she doesn't have to take naps anymore," said the mystery girl, who had now arisen from behind the chair. She stood facing Addie with a blue crayon in one hand a sheet of paper in the other. She was probably seven, with a pageboy haircut and a little dress that barely covered matching bloomers.

"Ah, you must be the older sister. What's your name?"

"Olga," she stated firmly.

"And what were you coloring back there?"

Olga walked over to the couch and stood next to the armrest so Addie could decide for herself. It was a test children have been giving adults forever.

"My, you've put a lot of work into that," Addie said patronizingly as a means of avoiding an answer. But Olga had been down that road before.

"Do you know what it is?" she challenged.

"Well, it looks like that is Fritter and he is playing outside next to your house."

"That's a dinosaur," Olga mocked before laughing hysterically. Madeline joined the laughter in support of her sister.

For the next few minutes the girls did most of the talking while Addie listened and occasionally prompted. Then Irene arrived and took Madeline upstairs for her nap. Madeline protested the whole way but Irene remained sweetly firm.

Finally, with two kids down and one quietly coloring, there was time to talk.

"I've never received a guest associated with my stepfather," Irene began. "And I'd have never expected a pretty young woman, besides. How did you two meet?"

"Oh, I'm just an admirer of his paintings, and being from Stout City myself, I looked him up."

"Interesting, since his art is older than you. Still, I'm pleased he has a fan. I guess I'm just surprised that after meeting him you still admire him. Or has he stopped drinking himself into a mindless stupor each day?"

"Um, no, he's still drinking, and I have to admit, it's rather sad," said Addie. "Not sure why he would give up on painting just to drink all day."

61

"How long have you known him?" asked Charlotte.

"Only a little while. I was actually hoping you might share some memories since he doesn't offer a lot of detail."

"Has he told you about his time in California—with my mother?"

"Not much," Addie admitted. "Just that he loved her. I got the impression some big event happened that broke them up."

"You got the right impression, but I can't shed much light on the big event, as you call it. I do know that they were truly in love until the end, especially in bed if their little winks and smiles were any indication." Irene waited for Addie to titter or look away. Addie did neither, knowing she was being tested for sturdiness.

"I could tell you their story from my perspective, if you have nothing better to do," offered Irene.

"That would be great. Like I said, he hasn't been overly forthcoming on personal matters."

"His life hasn't exactly been one to brag about," Irene said with a smirk. "Actually, I've only known him since I was eight years old. That's when we met him at the artist colony in Cambria. He described to you where that was?"

"The Central Coast, a few hours north of Los Angeles?"

"Exactly. But I should tell you, before that my mother and I lived in Washington, D.C. when my real father was alive. He was in the Navy, stationed at Fort Washington. When I was three years old he was killed while out at sea, although I don't know the exact details of what happened. Whenever I would ask, my mother would just say something about serving his country. I don't remember him at all and only knew him from a couple photographs she kept. After that, my mom worked at a florist shop and we lived with my aunt and uncle. Over time she saved up some money and we moved when I was eight years old. I'm not sure why exactly we went from the East Coast to an artists' colony on the other side of the country, but I think it had something to do with a coworker who had gone there previously and she had written to my mom about how fabulous it was.

"So anyway, here we are in this colony in California. The place was beautiful, with lots of pine trees and hills and then it opened up into a beach area where you walked down through huge rocks to the sand. I can see why the artists gravitated to this spot. It had a nice variation of natural scenes and the weather was lovely and it was so quiet. Inspiration was everywhere. Now, I was young, so I didn't really understand that my mom had these creative urges, but when we got there she turned into this carefree woman, full of imagination. It was wonderful and startling to me, but nothing out of the ordinary to this group of artists whom we lived among. There were all types of personalities in the colony, which meant constant laughter, debating, fighting, dreaming. For all the peacefulness of the setting, the group was darn near a circus, minus the elephants. But somehow, amongst all this careless living, they created art. That was the thing they all had in common, a hunger to create. Everyone that is, except Armstrong Perzie."

"Yes, he told me he didn't do any painting during his California years," Addie confirmed.

"If you had a few hours I could give you a long list of things he *didn't* do when he was out there," said Irene with a roll of the eyes. "It's still hard for me to believe that my mother ended up with him of all the men in the colony. Granted, half of them didn't go for women and the rest took themselves a little too seriously."

"What was Armstrong like at that time?" Addie asked.

"For all the grief I give him—and it's well deserved—he made a great impression when I first met him. Initially, he was just the man who sat in front of his cabin and smoked alone every morning. I didn't know his name or anything about him. He was handsome and had a little grin in his eyes, if you know what I mean, like he knew more than others. One morning I asked my mother if I could talk to him—she was intently writing and at this point I wasn't going to school, just a wandering girl entertaining herself. Anyhow, I remember walking up and sitting on the porch next to him. He was in a chair. I pulled my knees up to my chest and looked up at him and said 'Hi, I'm Irene.' He grinned at me and asked, 'Are all Irenes this pretty'?

"Oh, he was a charmer," Irene emphasized with a knowing look to Addie. "He asked questions about me and about my mom and where we were from. Unlike the others, he wasn't trying to impress me with his artistic genius. So, I kept visiting him every morning and we had fabulous conversations about why things were, or why things weren't, or what made people do certain things or act certain ways. I was convinced he could read minds and he swore me to secrecy where it concerned opinions of the others in the colony. Obviously he didn't want to make enemies. But what it did do was make me feel very special, and being a young girl living in some strange new world, I fell in love with him—in an innocent, daughterly way."

Irene stopped to glance out the back window as she recalled the period in her life.

"What happened next?" Addie asked, unable to tame her growing curiosity.

"Well, naturally, our budding friendship became a curiosity to my mother and she also began to visit with him, which led to the inevitable."

"Falling in love?"

"Yup. At first I was a little jealous because he'd been all mine, but as the weeks unfolded and their relationship grew intense, he still made time for me and our conversations were just as fantastic as ever. It only seemed to underscore the authenticity of our friendship. So when my mother told me he had proposed marriage to her, I was actually giddy."

"Just out of curiosity," Addie interrupted, "what did you make of the fact he wasn't painting? Or was he attempting some other type of art?"

"He attempted nothing, save avoiding effort. Being a kid, it didn't make much difference to me. I never questioned his goals. Heck, I just figured he was some sort of philosopher, which seemed like art to me, just not the kind put on paper or a canvas. It wasn't till later, when he and mother were married, that I overheard her talking to another artist about him. She was wondering when he would begin painting again, which was news to me. I had no idea he had ever held a brush. He never mentioned it once. But my mother seemed...not worried, but more...fascinated. She couldn't believe that he could be surrounded by so much creative energy and yet not be motivated to create. Wouldn't someone like that live elsewhere, where he didn't stand out? A few years later her fascination had turned to frustration. I remember my mother saying it was 'insulting' that he could have so much talent and yet do nothing except offer the same useless excuses about waiting for inspiration or passion. By then I was a teenager and I had learned that Armstrong was not only a painter, but that he had been a famous painter. I began to feel my mother's frustration, began to see that his charm was really a sad cover for being lazy."

"Was he drinking as much, then?" Addie asked.

"Yeah, he was drinking. They all did. There were impromptu parties almost every night in the colony. But he wasn't drinking during the day or anything like that. It progressed throughout the marriage and somewhere just before the divorce, he went off the rails. That was the end of the Armstrong I'd fallen in love with."

Irene stopped talking, seemingly lost in a trance as she stared at the coffee table. Addie waited, respectful of the vulnerability just shared. Then, just like that, Irene returned from the colony.

"I can't believe how much I've been talking," she apologized. "I guess I never really discuss that part of my life, not even to my husband."

"What does your husband do?" Addie asked after debating for a split second whether to change the subject.

"He works for the city, fixing the timers on those traffic signals, the ones with the lights. I don't understand how it works, exactly, but the timer makes it so that each direction gets an equal amount of time to pass. He says it's far more efficient than the days of traffic officers, although I sort of miss them with their whistles."

"Now I'll blame him every time I get a red signal," quipped Addie. They both laughed.

"So what do *you* do for a living, besides visit old artists?" Irene asked.

"I'm still looking for work, like a lot of people. My visits with Armstrong are just sort of a hobby," Addie fibbed. She didn't enjoy lying, but as an ex-mayor she had become accustomed to its necessity in getting things done. Anyway, unbridled honesty was overrated. Little kids and village idiots are honest. It takes skill to manipulate toward a greater good.

"So far I'm perplexed as to why he drinks so much and paints so little—as in never," continued Addie. "You said the drinking got worse around the divorce. What exactly happened between them that caused it to fall apart?"

"Besides his lack of interest in being remotely productive? I'm not really sure. That's something my mother never shared with me. At the end, it just got really strange, really fast. There were some arguments between them, and up to that point they had always been so perfect together. There were also arguments with neighbors. Armstrong began drinking heavily and right in the middle of it all, my mom got really sick and spent some time in a hospital. I'm sure it was from stress and lack of eating. Not long after that they split. Armstrong went down to Coronado, which is an island outside of San Diego. He can tell you about that part. I never heard from him again until I moved to Stout City."

"So, what made you move here?"

"I knew that'd be the next question. The truth is, I was eighteen and just wanted to be on my own. My mom was not the same emotionally and it caused us to become disenchanted with each other. She was mourning the past and I was dying to slay the future. So, I got it in my head that visiting Stout City would be a kick, sort of the opposite of what would be expected. You know, the teenage girl thing. Armstrong always talked about Stout City. It's where he made his fame and I wanted to see the place that was crazy enough to celebrate him. Remember I had never seen any of his art."

"And what did you learn about his past when you got here?"

"Nothing new, really. Just that he was an apathetic drinker with some womanizing thrown in for good measure."

They both laughed and Irene waited for Addie to ask more questions, but this was a spot where Addie was consciously holding back. She didn't want to guide Irene during this part where her prime feelings toward Perzie might be spelled out. Addie knew if she waited long enough, Irene would fill the silence with what she was really thinking. And she did.

"Actually, I expected Armstrong to be more famous here than he was. I was sort of young and naïve so I was expecting that there would be a street or building named after him. I finally asked a couple employees at the hotel about him and they knew nothing. It hadn't really dawned on me that his fame had been twenty years earlier. So then I went to the library and asked the woman about him, and found out his fame was short and wild. She showed me a book of his paintings and I was stunned. They were so beautiful that I couldn't believe it was the same man. I was so proud at that moment but so...ashamed, as well. Do you know what I mean? Here was this man with so much ability and yet he squandered it on meaningless living. I should have been bragging about the man who helped raise me but instead I left without telling the librarian I was his daughter."

Irene was instantly aware of the last word even as it came out of her mouth.

"Let me check on the children. I'll be back in a moment," she said before rising and hustling upstairs.

As she waited, Addie scanned the room, hoping she had missed something the first time, but there was still just one painting in the room and it wasn't *Number 17*. It was an oil work depicting some fishing boats bobbing in a harbor. The detail and the shadowing were excellent, the kind of skill which had intimidated Perzie.

"Why does my mom keep talking about drinking like it's bad? Isn't everybody supposed to drink?" Olga asked, looking up from the picture she was coloring on the coffee table. Addie had forgotten all about her, she'd been so quiet.

"Well, um, yes, everyone should drink, especially their milk. It will make your bones strong and help you grow."

"Then why is it bad that the man is drinking?"

"I guess he was drinking too much," Addie answered, unsure how Irene would want this question handled. She also noted that Armstrong's name hadn't had special meaning to the child and thought she'd probe a little.

"Do you know the man your mom was talking about?"

Olga shook her head. Embarrassed at not knowing, she changed the subject by holding up her latest work. Addie knew she was expected to guess the subject matter again.

"That's very pretty," said Addie as she stalled before speculating. "Is it another dinosaur?"

Olga smiled and covered her eyes to indicate that Addie was way off yet again.

"It's a zeppelin with a zebra driving it," she revealed playfully. "How can you not know that?"

Addie thought it was cute that Olga was so certain of her drawing. She also thought it was clever that she had mixed two Z items. Here was one of those moments that tugged a bit on her heart and made her want a child of her own. There was just something sweet and vulnerable about Olga. No one had judged her yet and she was brimming with awkward confidence. And she was so cute in her little dress with her skinny little legs.

Irene returned from her errand upstairs and it was obvious she had been thinking.

"So, you said you've known Armstrong just a short while?" she asked after settling down on the couch and fixing her skirt where it had bunched at her knees.

"That's true. Not long."

"Where do you rendezvous? Surely, not his pigsty of an apartment?"

"Actually, yes," Addie admitted with an embarrassed laugh. "But only before we go out to lunch." She wanted to emphasize the innocence of their relationship, thus the stress of the public daylight activity.

"So there is nothing of a romantic nature? I don't mean to suggest anything, it's just that you are such a pretty girl and he went through bushels of them in his prime, I'm told."

"As much as I like being called pretty, my interest is only in his art, I promise."

Irene continued to stare at Addie with a hint of curiosity.

"If you don't mind me asking," Irene continued, "what do you two talk about? I can't imagine that art alone is enough to carry these visits."

"Well, during my last visit, he told some of the story you just shared with me—about him going to California and getting married and how he got lazy and quit painting."

"Quite the lovely tale, huh? What did he say about me?"

Addie paused to create a favorable answer. The truth was, Perzie hadn't mentioned her at all until the speakeasy and that was only in connection with the location of *Number 17*. But the pause lasted too long and Irene caught it. She gave a polite, brave smile and Addie smiled sheepishly back.

"He hasn't proven to be too sentimental," Addie explained. "I can't seem to get many details on anyone in his life."

"I guess I just hoped I'd be a more than just an 'anyone,'" Irene admitted.

It was a painful admission and Addie knew it. She debated on how to proceed when an idea flashed in her mind. All along, Addie had wanted to know about *Number 17* but the right time to inquire never seemed to materialize. Now, an opening revealed itself where she could bolster Irene's hurt feelings and get her answer at the same time.

"Well," Addie began, "he's definitely mentioned you. It's the only reason I knew where you lived. And just the other day he was telling me that he'd given you one of his paintings as a wedding gift."

"He did give me a painting," Irene admitted with a wry grin. "It was about a week after the ceremony and Don and I had just returned from honeymooning. Armstrong telegrammed and asked if he could bring me a gift. It's the only time he has ever set foot in this house. The thing wasn't even wrapped. He walked in, handed it to me and said, 'This is a painting I did. It's not my best but thought maybe you'd want it.' Gee, thanks. Glad I could help you with your spring cleaning. He even mentioned that he hadn't signed it because it didn't measure up to his earlier work. I was pleased he had thought about me and made the trip and all, but it only made me feel bad about the painting—like between me and the garbage can I was the lesser of two evils."

"That makes sense," Addie agreed, secretly pleased that there was no sentimental attachment.

"Yeah, and I don't mean to sound ungrateful, it's just that he made it sound so...unspecial, if that's a word. So, after that the painting represented something entirely different than it should have. But that's standard with us."

"Really?" Addie prompted.

"I still make my annual trek out to his squalor and we talk, but we don't have the great conversations we did when I was young. Granted, he is usually too drunk for real thought, but there isn't much feeling either. Aren't drunks supposed to get more emotional when they are tight?"

She stopped and thought.

"I don't know, I guess there is a certain awkwardness to our relationship that's still unresolved. I'm still angry with how he grew distant from me at the colony; how he treated my mother at the end; how he just disappeared from our lives. Something happened between them that has never been explained. Whatever it was, it left our little family for dead and he has never apologized or explained and I refuse to make him. It's meaningless if you have to force the issue."

Irene stopped talking when she saw the comforting expression on Addie's face and realized she was being pitied.

"But it's only once a year," Irene added, trying to regain her dignity. "And it just makes me all the more grateful when I return to my little home and my loving family. You can't dwell on the past, you just have to create a new environment and move forward."

"I do love this house," Addie cooed while surveying the room as though for the first time. "Everything is so beautiful. You must keep that painting in a special spot."

Irene laughed with embarrassment.

"I was afraid you'd wonder where it's at. Now you're going to think I'm a complete heel."

"Impossible," Addie protested. "I'm already too impressed."

"You won't be impressed by this: I sold it."

Irene gave a sheepish look to Addie, who tried not to show her disappointment.

"After he gave it to me and basically explained why it was so bad, I stuck it in a closet. It stayed there for the longest time and I kept thinking I really should embrace it as a gift and display it somewhere but just never got around to it. Then Madeline got very sick and ended up needing surgery and we desperately needed the money, so I...sold it."

"You had to do it," Addie declared, wanting to comfort her host. "A sick child is more important."

"I've never told Armstrong, though," Irene confessed. "I keep thinking he'll ask about it. You think he'd be hurt? I mean, we hardly talk even though we live in the same city, and he did say that he hadn't signed the painting for a reason. Plus, he'd probably be too drunk to comprehend, anyway."

Addie could tell that Irene was talking about so much more than a painting, but it was the painting that had brought Addie here. It was the painting that would make her money and so it was the painting that she would keep the focus on.

"I'm sure he would understand with Madeline being sick and all," Addie began. "But just out of curiosity—being such a fan of his work and all—who did you sell the painting to? I'd still love to see it."

"This just gets more embarrassing. We went to an art dealer who thought it was a fake because it had no signature and because it looked a little different from his well-known works. Not only wouldn't he buy it, he looked at us like we were trying to run a con."

"Yikes!"

"Yikes is right. So we panicked and took it to a pawnbroker. He had never heard of Armstrong, and again it wasn't signed, but he liked it enough to buy it. I feel terrible knowing it's probably worth much more than we got, but we desperately needed money that day. He would understand that."

"I know he would," Addie assured her. "How long ago was this and which pawnbroker?"

"It was last year about this time. It turned out to be her appendix and we were already struggling because Don had missed two weeks of work with a horrible virus. Looking back I'm just glad we got the money in time."

"That's sounds frightening," Addie consoled. "Now, what did you say the name of that pawnbroker was, again?"

"I don't recall the name, although I can see it in my mind. It's down by the Orpheum Theatre, not quite to the corner. I think it's next to a typewriter repair place."

"Let's just be glad Madeline is fine," said Addie in summation, having gathered all the information she needed.

"I thought Madeline ate a mouse with sharp teeth," Olga interjected with a waiting smile, hoping to amuse the guest.

Addie appreciated the earnest attempt and rewarded her little friend with a big smile.

It wasn't long after that when Hugh awoke from his nap. His cry for Mom signaled the end of the meeting. The two women had enjoyed each other and promised to stay in contact. They hugged out of instinct, a female summation to a meeting where vulnerability was shared and not rejected.

On the way to the door, Olga caught up with Addie and gave her the picture of the zebra driving the zeppelin. Addie kneeled down to give her a little hug and Olga stood on her toes to wrap her arms around Addie's neck.

"Come back, OK?"

"OK," agreed Addie.

As Addie rode the trolley home she thought about Irene and her children and the power of maternal instinct. Then she snapped her fingers at a sudden thought: She'd forgotten to ask Irene about her mother, Julia. What ever happened to her? Was she alive, did they still talk? And what happened at this artists' colony that seemingly broke their family into pieces? The answers wouldn't get her any closer to *Number 17*, but her curiosity was growing.

10

Addie doubted that *Number 17* was still at the pawnshop. It had been more than a year since they'd purchased it from Irene, and because it was a purchase rather than a loan, they would have begun trying to resell it immediately. Still, Addie was anxious to get to the shop and see for herself.

Irene had described the place as being near the Orpheum Theatre. That would mean the southern part of downtown, on Broadway, the former heart of Stout City. As is typical of any large city, various parts of town rise and fall in stature as citizens constantly crave something newer and trendier. Broadway had been the place where important things happened in Stout City a generation ago, where people came to see and be seen. The original Wedlord's Department Store had been there before moving uptown. The *Stout City Sun* was still headquartered on Broadway but it was now the old fashioned newspaper, losing readership to more sensational papers like the *Star* and the *Times*, which were now housed near the university.

And the Orpheum Theatre had been the crown jewel of Broadway, opulent and storied. When *The Sky Seemed Green* had premiered in Stout City, it was the Orpheum that had hosted the red carpet event with floodlights shooting to the sky and Hollywood stars emerging from limousines. If you could spare an extra buck and wanted to impress your date, you took her to the Orpheum, the only theatre that featured a live band playing along with the silent pictures. And ironically, it was sound that had killed the stately queen. She was an independent theatre with no studio ties, and when talking pictures began to define the market, Fox Studios had built a modern, sleek joint in the West Park area, three doors up from the new Wedlord's. The constant crowd began to thin and Broadway seemed to get gray hair overnight. The Orpheum installed speakers and joined the talkie rage but it was too late. Now she just seemed like grandma, trying too hard to pepper her talk with youthful slang.

Addie arrived on Broadway and parked near the Orpheum at 9 a.m. Even this early, there had been a period when finding a vacant parking spot on this boulevard would've been difficult. Addie had a dozen choices today.

After parking, she stepped back into the street as far as was safely possible. She scanned the Orpheum's block looking for a pawnbroker near one of the corners, but couldn't step back far enough to get proper perspective, so she shrugged and went left. She walked to the end of the block but found nothing pawn-like, so she reversed course and headed for the other end. Near the intersection of 3rd Avenue she found the EZ Loan Pawn Shop. Irene had mentioned a possible typewriter repair place next door, but the pawnshop was between a coffee shop and a stenographer school. Addie debated the validity of Irene's clues but decided the Orpheum bit would be hard to get wrong. Plus, Addie had nothing to lose by inquiring, so she entered the EZ Loan Pawn Shop.

Little greeting bells rang as she pushed the front door open, but nobody seemed to care. There were no customers or employees in sight. Addie scanned the place and saw some paintings hung on the walls or resting on top of showcases but nothing resembling what she was seeking, so she walked straight to the counter and waited.

There were two men talking in a back office, visible through a large window. One of them glanced at her but they kept talking while Addie tried to be patient.

She had noticed over time that male customers rarely had to endure this, especially in less "ladylike" places like this one. She'd gone to a hardware store once and was completely ignored, the employees figuring she was just lost, looking for her man. Maybe being a male customer meant serious business, both in forcefulness and financial means. Maybe male employees thought transactions with other men would be more direct, simpler. There was probably some truth to all of it, but Addie hoped to change those notions if given a chance. She did wonder, however, if it was actually just a matter of being the right woman. Had she looked like Lily Gotem, those two men would be fighting to serve her.

Just thinking about it worked Addie into a simmer and she began moving along the counter until she was near the office.

"Excuse me," she called. "I'd like to pawn my purse full of rare diamond jewelry."

The two men stopped talking, looked at Addie then looked at each other with dubious expressions. Apparently the bigger of the men was in charge of dealing with livewires because he moved forward without discussion.

"Good morning," he said insincerely as he arrived at the counter. "Can I help you?"

"Why yes, you can," Addie answered with faux charm. "I'm looking for a specific painting that has great sentimental value and I have been led to believe it may be here."

"We get lots of paintings, ma'am. Could you describe it?"

"Um, well, it is not your usual painting. There isn't really a subject, per se. It's really more a montage of colors. Naturally, we in the family think they are striking colors. My cousin sold it about this time last year, if that helps you place it. She was very desperate at the time and, well, some in the family have just heard about it and we are so saddened at the thought of losing it."

A tiny glow of life showed itself in the big fella's eyes.

"Actually, I do remember that," he said. "She had a sick kid or something. It was an odd painting, although the colors were better than usual, I'll give you that. She tried to explain that it had been painted by a famous artist, but neither Oscar or me had heard of him and it wasn't even signed. I guess you know the story."

Addie offered a light laugh.

"My cousin can be dramatic and she was distraught about my niece. In all honesty, and she would kill me if she heard this, but she was pushing the bounds of honesty. It's a nice painting by a nice man, but no more than that. You see, it was purchased by our grandparents during a romantic anniversary trip. It has sentimental value."

"Well, listen, I'd love for your family to have it but it's been sold for months. An older lady from some nearby county bought it. I wanna say she was from Dellton but I ain't positive..."

He looked toward the ceiling and squinted, trying to remember a single transaction amongst thousands.

"Is there any way to look it up?" Addie interrupted. "I'm not sure how your establishment records things, I'm afraid."

"Oh sure, we keep lots of information like that. The cops require it in case we accidentally buy or sell stolen items. That way they can trace things back to where they oughta be."

"That's wonderful! So then you have a record of the painting's sale and you could tell me where in Dellton this lady lives."

The big fella made a sorrowful face.

"The problem with that is we don't normally give out that kinda dope to other customers. You can imagine how angry you'd be if you bought that painting fair and square and then somebody came bangin' on your door with a sob story—no offense."

"No, I understand."

"In our business, people like to remain anonymous. That might seem unfair to someone like you, but it's the nature of our dealings, you know?"

Addie nodded with reluctant agreement as she formulated her next move.

"I appreciate the concern for your clientele, I really do," she admitted. "That's how I'd want to be treated. On the other hand, you're running a business to make money, right?"

"Yeah," he agreed warily.

"I mean, it's just one painting and one customer," Addie continued. "And this is an unusual circumstance with my grandmother dying and all. I'm just wondering if you could make an exception for a couple dollars. This woman who bought it can't be so attached to that painting that she wouldn't be pleased to sell it to my family for a decent profit and you'd have made a little extra money the easy way. Everybody wins!"

The big fella now eyed her a little differently. This was no Pollyanna he was dealing with. She had an angle and wasn't afraid to pay. She definitely didn't give off the vibe of a cop or a detective, for that matter. Also, he'd dealt with any number of vixens who used their looks to sway some action, but this one was too refined and sincere sounding. The kind of gal his shop usually attracted was overtly sensual, leaving no doubt as to her lack of barriers. And another thing—the cousin of hers who had originally sold the painting was a bona fide housewife. She'd blushed just walking into a pawn joint. And the gal in front of him right now seemed like the girl next door. The big fella concluded that he really was dealing with a sweet but desperate girl who was looking to grant grandma a dying wish.

"I'll tell you what," he began, lowering his voice just a touch. "Give me a couple minutes and if Oscar don't mind me sharin' and you don't mind payin' maybe we can work this out—no guarantees, you understand."

"Sure, I understand. Thanks."

The big fella ambled to the back office and began sharing the story with Oscar. Addie watched nervously, trying to decipher something from their body language or expressions. Finally, the two men went to a file and began sifting through papers. After a time, they separated. This time it was Oscar who left the office and approached Addie.

"So, Lazy says you're looking for a family painting?"

"Did you call him lazy?" Addie couldn't help but ask with a surprised expression.

"Yeah, that's his nickname. Real name is Adam but nobody ever calls him that. Watch him operate for a couple minutes and you'll understand."

"Well, he was nice enough to discuss the painting with me."

"Yeah, he told me all about it. We both agreed this might be a case where we could help a little bit. We found the name and address but two things you need to know: this isn't for free and if she ever says something angry to us, we never met you and have no idea where you got your information."

"I understand, I really do. Our family thanks you."

"Not a problem. And you can thank us with a ten dollar contribution."

This was much more than Addie had anticipated paying. It was a week's rent, for goodness sakes. On the other hand, she was one step away from knowing the whereabouts of *Number 17*. *It's an investment in the bigger prize,* she explained to herself.

She pulled out her coin purse and extracted a five dollar bill and five ones, handing them over with a mixture of reluctance and anticipation. Oscar offered Addie a pencil.

"Here you go," he instructed, pushing a paper toward her. "Write this address down on something from your purse. Like I said, we don't want any proof linking us to your visit. Even at ten bucks we're doing a big favor here, risking our reputation."

Addie laughed inwardly at the thought of a pawnbroker being concerned about his reputation. She scribbled down the name and street but paused when she got to the city.

"I thought he said she was from Dellton."

"I'm sure he did. But you gotta remember, we make dozens of loans a day, six days a week. Anyway, he had the right county, just the wrong town."

Addie finished copying down the address for Cora Shafer in Fenton, Pennsylvania. She folded up the paper and stuck it in her purse.

"OK, that's that," she chimed. "Thanks again."

"Not a problem, but don't forget we've never spoken. When you write her asking about the painting, don't mention us."

"You have my word."

The bells above the door jingled as she departed.

Forget sending a letter, she was on her way to Fenton.

11

Addie returned to her car, parked in front of the Orpheum Theatre. Now she had a choice to make. Fenton, where *Number 17* now resided in Cora Shafer's house, was about fifty miles outside of Stout City. Driving her automobile there would give her the quickest start, but the single highway leading into Fenton was winding, hilly and one lane each way. Get behind the wrong truck and your travel time might be doubled.

The local train connection offered less risk but ran on a schedule, and who knew when the next one left? As she pondered her choices she noted a few raindrops that had fallen on her windshield while she was inside the pawnshop. That seemed to tip the balance toward taking the train. There was no real urgency anyhow. Cora Shafer had already owned the painting for many months. An hour either way wasn't going to mean anything. Addie just needed to relax and focus on how she was going to get Cora to sell. A train ride was perfect for thinking, and the train station was just a dozen blocks away.

Her decision made, she paused to look through the windshield at the Orpheum. She had watched movies there several times in her life. When she was in elementary school her dad had played hooky from work and surprised her on a few occasions. They'd snuck off to the theatre and watched Fatty Arbuckle movies. Mom hated Fatty Arbuckle and couldn't understand why anyone found him funny. Addie was only slightly amused by him but cherished the time alone with her dad, watching him carefree and laughing like he never laughed any other time. It wasn't that he overly serious or anything, just that he seemed to be lost in thought all the time, like he was always on duty. He showed emotion through acts, like teaching her to change a tire, or encouraging her to attend college ever since she was little. But in the dark of the theatre, his face lit only by the flickering screen, he laughed like a kid, and for some reason that made Addie happier than anything in the world.

The Orpheum was also the first place she had ever been slightly physical with a boy. His name was Thomas. He was a classmate. A junior when she was a sophomore. He had more money than most kids, and better looks, though he wasn't particularly popular. He seemed too smart and didn't know how to fit in by acting less smart. Their first date was allowed by her parents only because she was doubling with Lyla, a friend of hers whom they trusted. Of course, as soon as the foursome entered the theatre, the couples went their separate ways. Addie and Thomas sat near the back, and while waiting for the movie to start they made inane conversation about school, the only thing they had in common.

When the movie started and the band began to play they studied the screen but their minds thought only of each other. Something inside each of them, some instinct or voice, seemed obsessed with touching the other one, as though compelled by unknown forces. And yet, the fear of rejection hung heavily on both sides. Addie knew by convention that her part was to wait. He was the instigator. His part was to risk and hers was to accept or deny. The movie droned on and she "unknowingly" made her hand available, resting it awkwardly against her thigh. Soon his hand was on hers and they continued to stare at the screen, afraid to break the spell. After a while his hand released hers and rested on her leg, near her knee. Addie felt her breathing increase. This was the most monumental thing that had ever happened in her life. She was allowing a trespass into the gray area, but it felt so good. She put her hand on his to show him she accepted, but also to retain control should he seek higher ground. She wanted more, but not now, not here, and in her head she begged him to please not attempt anything that would make her have to say no. He didn't. He rubbed her knee some more and she ran her hand along his strong forearm and the movie played on and neither one had a clue what it was about. When the movie had ended they walked out without touching, nor saying a word about what had happened.

They went out two more times but the spark in their relationship never ignited. They were never officially a couple and so they never officially broke up. One day she saw Thomas playing with the fingers of Norma Walston at lunch break. The way they looked at each other made Addie know her time with Thomas was done. She was neither sad nor happy. She was only curious about Norma Walston and wondered, *why her and not me?* Eventually she decided it could easily have gone in reverse order, and she took comfort in that. Still, over the next two years she would see Norma and feel inferior. It was a female quirk, judging herself against Norma, wondering what Thomas saw or didn't see in her. To this day, she still battled the need to understand where she fit into the context of others' lives rather than where they fit into hers.

Those moments at the Orpheum could never happen again. They required a certain innocence that could not be recreated. It felt appropriate to Addie that the Orpheum she now looked at was empty. Having always visited at night, she'd never noticed the streaks on the glass, nor the scuff marks at the base of the ticket booth where a million feet had anxiously kicked while enduring the transaction that held them up from entertainment. A wave of sadness passed through her and she knew it was sadness at growing older.

Addie backed her car out and headed for the train station, hoping her daydreaming hadn't cost her the next train to Fenton.

***

At the terminal, the man behind the ticket counter told her the next train to Fenton departed in forty minutes. She bought her coach ticket and took a seat in the waiting area.

Addie didn't mind waiting. She liked to watch people. During her high school days, she and her best friends, Lyla and Polly, would spend summer afternoons sitting in air-conditioned lobbies around the city, watching people. It was their sport. Their observations led to great debates about perceptions and human nature. It was also a great way to ridicule all the other women of the world.

Addie was casually people-watching when a sight at the ticket counter shocked her into alertness.

It was Oscar from the pawnshop!

At first she couldn't comprehend what she was seeing. What were the odds of him arriving at the station right on the heels of them meeting each other at the shop? Her optimistic nature wanted to be thrilled with this coincidence, but the increasingly savvy part of her insisted this was not right. *Is he following me?* she wondered. *Does he think he can chat me up on the train where I have no escape? Or maybe he wants to talk me into a date while we are in a small town, cut off from familiar surroundings.*

All she knew for sure was that she didn't want to be spotted until she could figure out his motive. As he bought his ticket, Addie slowly got up and moved to a spot where she could spy from behind a column.

Oscar finished getting his ticket, checked his watch, and then paid a visit to the men's room. Now was her chance. She walked quickly to the ticket counter and stood in front of the man who had just helped Oscar.

85

"Excuse me," she said sweetly. "That man you just helped was my husband. I spied him just as I was exiting...well, after I'd finished freshening up. Now he's freshening up..."

Addie and the ticket agent exchanged embarrassed grins.

"Could you tell me which ticket he ended up buying? I need to call my mom and let her know when we'll be there."

"Yes, ma'am. He bought one ticket on the 10:45."

"To Fenton?"

"No ma'am, to Dellton. Do you, uh, need to buy another ticket?"

They shared another awkward smile.

"Yes, I guess I better," she said. "Apparently he has changed his mind and we're visiting *his* mother. I wonder what got into him. Can you exchange this ticket, please?"

She handed him her Fenton ticket, got her Dellton ticket and hurried back to her hiding spot behind the column.

You don't suppose this is about the painting? she suddenly asked herself.

12

The 10:45 to Dellton was light on passengers today, making Addie's job of tailing Oscar a little tougher. What really saved her, though, was that Oscar had no expectation of Addie being on the same train. Other than taking a second glance at a woman bent over, storing her purse, he was focused only on boarding the train and finding a seat.

Addie, on the other hand, was on edge with decision-making. For one, she couldn't decide if she should sit behind Oscar in the same car. It made sense to keep an eye on any movements he might make, but on the other hand she knew where he was going, so why risk exposing her presence? Therefore, she watched him take his seat and then moved into the next car back and took a seat of her own. She had to be alert, though. Should he suddenly decide to take a stroll she'd have to hide. After some debate she decided to hang her coat on her shoulder and if he appeared she would lean into the window and pull it up against her face.

Settled in her seat, she then began to wonder if she should just confront Oscar. After all, it was he who was traveling with questionable motives. Or was he? Maybe he really had plans for visiting Dellton that were coincidental. Maybe he lived there. Plenty of other people made the short train trip every day for their jobs in Stout City. But why would he be going home so early?

OK, let's say he is after the painting, she quizzed herself. *Would I be better off confronting him and scaring him off the hunt or would it be best to follow him to the painting? If I was going to scare him I should have done it at the station. Shoot, I doubt I'd scare him,*

*anyhow. He'd just say, "Lets walk to her house together
and make bids on the painting," knowing full well he
has far more cash than I do. He also knows the woman's
real name and address and could withhold it until I give
up. No, I think I'd better just tail him and hope the
woman isn't home. That way if he takes a break for
lunch I can get to her first if she comes home.*

Addie exhaled and looked out the window as
Stout City rolled past. She wished she could just sit back
and enjoy the scenery but she had to be ready if he came
walking into her car. Such was the life of a harried art
hunter.

At that same moment, Oscar had no thoughts of
strolling anywhere. This was an unusual midmorning
break from the shop, and he was content to be off his
feet, not dealing with any customers.

It wasn't that he hated customers; he'd simply
grown tired of the give and take. He and his brother-in-
law, Adam "Lazy" Riffle, had owned their pawnshop for
twenty-one years and had been its only full-time
employees. They worked six days a week from 9 a.m.
until 7 p.m., taking off only Sundays, Thanksgiving,
Christmas and Independence Day. Neither of them
minded the long hours and they loved getting a good
deal, but lord, the customers were a mess of trouble.
Granted, some of them were straight arrows re-
prioritizing possessions or needing a loan to survive a
rough patch, but the majority were riffraff of the lowest
order: drunks, prostitutes, drug addicts, pimps,
gamblers, and musicians. And that was in good times.
Ever since the economy disintegrated, even the straight
arrows were getting rough around the edges.

Oscar and Lazy were doing just what they were
meant to do, though. They'd bought the pawnshop
because they were conniving predators who had no
problem exploiting the down and desperate for a nickel.
They'd even tricked the former owner's widow into

paying transaction fees when she sold the business to them. They were the most dangerous type of men: clever and crude.

Their fingernails were dirty, they smoked cigars for breakfast and instead of tipping the paperboy, they demanded discounts for errant tosses. They had married Lithuanian sisters who spent their days complaining to each other on the phone while their kids terrorized animals, neighbor kids and each other. Were they ever to set foot in a church, the brothers-in-law would surely have taken from the collection plate instead of giving.

The concept of joy had never occurred to Oscar or Lazy. They saw life as a battlefield where some profited and the rest lost. Addie, for example, seemed like a decent gal, but why should she profit off a painting instead of them? She'd just spend it on a skirt she didn't need or buy milk for a kitten.

Actually, Lazy had almost blown the whole opportunity when he'd first spoken to Addie. He'd given her all the information she needed to find the painting except the buyer's name, and he'd have given her that if he'd remembered it.

It was only when he talked to Oscar in the office that the two of them began to construct a theory. For one thing, if this painting had such great sentimental value to Addie's family (a lie, though they didn't know it), then why wait a year before looking for it? Also, when the cousin (Irene) had originally brought it to the pawnshop, she had made no mention of its sentimental nature, only its connection to a famous painter, which they had no reason to believe at the time. One of them was lying and they doubted it was the blushing housewife.

They believed that Addie wanted the painting because it *was* valuable. As a final test, Oscar had upped the price for information to ten dollars. That was a lot of money, and he figured she would balk at the cost and begin pleading for a break if it was just a sentimental item she sought. Instead, Addie had willingly paid the exorbitant price because she knew it was simply the small cost associated with a much bigger profit.

Oscar wasn't fully convinced that Addie was art hunting, but his intuition was pretty certain. And if you wanted to survive in this dreadful economy you had to chase a pot of gold even when based on a hunch. For two bucks round trip and the chance to get out of the shop, Oscar wasn't risking much to try and buy back the painting. And if it turned out that the painting was essentially worthless and Addie really did want it for sentimental reasons, then he'd just add ten bucks to the new asking price and get that from her along with the ten bucks he'd already made selling her false information.

Not that the information was completely false. There was a real life Cora Shafer in Fenton, all right, but she was senile and it would take Addie quite a while to figure out the truth if she ever did. And just to make sure, Oscar had hinted to Addie about writing a letter to Cora instead of visiting her. That would gum up the works even longer.

All in all, Oscar was pleased with himself. Exploiting the down and desperate was standard business, but turning the tables on another person who thought she had a clever angle was as close to joy as he got.

His satisfaction was momentarily increased by the sight of a pretty woman passing down the aisle next to him. He gave her a Cheshire smile but she wisely ignored him and continued toward the next car. This small rejection did not prevent him from craning his neck to watch her walk away.

When the door to Addie's car suddenly opened, Addie jumped and almost hid behind her coat for cover. Much to her relief, it was the pretty woman continuing her stroll. Addie smiled politely as the woman passed and received a polite smile in return.

(Not surprisingly, had Addie and Oscar been summoned to court and ordered to describe the woman in the aisle, Addie would have mentioned her green eyes and brown hair, and guessed her to be a married woman approximately forty-five years old. Oscar would have shrugged and said she had nice gams.)

As the train climbed through the hills toward Dellton, Addie's thoughts turned to Zep. They had talked the previous night and reconfirmed their individual plans of attack. Addie would continue her pursuit of *Number 17* and Zep would visit Perzie in hopes of jump-starting his painting career.

She looked at her watch and determined that the two men were probably talking in Perzie's apartment right then. A look of worry crept across her face when she imagined a meeting between the two hardest drinkers she had ever known. How that would turn out was anybody's guess.

13

When discussing plans the night before, Zep and Addie had agreed that Zep's initial visit to Perzie should be unannounced. They felt that the drunken painter would likely reject a second caller if given a choice. After all, the old man had spent years avoiding people and he certainly wouldn't be keen on turning his den of iniquity into a social hub.

Thus, knowing he probably wouldn't be embraced, Zep was prepared for anything when he knocked on Perzie's door. At least he was armed with the knowledge that one must catch Perzie before noon if one wanted him to be reasonably sober.

"Enter," bellowed the old painter.

Determined not to show fear, Zep strode inside and swung the door closed behind him as though he were a long lost son returning home.

"Hi there," said Zep with the most disarming smile possible. "How you doin'?"

"I'm doing pretty well for a useless old man. Now might I inquire who the hell you are?"

Zep laughed softly, half out of embarrassment, half in an effort to keep things light.

"Well, I'm a friend of Addie's and it's nice to meet you. She said you were a marvelous artist and that I should stop by and say hello."

"Say, do you know what happened to her the other day?" Perzie asked, remembering he had lost her at the speakeasy. "Did she tell you? I came back from the men's room and she was gone."

"I think she was worried she'd had too much to drink and that she'd get sick or say something embarrassing. You about had her passed out. You gotta be more careful inviting rookies into your world of guzzling."

"You are correct. I probably scared her to death and that's why she sent you over here," confided Perzie. "She told you I was a has-been who was drinking himself to death and you should come by and tend to me. That's how women are. They just can't help wanting people to be better. Now, am I right?"

"I'd say you're pretty close," Zep admitted. "I used to be a pretty fair drinker myself, and she figured maybe I could slow down your destruction a little."

"How 'bout that? After two visits she is already going to the trouble of healing me. I either made a really good impression or a really bad one."

"Or, as you said, it's her female duty," Zep reminded him. "The things that really unleash maternal instinct are wasted potential, a sad situation and vulnerability. I'm thinking you meet 'em all."

"What makes you think I'm vulnerable?"

"You mean, besides being drunk and old in an unlocked apartment? By nighttime you couldn't defend yourself against a Camp Fire Girl."

Perzie picked up the bottle resting against his hip and guzzled enough to harm a camel, then he licked his lips in case any was missed. He looked at Zep, then the wall, then back to Zep.

"I'll be honest. I don't really want to be saved," Perzie finally declared.

"Neither did I," admitted Zep as he took a seat on the couch facing Perzie. "I still drink a little, and I gotta admit, I miss the days of being holed up alone, making my brain all foggy while the rest of the world scurried around. Truth is I'm taking a risk here. There's a fifty-fifty chance you'll get me to backslide instead of me saving you."

"If you liked it so much, then why'd you give it up?"

"A woman named Mabel."

"And there we are, right back to women wantin' us to be better humans," said Perzie. "I think we have reached an agreement on that angle, but the difference is you are young and have a woman worth stopping for, whereas I'm decrepit and really not worth saving."

"You make a valid point," Zep concurred, much to the surprise of his host.

"And you have a funny way of trying to save a fella," said Perzie with a bit of hurt in his expression.

"You said you didn't want to be saved and I was just respecting your wishes. Plus you really did make a valid point," said Zep. "Even if we did straighten you out, your prospects for a woman would be dim with such a bad liver and burned shirts and all."

"Wouldn't that make me vulnerable *and* a sad situation? That's two out of three, which ought to get me some sort of woman aiming to mother me."

"Another valid point. But then we are back to the start: you don't want to be saved."

Perzie nodded and demonstrated his agreement by tipping back the bottle and relieving it of its remaining contents. He placed the empty bottle back in the nook of the chair and offered an audible "ahhhh" for the enjoyment of his formerly hard-drinking guest.

"All right, let's stop talking about drinking for a bit," insisted Perzie. "Maybe you'll save me, maybe you won't. Frankly, I feel too wonderful at the moment to keep analyzing the thing that makes me feel so wonderful. And another thing: You've got to earn my consideration. I just met you. So let's start by learning about you and this woman Mabel. Are you married to her?"

"We're sort of engaged. What I mean is, I proposed and she said yes and I gave her a ring."

"But?"

"But, then I stalled her and started drinking a little and then I gave up my career."

"And here we were talking about what a mess I am. So, did she break it off with you or what?"

"Not exactly. She went to South Carolina to stay with her mom—to raise the stakes and show me what I was missing."

"How long ago was that?"

"Four months."

"And are you missing her?"

Zep leaned his head back and thought about an answer as he studied the far wall where it met the ceiling. It was one of those questions that made him feel bad, and therefore he hated to consider it.

"I love her," Zep finally answered. "I just don't know if that's enough. She deserves better than me."

Zep waited for Perzie to comment on this raw admission, but Perzie was now lost in his own thought, his expression a mixture of seriousness and defeat. Zep wondered if the old painter was sorting through his own emotions. He decided to make a mental note of the subject—a woman deserving better—and come back to it when Perzie trusted him more.

"Anyhow, she still wears the ring," Zep continued, referring to Mabel. "She told me the other day that some man commented on it."

"Yes, well, a statement like that is fully designed to shake you up, kid. She's saying she is still loyal, but still desired, and you better make your move before she does."

Zep nodded somberly. Her statement was indeed a call to action, but Zep was still paralyzed, unable to understand his vision of life and afraid to pull her into the unknown. Mable, of course, was dead certain she could help Zep solve his struggles, but only if invited. And so they sat, miles apart, waiting for Zep, the weakest link, to fight or surrender.

Unwilling to discuss this riddle any further, Zep turned to his two trusted friends, denial and subject change.

"So Addie tells me you lived in California for a long time. What was that like?"

"Well, I was there for sixteen years, so it's hard to summarize in a single sentence. And since you are here to save me—and assuming you have a few minutes to kill—I'll tell you about the portion of my stay in California where I lost it. That way you can see the depths of my depravity and know what you're dealing with."

"This sounds fun."

"I'm sure you'll be able to appreciate it. Now, let's see, where do I start? Well, I'd been living in an artists' colony on the Central Coast when an unfortunate incident took place, compelling me to leave. I had grown quite enamored with the weather in California—if you can really call endless sunny fluff weather—so I stayed in state and headed south to San Diego where I ended up living in a magnificent tent city on the island of Coronado. It was actually a summer gathering, an urban camping area where city folk could enjoy the ocean breezes while the rest of the world sweltered. It all revolved around the Hotel Del Coronado, a very large building which dominated the island. This is where the wealthy stayed. The hotel served as the base, and the tent city sprawled away from it in very organized fashion, with temporary streets and even mail service.

"Anyhow, that's where I landed, and for the next few months I wandered the beach during the day, drank highballs at the hotel bar as the sun set, and finished with straight liquor in the little tent I rented. I would get good and tight and then wander the tent city, listening to bits of conversations before returning to my tent and drinking until slumber."

"So far, so good," interjected Zep.

"Yeah, it was idyllic, in a sense," Perzie continued. "Had my mind not been consumed by the trouble I'd left at the colony, I'm sure I'd have counted this period as a life's highlight. Instead I was hiding from my pain and using the activities of strangers as distraction. But then the summer ended and the tent city disappeared. The island became quiet, just a few hundred locals and whatever guests were staying at the Hotel Del. This was in 1916, by the way. So, not really having a plan, I just decided to stay. I rented a tiny bungalow that sat behind a house owned by an ancient widower. He didn't care anything about me except the rent I paid, which was perfect and dangerous at the same time. I still wandered during the day but now punctuated my little outings with liquid refreshment, some at home and some at a drinking establishment."

"I'm telling you, this is not good for me at all," Zep added in complete seriousness. "Call me crazy or sick but that sounds like paradise. And that's what terrifies me about myself and it's what Mabel should fear."

"You make a valid point," agreed Perzie with a wry grin. "I get closer to her point of view with every minute I get to know you."

They both laughed. Men sharing informal truth.

"So I interrupted you," apologized Zep. "You were getting drunk on Coronado Island."

"Yes, daily, for well over a year. But even that wasn't enough after a while. The occasional pang of regret regarding the colony incident was still able to seep into my head, so I upped the ante. I met a fella at one of the less genteel bars who provided me with access to morphine. I know what you are thinking and even now it feels funny to admit to this, but I became dependent on this drug. Then again, if you think deeper, morphine is a byproduct of nature, just as alcohol is. At least that's what I told myself at the time. It was just another form of escape, but with a new feeling. It refreshed me in my battle to forget.

"Now, as a sidebar, I should mention that time itself is the only true healer. Each day is another layer, placing a bad event deeper into the context of life. The event is no longer front and center. It begins to blend in with other significant events. What I was trying to forget still hurt—and it does to this day—but its pain became cloudier, more memory than reality, as though I could blame some of the pain on a faulty remembrance rather than actual complicity."

Perzie stopped talking and reached for the bottle in the chair next to his hip. He'd forgotten that it was empty, though, only remembering when the bottle was halfway to his mouth. He stared at it for a moment trying to comprehend his misfortune, finally frowning and sticking the bottle back in his holster.

"I'm going to have to go shopping here shortly," Perzie warned his guest. "Now what was I talking about?"

"The morphine?" Zep offered in the form of a question, trying to be polite.

"Yes, the morphine. So, there I was in my Coronado bungalow, numb as a frostbitten toe, drifting in and out of stupor. Sometimes, I'd listen to records played on the Victrola I'd bought for two dollars from a fella in the tent city who didn't have enough room in his car to tote it back to Arizona. But music has a funny way of toying with one's emotions, so I had to be careful. The rest of the time I'd read magazines and newspapers. I bought them by the armful. My curiosity—my love of being alive—had not dissipated, which is important to note. It was only what I had done with my life that troubled me. So I ignored the past—with morphine and liquor—and dove deep into the present by reading, always reading.

"At this point—it was 1917 now—there was much being written about the war in Europe and I sat in my bungalow and drafted philosophical stances on the world's problems and solutions. My reality was becoming so isolated and altered that I truly began thinking I could solve the world. I'm not joking. My daydreams began feeling like real life, which created an altered state in which I would plan heroic deeds. In these drug induced fantasies I would fly to Europe and intervene with the world's leaders. Using my guile I would help them see the error of their misunderstanding and point out the foolishness of their posturing. Or I would hijack a small naval vessel and destroy German U-boats using crafty strategies that other mortals had not yet comprehended. And no matter the daydream, it always involved plenty of praise in the newspapers and women begging to gift their bodies to me. You're shaking your head in wonder, but I was going slightly mad between the ears in this little bungalow in California paradise."

"Sadly, I understand exactly what you are talking about," Zep conceded.

"Then you know that the tempest in your teacup becomes overwhelming. Not only that, I began to suffer from physical ailments. I had terrible constipation and my breathing was becoming difficult. I was forgetting to eat and losing tracking of time. A sense of doom was building and something deep in the back of my mind told me I needed to stop. So I resolved to quit morphine use and I did."

"Just like that?"

"Yep. It was three days of hell, I'll tell you. Especially the last two. I became agitated and then I was sweating profusely and my nose was running like a faucet. My body ached and my guts felt like they were being crushed. I began to vomit, and what food I could hold down went through me in no time. I desperately wanted to track my friend down and get more morphine, but I became so sick that even that became impossible. And here is the worst part: As it reached its miserable zenith I began to savor my punishment. Lying there on the floor in a ball, I felt like I was paying the price for my actions at the colony. It was the most pathetic moment of my life."

Perzie paused, unable to add anything further to such a sad admission, and Zep could only watch silently, sensing the sacredness of what he was hearing. He dared not comment.

"But I survived," continued Perzie, with a cavalier tone that suggested this story was over. "I just dedicated my life to drinking, instead. It's a much nobler form of self-destruction, and cheaper. It still takes a toll on the body, but not to the same extent."

"And what happened afterward...in Coronado?"

"Not much, really. I was still living off the money I made here with my paintings. Mostly I was drinking, wandering, reading. For sport I pursued the ladies, enjoying the rewards that often came with victory. I wasn't in it for love. I just enjoyed the challenge and the sweet smells. There is something about women that is the very essence of life distilled. All of its goodness and possibility packaged into a soft, breathing wisp of curiosity."

"And all of life's terror and suffering when she is displeased."

"Oh, lord, yes," agreed Perzie, "but at the time I wasn't involved long enough to earn any real scorn. I just wanted to pick the fruit and enjoy the sweetness. Some other jackass could water the tree and trim the branches. And besides, I still had love for another woman—sort of like you do for Mabel. The difference is that I had destroyed my future possibility with this woman. I hadn't destroyed my feelings for her, you understand, but I had ruined my chance to be part of her life."

"What was her name? Was she the one from the colony?"

"Julia, and yes she was. But as I was saying, the war came along. That is to say America became involved. I was a no-good drunk, but I was a loyal citizen, and even though I knew they'd laugh at me, I tried to enlist. Well, of course, they weren't going to take a fifty-two-year-old man with no military experience—one with more alcohol in him than blood. But I did land a position as a volunteer lookout, even if it was a pretty lame job.

"The whole north side of the island was used by the Navy as an air station. The place was crawling with military men who had better vision than me, but they claimed you could never have too many eyes scanning the waters for U-boats. So they scheduled a bunch of us rejects to take shifts walking the south beach, looking for suspicious movement. During the day wasn't bad, but at night everything seemed suspicious. Had a U-boat actually surfaced at night I'd have probably gone into a fright-induced coma. To make it worse, I tried to schedule my drinking so that it was heaviest right *after* a shift, which meant I was at my soberest—and thus jumpiest—when a shift started. So anyway, that was my contribution to the war effort. Basically, I rescheduled my drinking and stared at a bay that never received an enemy the entire war. It was a little more than a year after the war ended that I decided to return here, my hometown. That was early 1920, and I've been in this apartment taking up space ever since."

"Unbelievable," said Zep.

"What's unbelievable is that I've been talking this whole time with my bottle being empty," Perzie proclaimed. "I need to get out and find reinforcement. You're welcome to join me, if you'd like."

"Sure, I'll grab a little fresh air with you. I can't stay too long, though."

"Fair enough," agreed Perzie as he got up and moved toward the coat rack. "Am I to assume you will be visiting me regularly as you seek to save me from drink?"

"Until Addie gives up on you or until you've turned me back into a drunk."

Perzie laughed for a moment before his expression gave way to one of frustration. He was struggling with his coat. His left arm was fishing for the corresponding arm hole in his jacket without much luck. Zep almost made a move toward aiding his older, slightly inebriated host, but instinct held him back. It was bad form to assist another man unless there was imminent peril or a specific request. Both men were relieved when Perzie's arm finally slipped home.

"They used to make coats better," Perzie mumbled by way of explanation for his display.

"Isn't that the truth?" agreed Zep in dutiful support.

They moved into the hall and Perzie pulled the door shut without locking it.

14

When the train came to a stop at the Dellton station, Addie waited and watched from her seat. It wasn't long before Oscar could be seen outside, zigzagging through porters and passengers. He was walking more quickly than she expected, forcing her to throw on her coat and disembark in a rush. If she were to lose track of him she would have no chance at finding her painting.

She rushed into the little train station, anxious to spot Oscar, and in her haste she darn near ran into him. He had stopped to ask a railroad clerk for directions. The clerk had his arm extended toward town, pointing out the path Oscar should take. Oscar was so engrossed in listening he didn't see Addie throwing on the brakes out of the corner of his eye. She darted behind a wire swivel rack containing postcards, blocking a tourist who had been searching for the perfect card for her niece. The woman glared at Addie and waited, but Addie was too busy watching Oscar to notice she was being rude. Only when Oscar headed outside did Addie leave.

Away from the station, Addie quickly caught sight of Oscar, but now she had a new problem. The area immediately adjacent to the station was a quiet neighborhood made up of simple houses. It had been easy to hide from Oscar in all the hubbub of the train station, but now she had to stay hidden in plain view. This meant a much longer following distance, and it meant that every sound was magnified the deeper into the neighborhood they traveled. It didn't take Addie long to realize that her heels seemed very loud and she was forced to remove her shoes and carry them. Not only was the sidewalk cold, but now she looked conspicuous walking around in stockings and carrying shoes in the dead of winter. Well, as long as she remained unnoticed by Oscar that was all that mattered. Hopefully.

Oscar crossed over to the other sidewalk and at the next street he turned right. The street began with an incline and then crested before dropping out of sight. Unfamiliar with the area, Addie panicked when she could no longer see him beyond the crest and began running to catch up. She was glad she did because when she reached the top it was just in time to see Oscar turning left onto the first street below. Instinctively, she felt herself too exposed and jumped back just as he turned his head and looked back at where he had been. It was a close call and she waited an extra moment to be safe.

As she paused, Addie looked down at her feet and mourned the loss of her stockings. She was glad they were just a pair of cheap mercerized cotton stockings instead of her good silk ones, but still, that was another twenty-five cents expended on this adventure.

Addie peeked down the hill again and saw that Oscar was now gone. She gingerly ran down the sidewalk, needing to catch sight of him before he disappeared for good. Her momentum increased as she moved down the hill and she was moving at a healthy clip when she approached the corner Oscar had taken. This made it harder for her to stop, and boy did she need to stop. Apparently Oscar had taken a wrong turn and he was now headed back to the corner that Addie was nearing.

She had only a millisecond to change course, which she did, veering into the front lawn of somebody's house and hiding behind a big oak tree. Out of breath, she clung to the trunk, trying to become one with the tree. She could hear Oscar's footsteps as he retraced his steps along the sidewalk. He was only ten feet away when the steps stopped. Addie held her breath and waited, praying that she hadn't been spotted. She listened intently for feet moving across the grass, too afraid to risk exposure with even the slightest peek around the tree.

His steps began anew, but now there was a slightly different sound to them. It sounded like they were moving away from her. Ever so slowly, Addie poked her head around the trunk. With great relief she watched him crossing the street, the asphalt accounting for the different tone in his steps. Apparently he had turned left at the bottom of the hill when he should have turned right. Correct street, wrong direction.

Addie decided to stay behind the tree trunk as long as she could keep him in sight. That was when it dawned on her that she was hiding in front of a stranger's house. She turned and looked at the window directly behind her and nearly had a stroke when her gaze was met by another pair of eyes. Luckily the other eyes belonged to a fat, white cat sitting on the back of a couch. Addie offered a polite smile but the cat seemed to look back with contempt. *You don't have to be so mean about it,* she said telepathically.

She turned and looked back up the street just in time to see Oscar pause in front of a house. He consulted a paper in his hand before proceeding up the walkway toward the front door. He had found the place. Addie was both excited and alarmed. She wanted to run to the house and plead with the owner for a chance at the painting but knew she would look crazy, probably frightening the would-be seller. And Oscar almost certainly had more cash, she conceded once again.

The waiting game had begun and it was killing her. Continuing to stand in a stranger's front yard wasn't helping her nerves so she slowly moved onto the sidewalk and then a few steps into the street where she had a better view of the house Oscar had chosen. She hoped to memorize a feature or two of the house's exterior since she didn't have the actual address.

Much to Addie's surprise she spied Oscar still standing on the front porch. The front screen was pushed open and he was obviously talking to someone but he had not been invited inside. That was a good sign. Initially she had hoped nobody would be home but now she was hoping it was a maid or a child. Or maybe it was the owner, unwilling to admit they possessed the painting to such an obviously smarmy man like Oscar. Any of those scenarios might give her a fighting chance at *Number 17*.

And then it got better, yet. The screen door closed and Oscar turned and walked down the steps, along the walkway and back to the sidewalk. He had departed without the painting!

Addie barely had time to celebrate before noting that Oscar was walking back in her direction. Like a ballerina, she tiptoed across the lawn and back behind the tree trunk, her home away from home. She looked back at the cat, which continued to glower.

Oscar's footsteps echoed softly on the sidewalk and she guessed he was nearing the street. But something didn't sound right. She squinted and listened with all her might. It was an extra set of footsteps she was hearing! She turned her head toward the hill she had originally descended and caught sight of the interloper. It was the mailman. He was just three houses away. Two men were closing in from two directions as she stood barefoot hiding in a stranger's front yard.

She wasn't sure in which direction Oscar would go at the street, having made his visit, so she carefully peeked just in time to see him practically in front of her. He was walking down the same sidewalk he had retraced earlier. She jerked her head back and waited, watching the mailman who was now two houses away. One of them would spot her soon.

Oscar's footsteps stopped. So did Addie's heart. If he'd caught sight of the mailman and decided to get clarification on directions she was doomed. One of them would have a clear view of her as they walked toward each other. Oscar was apparently pondering as the mailman moved another house closer. Addie could wait no longer. She casually stepped away from the tree and walked quickly toward the opposite side of the street— toward the house from which Oscar had left empty-handed and away from where he now stood.

Her hope was that he wouldn't recognize her from the back, but to pull it off she needed to walk calmly and not look back. The last part was the hardest and she kept telling herself she would not look back until she had reached the house. *Please don't be suspicious of the woman walking barefoot in February,* she prayed.

When Addie arrived at the desired walkway, she turned and moved toward the porch. Just before reaching the steps she risked a glance down the street. Oscar was gone. So was the mailman. She breathed a sigh of relief.

But *now* she was standing on the porch of the home that potentially housed *Number 17*. Just like that, she had to change gears. She couldn't loiter, either. Whoever was home would have a bad impression of her if they happened to look out the window and see her just standing there. She knocked on the door and hoped inspiration would flood her brain.

The door swung open and there stood a woman in her thirties. A screen door separated them but Addie thought she noted a bemused look on the woman's face. She probably found it a bit interesting to receive two random visitors in the span of five minutes.

"Can I help you?" the woman asked nicely enough.

"Um, well, I'm sort of with the gentleman who was just here," Addie stammered. She was instantly mad at herself for such a dumb story.

The woman looked a little puzzled but she maintained a happy face, silently waiting for Addie to continue.

"Anyhow, we're sort of working on a project together and I didn't get a chance to talk to him yet and hoped maybe you would be kind enough to repeat the information you just gave him—about the painting."

She threw the idea of the painting in at the end as a bluff to see if the woman would deny or confirm it. In reality, up until now Addie had not been certain whether Oscar really was chasing the painting or whether he was merely conducting innocent business.

"Well, I was just telling him that the woman he is looking for doesn't live here anymore," the woman explained. "She actually died a few months ago, bless her heart. My husband and I had no idea when we bought the house, not that it makes any difference. It's just kind of sad."

"It really is," agreed Addie. "It really is."

Addie waited a respectful second in honor of the departed before she got back to business.

"So, this poor woman, what was her name?"

"Like I told your, um, friend, I only know that her first name was Minnie. A neighbor told me. I guess they had known each other a long time. It's just so sad."

"So sad, you're right. As for my, uh, coworker, do you know where he was headed next? I was supposed to meet up with him but got a little lost."

"He wanted to know more about Minnie, like what happened to a painting she'd owned. I told him maybe he could check at the courthouse and they'd have a record of next of kin. It's down that way."

The woman swung the screen open and stepped onto the porch where she pointed past Addie's tree to the west.

"Keep going that direction and you run into the business district," the woman offered. "The courthouse is just a couple blocks up and it's real obvious."

As this was being explained, Addie was trying to figure out a new plan. Following Oscar was too impractical, and besides, she needed a method for beating him to the next crucial bit of information, not joining him. That's when an interesting thought occurred to her.

"Say, you wouldn't happen to remember the name of the person who sold you this house, would you?" Addie asked. "You know, the realty person?"

The woman laughed at the question

"Believe me, he is not a man one would ever forget. His name is Max Mast and he is beyond colorful. Were you thinking of asking him about the previous owner? That might not be a bad idea."

"Exactly what I was thinking, yes. Know where I might find him?"

"Well, he has an office downtown, but from experience I know he often eats lunch with his widowed mother. She lives one street farther down the hill. Go back the way you came, take a right then a right on Aspen Street. It's about five houses down with pink roses all along the front of the house. No guarantee he's there, but if he is, he won't mind. He's crazy about his job."

"Great! Thank you so much."

Addie turned and gleefully descended the steps. While Oscar was busy working his way through the machinery of local government, she hoped to get the next of kin's name much quicker through Max Mast.

The race was on!

15

As Addie's pace increased in Dellton, Zep's pace was getting sluggish in Stout City.

Following his initial visit to Perzie's apartment, the two men had continued their meeting on foot as Perzie ran his daily errands.

The old painter stopped at the newsstand and purchased several magazines and newspapers (including *Le Petit Parisien,* even though he knew very little French). Then he stopped by the Greek restaurant and bought two bottles of ouzo. After that, the boys decided maybe they'd eat lunch together. Neither had any urgent matters to attend to that afternoon and both were enjoying the company.

Being men—meaning they had low standards and gravitated toward the path of least resistance—they ended up in the Bonus Basement. The joint was close, cheap, and...well, it was close and cheap.

Since they were eating at the scene of Addie's egregious intoxication, a discussion of the episode was renewed. At first, Zep had only meant to chide Perzie a little in defense of Addie. But Perzie defended himself saying it had all been in fun and she could have quit at any time. "Yes, but you must remember, not many people can handle liquor like you can," Zep reminded the painter, "and then they become disoriented and don't make proper decisions."

Perzie knew he had done wrong by Addie and he admitted it. But once again, he couldn't resist some fun. So, Perzie conceded to Zep that "anyone could have been incapacitated by that type of imbibing, even a supposed real drinker like yourself."

"Supposed?" asked an insulted Zep.

"Well, I just met you today when you came barging into my flat. For all I know your drinking problem consisted of a little extra sherry while you were cooking for your girlfriend."

"I drank a lot more than that. You can ask my bootleg connection. I'm sure I paid for his last vacation home."

"I'd let you prove you could handle a shot of gin if I didn't think your girlfriend would find out and scold you for getting a bit tipsy."

Zep laughed.

"You think you're going to get me tight like Addie, don't you?" Zep teased. "That's your game, to draw people into your world so you feel less bad about yourself. Well, I've been in your world and I know how it works."

"Yes, you're probably right about me. There is some psychological reason why I try to disrupt others. Then again, I'm out of practice being social. You two are my first friendly visitors in years. Maybe drinking is just a shorthand method for relating to people after years of self-confinement."

"Or you're just trying a different angle on me."

"Have a shot with me and I won't have to try angles. Coming up with these tricks is work for me too, you know."

Both men laughed.

***

Two hours later, they returned to Perzie's apartment, drunk as skunks. Perzie had enjoyed a head start, drinking for breakfast, but Zep had abstained for a while, so his tolerance was down. The result was that they reached the perfect pitch of drunkenness at the same time—that spot where everything is funny, duties are easily dismissed and poor choices make sense. For some, this spot in the drunken arc includes singing and overly loud laughter, but Zep and Perzie were old pros. They could hang around the edge of sloppy for hours without going over.

Today, however, they were pushing the bounds. There was a synergetic euphoria resulting from two loners downing drinks together. Their buzzes, usually self-contained, were now feeding off of one another. The height—or depth—of this phenomenon was reached immediately after they returned to the apartment.

Because they had finished their binge at the speakeasy with a slew of beers, both men were in desperate need of a bathroom by the time they reached Perzie's place. Sadly, he possessed only one such room and with Zep being the guest it was agreed he had first right of usage.

There are few things in life that feel better than genuine relief, and Zep was enjoying this newfound bliss as he exited the bathroom and wandered into the living room. His joy was short lived, however.

Standing in front of the open living room window was Armstrong Perzie, the famous painter of yesteryear. The great artist was creating his own relief at the expense of an unsuspecting world three stories below.

For just a moment, Zep felt a wave of sobriety rush through his veins. He wanted to halt what was an obvious breach of etiquette—if not law—but it was too late. What had started could not be stopped. Furthermore, by saying something, Zep would have only startled the painter, which in turn might have caused more problems than it fixed. So, Zep stood, his mouth hanging half-open as he watched this tragedy unfold. He wanted to look away, he really did, but the shock was too great.

That the old man had such a mischievous grin on his face made the whole sordid act even worse. And oddly enough, the grin only broadened when someone hollered from the alley below.

"How would you like me to come up there and stick my boot where the sun don't shine?" an angry voice bellowed upward.

"Try it, you wet little weasel," Perzie yelled back with full drunken boastfulness.

Zep's eyes darted back and forth as he listened intently. When no reply was heard he relaxed a bit, even chuckling at the absurdity of the whole thing as Perzie finished with his zipper and took a seat. Hearing Zep laugh, he began to laugh along. Soon they were beside themselves with tears in the corners of their eyes.

Then they heard steps on the stairwell.

They were loud, quick, angry steps and they were getting closer. Both men stopped laughing and looked at each other with alarm. There was no boast now, just the pending price for too much alcohol.

The footsteps reached the hall and paused. The recipient was trying to determine exactly which apartment contained the rogue sprinkler. The winding staircase had disoriented him and he was no longer sure which apartment faced which direction. He could be heard taking a few steps in each direction trying to find a clue, maybe a voice or a shadow moving under a door.

Zep glared at Perzie to convey the seriousness of their dilemma and he held a finger to his lips to indicate the importance of silence. Perzie nodded his head like a boy in trouble.

"Why don't you come out here and settle this like a man?" the fella in the hall finally uttered for all to hear. "You think you're funny but I'll show you funny."

When men are angry, they often declare nonsensical things, thinking they sound valid if spoken with enough threat. This was such a case.

"Afraid, are you?" the man challenged after hearing no answer. "Afraid somebody will show you what a joke really looks like?"

Zep and Perzie continued to look at each other, bug-eyed with concern.

"If I ever catch you letting loose again I'll be back here to rearrange your face," the angry man threatened in closing. A moment later, footsteps pounded down the staircase. It was soon followed by the sound of doors opening along the hallway as various tenants determined it was now safe to assess what had just happened. But seeing nothing, they closed their doors one by one.

The frightful episode had effectively ruined Zep and Perzie's pitch-perfect buzz. It sent them straight to the other side of the drinking arc: drowsy silence.

It was just as well. Neither man wanted to discuss the window incident after handling the threat to their manhood with cowardly hiding. Had they used their combined force to beat or chase the damp man, they'd have rehashed the conquest for an hour. Bragging was the spoils of victory. Cowardly silence, on the other hand, was treated with more cowardly silence.

After a couple awkward minutes, a small discussion about lunch was introduced and both men gave it a half-hearted attempt, but it had no legs and died quietly.

Desperate to regain what they had lost, Perzie introduced one of the fresh bottles of ouzo he had picked up during their outing. Zep knew he should decline but instead surrendered to finishing what he'd started.

They took turns with the bottle, each time wiping the opening with their shirtsleeves. In the case of Perzie's shirt, it was likely that such "cleaning" only worsened the sanitary conditions.

They plugged along, determined to regain some jocularity. What they encountered instead was the side effect that has tripped many a man in the throes of drink:

honest, heartfelt emotion. It can seep out without warning, and it did.

"I really miss Mabel," Zep declared glumly without any prompting.

"I bet," Perzie agreed with equal sullenness.

"I'm serious. Right now I feel kinda sad and ashamed, if you want the truth. I need her to take care of me. I hate to admit it, but it's true."

"No shame in that," Perzie agreed.

"Well, a little shame," Zep countered. "I should be able to do better on my own, instead of moping about life and getting drunk every time I don't know what else to do."

Perzie was too tired to guess whether to help or argue so he just nodded solemnly. Then he took a big swig. Liquor always filled the silence that nothing else could.

"What about you?" Zep finally asked. "Whatever happened to that wife you loved so much?"

"I told you, something occurred. It killed us and it's done."

"What do you mean killed? Unless you really killed someone there is always a way to fix things. And even if you did actually kill someone, well..."

"I didn't kill anyone, exactly. Some things just happened. You wouldn't understand unless I told you the whole story and I'm not gonna."

"Now you're saying *things* happened. Plural. *Things*. What could these things be that are so bad?"

"Do you always ask so many questions when you drink? Let's talk about something else. You like baseball?"

"Followed it all my life," Zep answered. "Having grown up here I've always been a big fan of the Stout City Rakes."

"Me too, for the same reason. Hell, I was attendin' Rakes games before you were born. Ever heard of Elmer Auzen?"

"Of course I've heard of Auzen. Supposedly the best pitcher that ever lived."

"Well, I saw him pitch when I was a kid. Several times. He threw so hard that you sat on the edge of your seat fascinated by the blur. Boy, would that pill pop into the catcher's mitt. You could hear it echo in the stadium. Pop!"

"That would have been something to see," Zep agreed in wonder.

"I still listen to all their games on the radio there," Perzie said, motioning toward a console in the corner. "Every afternoon. And when they aren't on I listen to the Cubs or Cardinals. Can't really pick up the White Sox games too well. Too much interference or a weak signal or something. But anyhow, baseball is what keeps me sane. The winters are tough, but when spring rolls around I'm saved again."

Zep nodded but he hadn't been listening closely and Perzie could tell.

"You're still thinkin' about Mabel, aren't you?"

"I can't help it, Armstrong. She really is perfect for me and I'd do anything to have her squeezed up beside me right now."

"You could snuggle up to me," Perzie offered before the two men burst into laughter.

They had survived the side effect of heartfelt emotion and now the ouzo reinforcements were kicking in, moving them back along the arc toward jocularity.

And somewhere a few blocks away, an angry man tried to explain his damp condition to a horrified wife.

And many miles northwest in Dellton, the race for *Number 17* was in full swing.

16

Upon finding Max Mast at his mother's house, Addie was invited inside like a family member. Momma Mast, horrified to see a young girl in stocking feet, insisted she sit and eat some soup while wearing a spare pair of slippers.

When they heard Addie's story they were beside themselves with excitement. Such drama falling into their laps without warning? It was a marvel straight from the heavens. They were only too glad to help a sweet young woman trying to find her dying grandma's favorite painting.

"So, do you know much about this Minnie who used to own the house?" Addie asked between spoonfuls of vegetable noodle soup.

Max rolled his eyes, all with a great big smile.

"I have been buying and selling residences in this town since I was nineteen years old," he declared, "and I can tell you the details on every one of them."

"It's true," swore Momma. "Pick an address and see if he doesn't know all about it."

"I...I don't really know this town..." Addie stuttered.

"All right, I'll choose one," Momma decided. "Um, how about 3767 Franklin Street?"

"Nice try," Max grinned. "There is no such number on Franklin. I'll tell you about 3762 Franklin, though."

"Actually," Addie tried to interject. "I was hoping..."

"Tell her about that one," Momma interrupted with proud anticipation.

"That particular house is owned by Chet and Jeannette Pederson—don't you just love to say that, Chet and Jeannette? Anyhow, they bought it from the Ralinfords for $2,800 in 1927. He'd been transferred by the railroad. Nice, nice couple. The house is 1,600 square feet upstairs with an 820-foot basement. There is actually more space down there including closets and whatnot, but you know, 820 feet of useable space. The home has three bedrooms and a bath, plus a bonus room that could be used as a guest room or a sewing room or an opium den, I suppose."

Momma and Max giggled, leaving Addie to fake a confused chuckle.

"No, seriously," he continued. "It is a nice house. It used to be green with white trim but Mrs. Pederson hates green so now its robin's egg blue with a yellow trim that looks like butter mixed with sunshine. Really love it. Oh, and the architect who originally designed the house was...um...gosh darn it, I can't remember his name."

Momma's eyebrows furrowed with concern as Max battled his memory bank.

"Delvin Scott Richards!" he finally blurted. "I always want to confuse him with Richard Dover Stinson, but it was Richards who created that house."

Momma's face relaxed as her son successfully proved his extraordinary memory once again. Ever since he was a little boy he had exhibited a mind capable of wonderful and inexplicable things. Not only that, but he had always been such a cheerful person. She had always been so proud, unable to ask for more from her only son—except maybe a daughter-in-law and kids, but that could wait a tad longer. He was thirty-seven and still in the prime of a busy career.

"Your memory is mind-boggling," confessed Addie, "but I have to be honest, time is of the essence and I need some information as soon as possible."

"Of course you do!" seconded Max. "So let's get down to it. That house was owned by Minnie Upton. She was never married, but had one son..."

"It was a tough situation," Momma explained in a lowered voice. "A fella that worked for the railroad came through here and made a lot of promises. Minnie never regretted it for a moment. She adored her boy."

"So, anyhow, Minnie died suddenly last year," continued Max. "She was seventy-four years old but looked grand for her age. No health issues that anyone knew about."

"None," confirmed Momma.

"And then she was gone just like that," he said with a snap of his fingers. "Thank goodness she left a will. Some people don't, you know?"

"Always a shame," Addie agreed dolefully, even though she had never once considered the idea of making out a will.

"Everything went through her attorney who was the trustee," continued Max. "He and I have a long professional relationship and he had me sell the house and turn over the proceeds to the estate. The money and nearly all of the possessions went to her son, Victor, or Vic, as he has always been known. Last I heard, he lived in one of the Dakotas or some such place. Anyhow, I don't know any more details than that since I wasn't the trustee. That was her attorney, Lloyd Bigelow. He is the man you really ought to see in connection with that painting. He'd know exactly where it went, though I'd expect Vic has it."

"Definitely," concurred Addie. "That sounds like the man I should visit. Where might he be located?"

"He should be in his office," Max informed her while arising from the table. "Let me just call him real fast and make sure, though. If he's there, I'll run you down there myself."

"That's so kind of you," said Addie sincerely.

"And please wear something on your feet," Momma Mast implored. "You can even use those slippers if your regular shoes aren't working out. Might look peculiar, but better to have warm feet than worry what a bunch of others think."

"That is so sweet. Maybe I will just borrow them. My feet aren't quite thawed yet."

"Don't be ridiculous. Keep 'em. I have plenty of slippers. Max takes me down to Stout City four times a year and I can always get whatever I need there."

Max, who had been talking on the kitchen wall phone, hung up the mouthpiece and announced that Lloyd Bigelow was in his office and would be glad to see Addie. Max was as excited as if he were the art hunter himself.

He clapped to signify an exciting new urgency, kissed his mom on the cheek and helped Addie into her coat. The two women hugged and promised to see each other soon. A kindly debate was reignited regarding the future ownership of the slippers and it was once again decided that Addie should keep them. Parting cries of "thanks" and "good luck" rang out as Max hustled Addie through the front door toward his car in the driveway.

She hoped Oscar hadn't made any headway. What if he were also directed to the attorney's office?

17

Max Mast seemed to keep forgetting that Addie was in a hurry to get to the attorney's office. He drove slowly through the residential streets of Dellton, pointing out houses he had sold and telling stories involving small town minutia. It was hard for Addie to be upset with him because he was such a genuine, likable man. Any other time, and she'd have gotten a kick from listening to the absurd things he found fascinating. But today she was on a mission. She was chasing a painting that seemed to slip further from her grasp the closer she got to it.

As Max told the story of the McCoreys' special fenced-in front yard (three-year-old Paul had a habit of biting people), Addie was trying to figure her strategy should she cross paths with Oscar.

To this point, she had been able to explain Oscar as a husband or a coworker whom she had just missed. But what if they met at the attorney's office? The gloves would be off and the overt competition for the painting would be on. Addie would stick to her story of needing the artwork for sentimental family reasons and Oscar would probably...what would Oscar do? He certainly had more money and could outbid her for information leading to the painting, as well as for the painting itself. Then again, Oscar had no true idea of the painting's value or he wouldn't have resold it. He was operating on a hunch based on their pawnshop conversation, and now he was hoping to get it back on the cheap before Addie could throw her sad story in the ring.

There was also the possibility, if confronted by Addie, that he would simply lie and say he was chasing the painting down for her. That was highly unlikely, however, since he'd gone to the trouble of giving her a phony address. No, this was a pure battle for *Number 17*, and it really came down to who could get Vic's phone number first.

"See that dog over there?" he asked, his arm pointing straight past Addie's face. "The one with the shiny black coat? That's Waldo, although technically he has some long, official name registered with the Kennel Association. I believe he's a Turkish sheep hound. Anyhow, he is an actual show dog, no kidding. He made it to the regional finals in Gibbsville last year and took second in his breed."

"Good for him," offered Addie mechanically. "Who won?"

"The dog who didn't break loose from his handler and chase a female miniature Klietzer named Party Favor."

Max laughed so hard at his own joke that he nearly brought the car to a halt. Addie smiled and stared ahead, hoping she could subliminally influence him to get moving. *Please,* she begged in her head, *take me straight to the office.*

And it worked. For almost three blocks. That's when he noticed multiple newspapers on the porch of the Tensons.

"I wonder if they are on vacation. I don't recall them ever going in February, though. Maybe we should put those behind the planter on their porch."

Addie wrung her hands with impatience. She'd have gotten there faster walking in her new, used slippers.

18

Oscar sat and waited, trying not to fume. After a lifetime of surviving the hustle and bustle of a metropolis like Stout City, he was unprepared for the ways of Dellton.

It had been charming at first when he'd entered the courthouse building. He was directed to the Records Office by an ancient security guard who was so frail that his holstered pistol threatened to topple him. Oscar doubted the guard had actually fired a shot since Gettysburg.

Down the hallway, which squeaked softly under his feet, Oscar found the Records Office and entered. He was amused to find only one other customer being served. In Stout City such an office would resemble Ellis Island on arrival day. Also notably different was the number of clerks helping. There was just one. Oscar contemptuously eyed the two empty counter spots with signs that said, "See other clerk." Resigned to fate but glad he was next, Oscar took his place in line.

From what he could gather through eavesdropping, the old fella being helped was a homeowner trying to resolve a dispute with his neighbor regarding property lines. Apparently he'd been sent to Property, and they sent him to Civil Engineering, who, in turn, had sent him to Records. It seemed that the deed with the original property dimensions went back several owners, which sent this case into lengthy historical mode.

Because he had no idea Addie was in town, Oscar was maintaining patience, but this was tested as he heard more. Details emerged regarding the genesis of this neighborly dispute and to Oscar's dismay he learned that six inches of ground were at issue. And furthermore, these six inches were of importance because they would determine the fate of a honeysuckle bush. Madge, the fella's wife, had planted it when their second child was born. This was all well and good for forty-three years until one of the bees attracted to this bush went rogue and stung Stella, the wife next door. Her arm "swole up like a grilled weiner," the old customer admitted to the clerk, but "geez Louise, one bee sting every forty-three years ain't the end of the world." Stella, however, had taken the hard-line tactic of insisting that the ground which housed the bee bush actually resided on their property, and they intended to remove said weed. "Not before I get proof from City Hall," Madge's husband had warned, and here he was.

A Stout City clerk would have chased the man away from her counter, threatening a hefty fine from the fictitious Garden and Wildlife officers for wasting her time. In Dellton, however, where a clerk had an eighty-three percent chance of somehow being related to the inquirer, such small matters were dealt with seriously.

Not wanting to create bad will with the clerk who would be assisting him, Oscar decided it best to take a seat away from the fray. After signaling his intentions to the clerk—not wanting his place in line to go unnoticed in case another relative arrived—Oscar received a nod from the clerk and sat in one of the five wooden chairs along the back wall.

The dispute at the counter dragged on for another ten minutes as documents—each one older than the last—continued to support Stella's belief regarding the property lines. Finally, some additional paperwork was found based on realignment following the French and Indian War in 1763. It appeared that a number had been transposed, giving the fella the upper hand. He slapped the counter triumphantly, thanked the clerk profusely and left to confront Stella.

Relieved beyond measure, Oscar claimed his rightful spot at the counter. He explained his desperate need to track down a painting that meant the world to his family. Grandma was dying and it would lift her spirits.

The clerk was very sympathetic and even took the time to tell a long story about how her grandmother had passed away. This death she described was sudden and involved no painting, but she seemed to believe there was enough relevance to keep talking without a breath.

At least Oscar had appealed to her emotional side and he calmly awaited the fruits of his auditory suffering. Unfortunately, she informed him after wrapping up her tale, Oscar needed a next-of-kin record and that was only available in the Probate Office. The good news, however, was that this office was only two doors down.

Worn but progressing, Oscar exited Records and found the door for Probate. Sadly, it was locked. Hanging from the door was a sign with a little pretend clock whose hands promised the office would reopen after lunch at twelve thirty.

Oscar could hardly comprehend the awful truth. In Stout City the only thing that closed for lunch was breakfast.

Despite the setback, he had to admit this beat another day in the shop, so he calmly walked outside, past the guard doing the crossword puzzle, and took a seat on the steps of the Dellton Courthouse. He squinted against the cloudy sunshine and marveled at the lack of activity around him. The only sound to be heard was the heavy cloth of the American flag buffeted by the breeze. He was a pawnbroker trapped on another planet. Did this place even have pimps and musicians?

If so, they were undoubtedly at lunch.

19

When they finally arrived at the attorney's office, Max insisted on escorting Addie inside. After all, the Realtor and the lawyer were old friends. But more importantly this was too exciting for Max to miss.

They walked up the stairs of the town's one and only professional building. When they reached the second floor landing a door on the right opened and an elderly man emerged, stooped over and moving slowly.

"Lunchtime, Dr. Heston?" queried Max.

The doctor mumbled something without looking up or stopping.

"That's his office," Max explained to Addie. "We had a second doctor—a much younger one that came here from Ohio—but he just retired."

Normally Addie would have had many questions regarding the health and welfare of Dellton, but right now she was focused on the lawyer. His door was on the left, sporting a nameplate which said: Lloyd C. Bigelow, Attorney at Law.

Max knocked on the door while simultaneously entering. Small-town protocol. A thin, middle-aged man rose from his desk chair with a big smile and greeted his guests.

"I was wondering if you two were actually coming," he chided half-jokingly.

"Sorry about that," Max apologized. "Addie was curious to see a little of the town on the way in."

Addie smiled politely, but with long-suffering eyes which Lloyd understood.

"Well, it's a beautiful day," Lloyd reasoned. "Might as well enjoy your visit to Dellton—I did hear you're from Stout City, right?"

"That's right," Max answered for her, feeling compelled since he had provided the information during their phone conversation.

"So, according to Max you are here in search of a painting...um, please have a seat."

The three of them sat down in unison. Both men smiled at Addie and waited.

"Yes, my family has sent me. The painting in question means a great deal to us, and it was lost under some unfortunate circumstances. With my grandma so sick—dying, possibly—it's become an urgent matter...my finding the painting, that is."

"I'm terribly sorry to hear about your grandmother. I know just how that feels."

"Thank you," responded Addie in a sorrowful tone befitting the story.

"What is her name?" Max wondered randomly.

"My grandma's name?"

"Yes, unless her real name is Grandma," he answered, much to his own amusement.

Addie and Lloyd exchanged a good-natured look and chuckled softly.

"Her given name is Mary. She's the last of her brothers and sisters."

Addie frowned to herself. She wasn't sure why she felt compelled to add the extra lie. It just seemed needed after she was challenged about the name, even if it was Max just being Max.

"I really appreciate your problem, Miss Sumner, I really do," continued Bigelow, "but I need to ask a couple more questions so that I can assess the situation for my client. As you can understand, I have a duty to him first, although I look forward to helping you if I can."

"We understand. Makes total sense," Max agreed for all involved.

"Now, Miss Sumner, is it your family's intention to try and purchase this painting or were you seeking to maybe borrow it?"

"Um, well, I'd have to say purchase. It has strong sentimental value. My grandparents purchased it on their anniversary vacation. The true value of the painting is minimal based on the few dollars they paid for it."

"Of course, and I wasn't trying to insinuate a motive toward profit. I'm late to this story and I'm just trying to see the big picture."

Max laughed and clapped at the unintended pun, momentarily confusing the other two.

"How did this painting become disowned?" Lloyd continued.

"My cousin, bless her heart, needed some money for a family emergency and sold any items she thought might have value. She got very little but her child was saved, thankfully. She was too embarrassed to say anything about the painting for months."

"What a shame," Lloyd acknowledged. "Well, anyhow, let's see if your painting is even part of Minnie's estate, shall we? I have a final reckoning of her belongings here which I pulled from the file after Max called. How would you describe this painting?"

"This is always where it gets difficult," Addie confessed with a light laugh. "Basically, this painting has no particular subject. It's more of an abstract thing made up of lots of colors. Think Monet, but wilder, less distinct. Very unlike my grandparents, really. That must have been some vacation."

"Good for them," Max interjected with a slightly devilish expression.

Addie watched as Lloyd pored over the stapled paperwork in front of him. His head scanned back and forth ever so slightly as he read the top sheet. Not finding an answer, he flipped that page and held it upright while he scanned the second page. It was a long silence, and while Max looked around the office Addie tried to casually read the first page which Lloyd held upright. It was difficult to decipher because it was small print and it was upside down.

"Minnie accumulated a great many small possessions in her lifetime," offered Lloyd as an explanation for the long silence. "And art was her favorite vice so there are dozens of items listed: figurines, vases, paintings and so on."

He said this without looking up from behind the first page, which he still held upright. Emboldened by his perceived concentration, Addie squinted at the writing. Then, she pretended to fix her slipper, thereby giving her an excuse to lean closer and to crane her head at the upside down writing.

"Your feet warmed up yet?" Max whispered.

"Oh yes, much, much better. Just have a little itch."

"Need a ruler or something? I have a pencil you can use."

"No, that's quite all right, I got it. Thank you," she said.

Lloyd flipped over a second page and slowly his hand let the two pages wilt to the desk.

"Hmmm," he moaned to signify his perplexity. "I don't see a specific piece listed like the one you want, however at the end there is a line item that says: 'Paintings (4), unspecified.' Did yours have a title or an artist's name or any sort of specific marking?"

"Nope. It wasn't even signed."

"Not signed? That's unusual."

"Hence my belief that it holds little value monetarily."

"Unless the artist signed it in a clever way," Max added. "I've heard of painters that make their name tiny, or blend it in to the paint or incorporate it into the subject, like a clown's collar."

"I'm sure her family would know," Lloyd explained.

"Yeah, we've studied it over the years," Addie confirmed. "It was a cherished item."

"Well, listen," Lloyd calmly offered, "with this painting being so hard to describe and having no subject or unique markings, it might make sense that it would be listed as 'unspecified,' *if* she had it."

"That's a good point," Max agreed, nodding at Addie to reassure her.

Lloyd leaned back in his chair and pondered the possibilities.

"Do you know for certain that Minnie would have had that painting?" he asked.

"I have a very strong reason to believe so," Addie answered. She hated sounding vague but really didn't want to introduce Oscar into this equation.

"Tell you what, let me give Vic a phone call and see if he has what you're looking for," Lloyd decided. "I'm not in the habit of spending for long distance calls, but this sounds like a worthy cause. And here you thought attorneys were heartless."

Addie and Max chuckled softly but neither bothered to dispute his claim.

"Keep in mind he has every right to retain possession of it," Lloyd added, "and I will not be party to any pressuring. If he has it, I'll tell him your story and then it's up to him. Should he want it, he keeps it. End of story and I'm very sorry for your grandma. Sound fair enough?"

Addie nodded, trying to look sad but brave. She needed to inspire Lloyd on her behalf if he was doing the pitching.

"I'm crossing my fingers, Addie," promised Max.

Lloyd pulled an address book from his desk, found the right page and studied it as he dialed the phone.

"What is the primary color used in the painting, so I can describe it?" he asked while waiting for the long distance connection.

"Um, I believe purple, or maybe red. Primary is hard because he used so many in abundance," she explained, having never seen it.

"Sure, sure. Sounds like maybe it one of those deals where a person would know it when they saw it."

"Exactly, that's..."

Lloyd held up a hand to indicate he had a connection.

"It's ringing," he half-mouthed, half-whispered.

Silently, Max showed Addie that he had crossed his fingers on both hands. Addie acknowledged his sweetness with a smile before fussing with her skirt and staring intently at Lloyd. It seemed to take forever. Then, just when they couldn't stand it anymore, Lloyd hung up the phone. The handset made a sad click as it returned to the phone's cradle.

"No answer," Lloyd declared matter-of-factly. "I'm sure Vic is at work and I don't know about his wife Gladys. Could be running errands, could be at her sister's who lives a little out in the country. Matter of fact, last time I talked to Vic—oh, about three weeks ago—he said something about his sister-in-law expecting a baby any time."

Addie exhaled dramatically and Max gave her an empathetic sad face.

"All right, here's the plan," said Lloyd with renewed optimism. "I'll try back later. Unless he has to work a little extra, Vic should be home about suppertime. If and when I get an answer, I will contact you immediately. Could be today, could be tomorrow. I have an engagement later, but will try again from home if I need to. Not sure how you want to handle that, but it's the best I can do."

"And don't think I don't appreciate it," Addie assured him.

She looked at Lloyd and Max without really seeing them as she considered her options. She could wait around, but it wouldn't help anything. If Vic had the painting and was agreeable to selling it, she could arrange for its delivery as easily in Stout City as she could in Dellton. And if he refused, well, she couldn't change his mind here. She'd just have to regroup and decide whether to pester him more later or whether to focus on getting Perzie to create new paintings.

The thing that still troubled her was Oscar. If he had gotten Vic's number through the courthouse, she could only hope Lloyd got hold of Vic first. And what if Oscar's hunt led him from the courthouse to this office? Well, that was just a chance she'd have to take. There was no good way to warn the attorney or explain away Oscar. She would just have to hope that Oscar followed a cold trail or gave up. After all, Addie wondered, how far was he willing to pursue this painting on just a hunch that it held value? Not very far, she figured. Either way, there was nothing more to do about him.

"I think maybe I'll just head back to the city," Addie announced. "When is the next train?"

Lloyd looked at his watch, but Max already had an answer.

"The 2:05 is direct. If you wait until the 3:40 it stops for mail twice on the way down."

That made the decision easy, but it didn't leave much time.

Addie wrote down her contact information, then stood up and handed it to Lloyd before shaking hands with him.

"Please make Vic understand what that painting means," she implored one more time. "I will pay a fair price for it and arrange all the details for delivery. I'll even find him a replacement painting with no subject."

Max laughed at her joke.

"Don't worry, Miss Sumner, I'll be in touch soon. And between you and me, I don't see a real problem in you getting that painting, though you never heard me say that. Vic is a good fella. It's just a matter of him having it or not."

Addie and Max smiled the smile of great relief. They bade the attorney goodbye and hustled out to Max's car.

"We better get you to the station, pronto," he announced while backing out of the parking space. "And I know just the route. You ever seen a pygmy oak tree?"

Addie got to see a pygmy oak and she still made the 2:05. It had all worked out.

Except for the part where Oscar showed up at Bigelow's office at 2:20.

20

Although Addie was aboard an express train from Dellton to Stout City, there was actually one stop made just inside Stout City's northern limits at the Kelsipher station. It was a quick stop similar to one a trolley would make; passengers got on and off but no luggage or goods were transferred. The railroad had figured out that because they got downtown twenty minutes faster than the trolley with its many stops, enough people would pay twenty cents extra to take the train.

As a couple dozen passengers scrambled on at Kelsipher, Addie decided on a whim to get off. There was a task she had been avoiding and this afternoon she would cross it off the list. She was going to see her parents.

Addie had grown up in Kelsipher and her parents still lived there. They had been begging her to come visit, but she had been stalling for weeks, not wanting to have the tedious "out-of-work" conversation. They meant well, but it was discouraging. So, even though she loved and missed them...

After disembarking she stopped by the station's telegram booth and had a message sent to Zep. In it, she suggested they meet the next morning at the Bonus Café where they could compare notes from their visits and readjust plans. That done, she exited the station and enjoyed a leisurely walk to her old home, half a mile away.

A smile crept over her face when she arrived. Except for a plant here and a bush there, the place had hardly changed in recent years. Her parents had purchased the house when Addie was a toddler. At the time, their home was part of a brand new subdivision catering to those somewhere between upper poverty and lower middle-class. It was built to alleviate a housing crush in Stout City, the result of a huge industrial expansion. The suburb was named Kelsipher in honor of the billionaire who was kind enough to profit immensely from its development.

At the time, Addie's father, Walter Sumner, was a young engineer beginning his career at Stoutco Petroleum. Twenty-five years later, he had risen to a supervisor position within the Secondary Distillation Department. And during those intervening years not much had changed at the Sumner household. There was a younger son, Gary, who had arrived seventeen months after another baby boy was delivered stillborn to Maggie Sumner. The flowered wallpaper in the dining room had been replaced by yellow paint, which necessitated the purchase of a new table and chairs. Five different cars had come and gone, none of them particularly noteworthy. And Hatter, the spaniel Addie had begged for and received when she was seven, was now buried in the backyard under an elm tree.

Addie entered the house using her spare key and hung up her coat on the peg above the one she had used as a child. Growing up she had never noticed that the house had a certain smell, but now when she visited it was unmistakable. It wasn't good or bad, it just was. As she left the entry and moved toward the kitchen another smell became evident: lasagna.

"Hon-eeey," Maggie Sumner cooed upon seeing her daughter enter the kitchen. They hugged and then separated enough to inspect each other.

"I'm surprised you aren't thinner after being out of work," Maggie declared, dealing her daughter a sweet-sounding double blow as only a mother can do.

"Yes, well, I still manage to eat," Addie explained sarcastically, "and the pounds don't magically disappear like they used to."

"Well, you look beautiful and that's all that matters," Mom declared, reversing course. She had hinted at the few extra pounds because as a mother it was her duty to ensure her child wasn't ignorant of a potential problem. On the other hand, it was also a mother's duty to instill confidence in her offspring, facts be damned. As a teenager, Addie might have challenged the last statement ("You only say I'm pretty because you're my mom"), but nowadays she just changed the subject.

"So, where is Dad?" Addie inquired.

"In the living room, working on the vacuum cleaner," Maggie said with a shake of her head as they headed in that direction. "He was supposed to help me get everything tidy—I was running behind after an appointment with Dr. Wells today. Nothing serious but he thinks maybe I need more Vitamin D. I've been so tired lately and I'm hoping this is the simple fix. So, anyway, he was vacuuming and heard a funny sound— the same one I've been telling him about for two months—and you know him, he stopped vacuuming and started tinkering, so ignore the carpet if it looks..."

"Addie!" cried her father as soon as she entered the living room. He rose to his feet and gave her a hug and a kiss on the cheek, his arm outstretched so he didn't accidentally stab her with the screwdriver he was clutching.

"How are you?" he asked with optimistic enthusiasm. Unlike moms, who are proactive fixers, dads tend to be reactive fixers, never really wanting to hear problems.

"I'm great. Everything's good," she lied, for his benefit.

"That's great. I'm so glad to see you, pumpkin."

Addie had outgrown the little nickname of endearment but still glowed inside when her father used it. She smiled and watched him return to the stricken vacuum cleaner, which lay helplessly on its side, atop laid out newspaper.

The two women sat down on a nearby couch.

"Is this slipcover new?" Addie asked as she ran her hand across it.

"Sort of. Your Aunt Bessie gave it to me a few years ago. I had commented on it once when we visited them. You remember that trip, don't you? It was in the summer and Uncle Hal was at a convention or something..."

"It was a shareholder's meeting," Walter corrected without looking up.

"Whatever it was, I had mentioned to Bessie how much I liked this cover and lo and behold when they came to visit last year, they'd brought this with them and gave it to us as an anniversary gift. I was so excited and I immediately put it on the old couch we had—the one your brother confiscated for his fraternity—but it didn't fit well so after they left I put it in the closet downstairs and forgot about it until a couple weeks ago when I saw it and thought, 'A-ha, this will work perfect on the new couch.' You like it?"

"It's very nice," Addie agreed.

"So how is your job search coming along?" asked Mom with attempted nonchalance. It had taken every ounce of willpower to make it this deep into the visit before asking the question that kept her up at night.

"Nothing yet," answered Addie with matching ease. "I have a prospect or two, just waiting to hear back from them."

"What sort of places? You are so smart I can't imagine any company wouldn't have a place for someone like you."

"Just regular firms. Bookkeeping, secretarial stuff. That kind of thing."

"How many others were applying? It just seems like everyone is out of work these days. Mrs. Owens told me the other day that all three of her children were looking for jobs. It's terrible. Although honestly, the youngest one—you remember Stan who pinched you during Vacation Bible School when you were little—he has always been a bit different and I'm not surprised he is struggling."

"Is that the kid that pretended he was an explorer and would just show up in our backyard?" asked Walter with remarkable clarity of speech for a man who had two vacuum screws sticking out of the corner of his mouth.

"That was Dave Burford," Addie answered with a laugh. "You always think he's the boy in every story."

"By the way," Maggie whispered to Addie, "I heard that Dave's sister is in the middle of her second divorce. Makes you wonder what her problem must be."

"What makes you think it's her fault?" Addie admonished. "Maybe she just has bad luck."

"One time is bad luck, two times is something else," Mother insisted.

"Maybe her appetite for love making is too much for these toads," Addie teased.

"Addie Sumner! That's horrible. And Walter, stop laughing, it's not funny and you'll only encourage her. I've tried so hard to raise her right, and you go and undo everything."

"Wait a minute," protested Walter, looking up for the first time. "How is it that I'm suddenly involved? She probably picks that up from the movies."

Addie and Father exchanged a quick grin, satisfied that they had outraged Maggie. She, of course, continued to look disturbed, knowing her role of straight man in the family.

"Well, I'd hate to reunite you two," Maggie continued, "but I've been wondering if you shouldn't just move home for a while, Addie. Just until you get settled in at a job."

Addie frowned and rolled her eyes. She didn't want to have this discussion. She didn't want to defend her logic, even if it was illogical.

"I know, I know," responded Maggie to her daughter's sour expression. "After being a mayor it's hard to reduce yourself to living at home."

"It's not even that. The mayor thing was a stunt and I have no illusions about it. I did a good job—and it was a real job—but we all knew it was a temporary detour before my real life began."

"You were a national trailblazer," Walter declared, unable to hear his daughter diminish her accomplishments. "No female so young had ever been mayor of a small city like that."

"Yes, Father," Addie begrudgingly agreed. "I did something wonderful, even if it really was a large town rather than a small city..."

"What's the difference?" he asked.

"...but the point I was trying to make was that I don't want to move home unless I have to. It would be surrender and I'm not ready for that."

"Oh honey, that's nonsense," Maggie interjected. "Moving home would simply be practical. No one else would care. There are generations of families living together these days. The economy almost demands it."

"I don't know," argued Walter as he sat up and leaned back on his heels. "When you're that age you have pride. You want to be an adult and make it on your own. I was the same way. I did what it took to survive, though you might consider a boarding house or a roommate. For six months after college I slept behind an upright piano in a tiny place I shared with some buddies who'd also just graduated."

"So your solution is for Addie to sleep behind a piano?" Maggie asked with contempt. "Sounds like the perfect place to be chewed on by a rat."

"You know, I actually did catch sight of a critter or two," Walter recalled wistfully. "John Hinzo, one of the other guys, told me he could hear mice living in the walls where his bed was. Said he didn't sleep well the whole time. That place was something else."

"Thank you for proving my point," Maggie countered triumphantly. "There is no reason why Addie needs to follow in your footsteps when she has a fine house to live in, with lots of food, hot water and no mice."

Addie listened to the interaction between her parents, wanting to correct their misrepresentations, but she knew it was pointless. It was better to just let them offer advice and then ignore it.

Walter made a sound and grimaced as his screwdriver slipped. The conversation halted as both women waited to see if Father's setback would lead to a small tantrum. He was a very patient man for the most part, but inanimate objects were his weakness and often led to him becoming irrational when they refused to work properly. This time, however, there was only some grumbling as he reinserted his screwdriver, unaware that he was being observed and unaware that his two girls shared a silent giggle. For some reason, his little battles amused them.

With a start, Maggie jumped up and hurried into the kitchen, returning a moment later.

"Five more minutes on the lasagna," she announced while reclaiming her spot on the couch.

"I've got a question for you two," said Addie after a pause.

"Go ahead," said Walter as he squinted into the bowels of the vacuum.

"What is the very worst thing Father could do to disrupt your marriage?"

"What do you mean?" Maggie asked, unsure if she liked the direction of this topic.

"I mean, what is the single thing he could do that would make you not want to be with him anymore?"

Walter looked up from his work and locked eyes with Maggie. They were both curious about this answer, but neither wanted to go down the path. Thus Walter turned to humor as he always did when confronted with awkwardness.

"I guess she'd be done with me if I ever took up with Miss Donaldson," he speculated, referring to an attractive divorcee who lived a block away.

"It didn't take you long to come up with such an exact answer," said Maggie with defiance. "How long have you being thinking about that one?"

"Is she that pretty?" Addie teased, enjoying the spotlight being shifted.

"She's attractive," Mom admitted. "But it's the way she dresses that gets men's tongues wagging. She knows what she's doing."

"Never judge a book by its cover," Walter theorized.

"Baloney," declared Maggie. "Don't judge the book, maybe, but you're stupid if you don't note the clues."

"Exactly," agreed Addie. "There is meaning behind every woman's decisions when dressing."

"Even the ones who dress plainly?" Walter inquired.

"Their statement is they are not competing."

"What about the ones who dress oddly, almost costume-like?"

"Some of them are just zany and think it looks good," Addie answered. "Most, though, don't think they are pretty and want to distract or undermine their looks to give the illusion that their lack of beauty is a choice.

They are choosing not to compete, rather than losing the competition."

"What about men? What do our choices say?" he challenged.

"They say I'm at work or off of work or going to a wedding. Men don't compete like women."

Mother and Father both nodded. They had always enjoyed listening to Addie's views on things. Both wanted to ask the next logical question—why don't men compete like women?—but that was one layer too deep for a happy, surprise visit from their eldest child.

Addie, however, seemed determined to get back to her line of questioning.

"Now, I'm serious," said Addie, sternly. "What is the worst thing Father could do?"

"Why are you asking this?" Maggie demanded.

"I'm just conducting a social survey. This is pure speculation and means nothing."

Maggie was still not enjoying this game, but hated to disappoint her daughter during the same visit in which she was trying to sell her on returning home. So, Maggie sighed, then closed her eyes dramatically as she considered an answer for Addie.

"Well, I guess the worst he thing he could do would be to kill someone in cold blood," Maggie decided. "Although I don't see him capable of it so I'm not sure if that satisfies your survey."

"Wait a second," Walter complained as he sat up again. "What makes you think I'm not capable of killing someone?"

"In cold blood," Maggie repeated emphatically. "I have no doubt you could kill another man if you caught him with your girlfriend on the next block."

The fact that Maggie refused to say Miss Donaldson's name amused Walter. It was her way of retaining dignity and keeping the young thing in her place. Still, it bothered him that she didn't think he was capable of severe danger.

"I've fought a man or two in my life," Walter disclosed. "Now, if you were to extrapolate the pummeling by removing my good sense as an ending point, there is no doubt that either of those men would be dead, the result of force beyond the scope of reason."

"Spoken like a true engineer, which, in itself, makes the whole thing a little unbelievable," mocked Maggie. "Who knew I lived so close to danger?"

Addie was only trying to understand what Perzie might have done to cause his marriage to end so badly. Instead, the only good that had come from this exercise was that her parents were no longer focused on her living arrangements.

There was silence in the living room as everyone recovered from the awkwardness.

"So, besides looking for work, have you found time for anything interesting, honey?" Maggie wondered mildly. "Met any new gentlemen, maybe?"

"No, I have not met any new gentlemen," Addie answered with some annoyance. "And can we stop calling them gentlemen? That sounds like some dandy in a tailcoat and spats who smells like talcum powder. It would be like kissing another girl."

Much to the surprise of husband and daughter, Maggie Sumner giggled at being reprimanded.

"I've always thought the same thing," she admitted. "But it doesn't feel right asking my own daughter about 'fellas' or 'guys' or whatever you girls call 'em anymore."

"Mostly we just call them men," Addie informed her mother.

"Or suckers who fall for soft curves and end up fixing vacuum cleaners," chimed in Walter to an audience who didn't appreciate the joke.

"I'm sure you'll get over being a sucker as you gladly devour my lasagna," responded Maggie with a smirk. "Oh, before I forget," Maggie said, turning to Addie, "when you move home, there is a nice teller at the bank that you should meet. He's a little bit older, and..."

**

After supper, after hugs, and after promises to consider moving back home, Addie departed her childhood home. The evening air had never felt so fresh and liberating. It made her feel like hope was still alive, like anything was possible, even daydreams. She walked slowly, wondering what her husband would look like, how they would live. It felt good having it all in the near future but none of it defined. That way she could fill in the details as she desired them, which she did all the way to the trolley stop.

21

Addie arrived at the Bonus Café right on time for the 9 a.m. meeting she had arranged. She was surprised to see Zep already waiting in a booth, working on a cup of coffee. Maybe this timeliness was a trait of the improved, sober Zep, she surmised, not knowing he had been toasted the day before.

"Hey," she said, sliding into the booth.

"Hey, how you doin'?" he greeted back.

"Not as good as I'd hoped," she admitted. "Got a telegram last night that probably puts an end to the search for *Number 17.*

"What did it say?"

"It's from the attorney of the Vic fella who it turns out had the painting after all. I don't have the details, just that it was sold by Vic at a yard sale."

"I'm lost. Who is Vic?"

"All right, I'll start at the beginning so you can get caught up."

Addie proceeded to recite the entire tale, from her visit to the pawnbrokers to the discouraging telegram. Like any woman worth her salt, she included details, asides and commentary beyond what was necessary. And as often is the case, this abundance of information proved valuable. Despite a slight hangover, Zep listened intently, fascinated by Addie's adventure. He was particularly intrigued with Oscar's appearance in the drama, causing his instincts to wonder if this whole painting story was a square deal.

After her detailed report was concluded and they had commiserated over the telegram, Addie asked how Zep's meeting went.

"It was good," he offered lukewarmly.

She waited for him to continue but knew better. She turned her hands over, palms up.

"So, what happened? Was he upset you showed up? Did he admit he had a drinking problem? Did you get him to say whether he would consider painting again?"

"We had a good conversation. He figured you sent me but he wasn't bent out of shape about it or anything. We talked about drinking and then we did some drinking, then..."

"Wait a minute, Zep. You were drinking with him? Seriously?"

"It's nothing. I needed to gain his trust, show him we were the same kind of men. That way I could explain to him what he was capable of if he dried up a little."

"You could explain the joys of sobriety by getting drunk?"

"Well, in this case, yes. I wasn't going to change his life in one visit, Addie. It may take a couple visits just to make a dent in his habit. He's been drinking steady for over fifteen years."

"You're right," she admitted. "I just worry about you returning to your old self. Not that you were a complete mess or anything, but it wasn't helping you, either."

"I know, and we discussed that a little. I mentioned Mabel and how much I wanted to get it together for her sake."

"Wow, you two actually discussed something involving emotions? I'm very impressed."

Zep gave her a fake, don't-patronize-me smile.

"I'm just teasing, Zep. And I'm glad to hear you are still feeling something for Mabel."

"I still love her."

Addie grinned. Hearing men confess love was so adorable.

"The problem is," he continued, ignoring her smile, "she is so worried about what I'm capable of. I know I have potential, but I'm afraid I'm just not capable of reaching it. I don't even know how, or what it is. Doesn't everybody think they are better than their reality—that they'd be rich or famous or happy as a lamb if they had better luck or just knew which path to focus on or where to start?"

He stopped, exhausted from preaching the same old theory of hopeless confusion. But just like Mabel, Addie had no magic answer.

"Listen, Zep, I really care about Mabel and the last thing I want to do is talk you into marrying her out of obligation. And I know you. You would sabotage your own life just to prove to her that she was wrong in being loyal to you. I will tell you this though: She isn't obsessed with your potential because she needs to be wealthy. She just wants you to be happy because she adores you and the only way you'll ever be happy is if you are succeeding at something important to you. Although, it would be very helpful if that thing paid..."

They both laughed softly.

"But even if it's a hobby or a dream it has to start somewhere," she continued. "It's the only way, Zep. She would be your biggest supporter, just like you believed in her skill with finances when you worked together at the college. She was good at that job and loved it and you were proud of her. That's how she wants to feel about you, only it's stronger in us women. Your happiness is her happiness. It's how girls work, you dope."

Addie could tell she had delivered some sense to Zep by his thoughtful expression. She also knew he would be offering no rebuttal. He needed to absorb what she had said. Maybe it would take, maybe it wouldn't. In the meantime, they had unfinished business.

"OK, so you two got drunk and Mabel came up. What else happened? Any hint as to whether he might paint again?"

"Not really," confessed Zep. "I was careful not to show my hand. If he'd had an inkling that I just wanted his art, he'd have told me not to come back. It begins and ends with fixing him, kinda like what you were just sayin' about me. But, as far as getting him to stop drinking, that's a pretty tall order, and he doesn't seem motivated, which he has to be for it to work. There was *one* thing that seemed to affect him, though."

"What was that?"

"When we were talking about Mabel deserving better than me..."

"Agreed," Addie interjected mischievously.

"...I noticed that he was sorta lost in thought, and this wasn't long after talking about his ex-wife in California. May have been coincidence, but that look on his face was real. There is something about that situation that's at the heart of his drinking."

"Yeah, I got that impression, too," Addie confirmed. "Irene also seemed to change a little when that time period was discussed."

It was becoming clear that something fairly traumatic had destroyed the relationship between Armstrong and Julia. Addie had sensed this from the beginning, but Zep's observation seemed to underscore the significance of the unknown event.

It now dawned upon Addie what she must attempt. She had to somehow resolve the fractures in that family. There was obvious pain in Perzie and hidden pain in Irene. But what of the mother? She held the key and Addie didn't know anything about her.

As Addie turned this over in her mind, Zep was also trying to solve a riddle. There had been some things about Addie's adventure in Dellton that gave him pause. The painting had changed hands several times in the past year, with the final transaction coming at an untraceable yard sale to an untraceable customer. That in itself was awfully convenient. And why would this Vic fella have suddenly decided to liquidate some of his mother's possessions when he could have done it as an estate sale while it was all in Dellton? Done that way, he'd have sold it easier and had less to transport home. Minnie's friends and neighbors might even have paid a little more out of sentiment.

Granted, none of this made a counter-scheme conclusive but it was enough to make Zep think that *Number 17* might still be in play. Was Oscar involved in this? Had he talked Vic into saying it was sold in order to get Addie off the trail?

At almost the same moment, Zep and Addie broke the silence by declaring they had an idea. This made them laugh before they continued. Then it got funnier.

In perfect synchronicity, their separate ideas involved switching roles. Zep would now take up the hunt for *Number 17* and Addie would find a way to get Perzie painting again.

Zep's first move would be to visit Vic. He would pretend Oscar sent him to pick up the painting and see where it went from there. If Vic truly had sold the painting at a yard sale, Zep would be able to ascertain it from Vic's expression, his words and his facts. Zep might even get a clue as to the buyer. It all involved slim odds but there was nothing to lose.

"Where exactly does this Vic live?" Zep asked Addie.

"Max thought it was one of the Dakotas but didn't seem too sure. Then when I was trying to read that upside down document at the attorney's office I could swear I saw something about Decorah. That might explain Max's belief; he just heard wrong. And the attorney mentioned his phone call was long distance so that eliminates anything too close."

"If I'm going to gamble money for a train ticket to see Vic, I really should call the operator in Decorah and see if there is a Vic or Victor Upton."

"I know he works at a mill or a plant of some sort, if that helps."

"One more piece of information can't hurt. So, what's your next move?"

"I think maybe I'll run over to Irene's and get some details on her mom."

"How are you going to explain your interest in her?"

"I have no idea."

They both laughed. It was a satisfied laugh, the kind that happens when two people are enjoying themselves and obstacles are just adding to the joy of the adventure. Their prospects were disappearing as fast as their money but they were having the time of their lives. Full of blind optimism, they wished each other good luck and promised to stay in touch as events unfolded.

Zep left a dime on the table and the two art hunters walked outside together. They stopped at the first street corner and huddled against the frigid winter wind, rehashing their plan and waiting for the trolley. When it arrived, Addie waved goodbye, looked both ways and ran into the middle of the street where the trolley was paused. She climbed aboard and waved one more time, a young woman in love with life today.

Zep waited until the trolley was gone, then retreated into the Bonus Café to make a phone call.

22

Riding the trolley, Addie tried to formulate a plan for when she arrived at Irene's. Part of her wanted to open up and be honest with Irene about her motivations, to tell her that her ultimate goal was to profit off of Irene's stepfather. But really, that had ceased to be completely true, anyway.

Since meeting Armstrong and Irene and learning of their broken relationship, Addie had been unable to shake a feeling of sadness. Here were a father (practically speaking) and daughter living in the same city but only seeing each other once a year. And those visits sounded tepid and uninspiring, at best. Most men Armstrong's age were doting on their grandchildren, yet he had never seen his.

But the strangest and possibly saddest part was that they didn't dislike each other. There was no genuine hatred, just an unspoken impasse related to decisions made long ago. They were still thinly connected out of habit, or duty, or hope, but neither was willing or able to break the stalemate.

Addie had a strong hunch that Julia, the ex-wife and mother, was the...something. The problem? Lynchpin? Solution? Whatever her role in this broken family, it was a primary one and suspiciously silent. Neither Armstrong nor Irene had spoken much of her, yet in passing both had professed that the other one had loved Julia deeply. Nothing was fitting cleanly and yet nothing screamed disaster.

Addie's thoughts were interrupted when the trolley stopped at Harrison Street. Two women in their twenties boarded and took a seat directly across from

Addie. The women were obviously friends and their enthusiastic conversation never wavered as they boarded. They never even looked around them as they took seats. Had they accidentally boarded a circus trailer containing lions, they'd have not discovered their mistake until eaten.

Because they were so fervently engaged in their discussion, Addie was able to openly study them without fear of being caught. It was her favorite form of entertainment.

Regrettably, the topic she overheard was less than dynamic. Having already bashed their boyfriends and lamented their jobs while waiting for the trolley, the subject had turned to the motion pictures they had recently seen.

Bored, she began to listen less and look more. She observed their clothes, not so much critically, but out of curiosity.

Addie noticed that the one on the left had a large scuff mark down the outside of one shoe. She also had a quarter-inch thread hanging down from the hem of her dress. The hole in her belt, *next* to the buckle, was worn, indicating she had lost weight or gained a better corset. And one collar on her blouse was bent under ever so slightly.

Did any of this detract from the woman's appearance? Barely. Did Addie note these issues out of pleased spite? Not at all. Would any man have ever noticed these infractions? Never.

And yet, Addie felt a vague sense of embarrassment for this woman, as though the woman were painfully unaware of her compromised look. Her appearance was less than it could be, meaning she was less than she could be. It was hard enough for a woman to maximize the looks she was dealt by Mother Nature without accidentally sabotaging them.

But why this standard, Addie wondered. *I'm not exactly judging her, yet I'm expecting her to be as perfect in appearance as possible.*

She looked herself over. Everything seemed to be in order, except for the flap on her purse, which had already begun to wear at the edge. She hadn't even owned the purse *that* long. The imperfection wasn't out of wanton neglect on her part, she argued to herself, it was the purse manufacturer's fault. But did the string on the woman's dress get the same benefit of explanation?

Addie looked across the aisle at a man in a suit and straw boater hat. He was obviously listening to the two women chat. He was also observing their clothes, although Addie doubted he was noting the imperfections as much as he was imagining the possibilities.

There wasn't much to note regarding his suit. It was just a suit. It had its own problems—most notably a tiny stain on the tip of the necktie and some puckering at the coat seams as though he had tried to machine wash it—but such things were to be expected from a man.

But why was that? Because women let them skate on standards? Because it was understood that men's primary offering was something else—guile, power, force? Because men didn't need to care as much about appearance in this arranged gender dance?

The strangest part, thought Addie, *is that I don't really want to change the dance. I like being a woman with physical appeal. I just don't like the standards. Maybe if all women are less critical of each other then the standard can be lowered. But is that possible? And should some women work to lessen their appeal out of fairness for those lacking in appeal?*

All Addie knew was that being a woman meant she never felt good enough. A man earned his place in the world by virtue of birth (from out of a woman!), but a woman was constantly scrambling to prove she was better than other women or that she was worthy of being heard and respected by men.

And here I'm doing my part by pitying that woman for the string on her hem, Addie admitted.

Freshly inspired, Addie fumbled with the hem of her coat sleeve and worked a thread loose. She pulled it out until it hung to the back of her hand. *Women unite in imperfection,* she declared triumphantly in her mind, but the triumph felt empty.

It's rather silly if I don't include those women in my little cause, she decided. *But it would be even sillier trying to explain to them that I just maimed my coat in an act of solidarity. Plus, I'd have to point out to the one gal that the solidarity was in relation to her shoddy dress hem and instead of joining my cause she'd just glare at me. Then she'd glare at her friend for not telling her earlier.*

Addie was relieved when the two women got off at Hillyard Avenue. The man in the straw boater was a little disappointed.

23

It wasn't until Addie stepped off the trolley in Maple Hills that she realized she hadn't called Irene to warn her of an impending guest. Her previous visit had been a surprise for a reason, but now that they were friendly, it felt wrong to do it again. So, after Addie disembarked, she stepped into a café and called. Irene answered and told her to wait about fifteen minutes. That would give her time to get the two younger kids down for early naps.

Addie laughed when she overheard Madeline moan in the background upon hearing the mention of a nap. Even without being mentioned by name the little girl knew her time was up and began a whiny campaign against it.

"Tell her to give it twenty years and she'll be begging for a nice nap," Addie offered.

"I'm pretty sure our mothers told us the same thing and we didn't buy it then, either," Irene countered.

After exiting the phone booth in the back corner, Addie took a seat at the café's counter. Since she was only a couple blocks from Irene's, she decided to kill some time by getting a bite to eat. Her peanut butter toast needed reinforcement today.

"What can I get for you?" an older waitress asked with feigned happiness.

"Um, maybe a small bowl of oatmeal. With some honey mixed in."

"Coffee?"

"Water, please."

"Coming right up."

These small orders used to make the waitress weary, but with the economy in shambles, she was glad to have a job.

"Anything else?" she asked upon returning and placing the bowl in front of Addie.

"Yeah, one thing. Do you notice anything different when you look at me?"

The waitress sighed. This was going to be a lot of work for a small bowl of oatmeal.

"Not really," she confessed.

"Nothing stands out at all? Not one little thing?"

The waitress squinted and studied.

"I don't know. I guess your eyebrows could use a little work."

"What?!"

"You asked. I'm not saying they're that bad..."

"OK, what about this thread on my sleeve? You didn't notice it at all?"

"Nope. But if you know it's there why don't you just cut it?"

"I'm trying to make a point. Women feel obligated to look perfect and yet when we don't it shouldn't make any difference. You should be able to notice this thread and not feel like I'm failing as a fellow woman."

"You're talking to a gal who wears a uniform with permanent gravy stains. Now do you want to borrow a pair of scissors or not?"

"No...and I think you look wonderful in gravy stains. I bet any man in here would agree with me."

"They already agree. I get propositioned every day and I don't mean for marriage. Heck, around here men love stray threads and gravy stains. It just means you're poor and vulnerable. Walk out of here with a limp and I guarantee you at least two of 'em will follow you."

"So it is your expert opinion that men don't set standards for feminine appearance?"

"I'm not sure exactly what that means, but I know when it comes to men the thought of us bare is all that matters. The clothes are just the gift wrapping on Christmas morning, something to add to the surprise. Listen, I gotta help the others. You want scissors?"

Addie shook her head and dug into her oatmeal, all the while fighting the urge to pull out a compact and check her eyebrows.

***

By the time she got to Irene's the two youngest were halfway through their naps.

"Sorry it took so long," Addie apologized. "I stopped for some late breakfast."

Technically, it was her second breakfast, but there was no chance she was admitting to that. Unless you were stick thin, it only gave the other woman ammunition.

Irene invited her inside and they moved to the living room and took the same seats as previously.

"Where's Olga?" Addie asked, craning her neck to see if she was sitting in her hiding place.

"She's in her room changing," Irene whispered, not wanting to embarrass her daughter. "When I told her it was you knocking she wanted to put on her new dress."

To say Addie's heart melted a bit would be an understatement.

When the six-year-old finally emerged, Addie pushed the bounds of patronization by cooing and complimenting with gusto.

"What do you want me to draw this time?" Olga asked.

"Surprise me. I like your imagination."

They smiled at each other.

"Listen, I don't want to waste your entire nap time," Addie said, turning to Irene, "but I wanted to ask you something."

"OK."

"I wanted to ask about your mother."

"What do you mean?"

"Well, I was hoping you would tell me about her and then I'd be able to explain. Its nothing bad, I promise."

"All right, although I'm not sure what exactly you want to know. She lives in Greeley, Colorado, and used to work as a bookkeeper at a jewelry store before she got sick this last time..."

"Oh. What's wrong?"

"Some form of anemia which I can't pronounce from memory. It's just the latest illness for her. She's been sick with various things over the past few years. I think it's stress from lack of money, and of course missing work because of illness doesn't help much. It's a rough cycle."

"How does she survive? Is she married?"

"Not any more. She was married for a few years to a man named Paul, but I guess it just sort of fizzled. I never actually met him. I haven't even seen her since I moved here as a teenager."

"Wow. That's terrible."

"I know. It just never worked out, and then she couldn't afford it, and then we couldn't afford it, and then the kids came along..."

Addie silently gasped.

"The kids have never seen her?"

Irene shook her head with a sad, knowing smile.

"It's hard," she conceded. "My mom would love to see them. She tells me all the time."

Before Addie could inquire further, Irene motioned for her to follow. They walked down the hall to a closet door. Inside, on a shelf, were several shoe boxes. Irene pulled one out and showed it to Addie without saying a word. There must have been hundreds of letters, bound in bunches by rubber bands.

"All of these boxes are letters from her?" Addie asked with astonishment.

"Mmm hmm. I'm lucky to write one back for every ten she sends. I think the amount of writing is her way of trying to compensate for us...I don't know how to put it...our not having a traditional relationship, I guess."

"Because you haven't seen each other for so many years?"

"Yeah, that's a big part of it. There's also the fact that we don't discuss the past much, at least in detail. She asks occasionally how Armstrong is doing, but I've learned she doesn't want to talk about him beyond that. Since my childhood was sort of wrapped up in her time with him, it just makes it—I don't want to say taboo, but it leaves a lot unspoken."

"Let me ask you this: Do you feel like that period of your lives could be resolved? Or would everybody prefer it just stays sort of buried?"

"I was too young to understand so I can't say for sure. There is something there, though, and I guess it makes me feel a little left out."

"Oh, look at this," Addie exclaimed as she pulled out a photo. "Is this your mom?"

"Yes, I begged her for a photograph so she had one made."

"She's quite pretty."

"She really is. I was so pleased that I called her long distance to thank her, which neither of us can afford to do very often, but I had to after this, and it always feels so good to hear her voice."

"I bet you would love to see her in person."

"I really hope to one of these days. She's practically begged us to come visit lately and I keep telling her we will soon. It would be so much easier if she was well enough to travel here, but...it will work out one day."

Addie didn't want to push any harder so she changed the subject to the children. Moms need very little prompting, if any, to discuss their kids, and Irene was no exception. Hugh was teething and Madeline "helped" make a cake the other day. Olga was excited about returning to school after vacation.

"So, did you tell Armstrong I sold his painting?" Irene asked.

"No, I haven't seen him since our last visit."

"I just hope he won't be angry," said Irene with a sheepish face.

"And yet you're afraid he won't be," Addie added with a sly smile.

Irene shrugged, unsure how to respond to her vulnerability being exposed.

Addie wanted to pursue the relationship between stepfather and stepdaughter but thought it best to leave it alone. There was perceived apathy on both sides, and neither was brave enough to push for more. Perzie busied himself with booze and Irene occupied herself with children while each waited for the other to make a move.

"Well, I guess I'd better be going," Addie proclaimed.

"Wait, you never said why you were asking about my mother. Trying to understand Armstrong?"

"In a way. It's not really my business but I thought maybe I could help, somehow."

"I think maybe you've already helped me just by listening," Irene said sincerely.

"Actually, what I'd like to do is talk to your mom, if it's all right. I promise I'm not trying to start trouble. I'll just mention my concern for Armstrong and maybe she'll have some words of wisdom and maybe she won't."

Irene nibbled on her bottom lip, trying to decide if this was a good thing. The idea of sharing her mother was frightening, but she trusted Addie, and so she finally nodded in assent.

Addie felt honored by Irene's trust, which in turn made Addie feel like dirt because of her true motive. Still, she was beginning to believe she could secure multiple victories, enabling everyone to win. There was a reason she had been elected mayor once upon a time. She had the ability to help people see things differently and to make them believe it was their own idea. And hopefully, she had the ability to make money from someone else's art while helping a family heal at the same time. Even Nancy Drew couldn't pull that one off.

Before Addie left, Olga gave her a new drawing. This time she didn't make Addie guess, telling her up front it was Fritter on the moon. Just like last time, Addie kneeled and enjoyed a hug with her little friend.

"You have a string coming out of your sleeve," Olga shared sweetly.

24

Zep really wished he hadn't eaten that hot dog while waiting in the Stout City train station. He felt lousy during the entire trip to Decorah and his first stop upon disembarking was the station restroom. He emerged a better man, but his stomach was still fragile, so he sat and read the local paper for a few minutes. As long as he made it to Vic's job before noon he'd be all right.

Before leaving Stout City he'd called the Decorah phone operator and not only confirmed Vic Upton's existence but learned of his workplace. The operator also informed Zep that she occasionally played Bridge with another group that included Vic's wife, and that when he visited, Zep should eat at the Crater Grill. Zep had hated spending on a long distance call but he had to admit he'd gotten his money's worth.

Fortunately for his tender tummy, the walk from the station to the gypsum plant where Vic was employed was only a few blocks. Inside the main office, Zep stopped at the first desk he encountered and asked the woman how he might get in touch with Vic. She directed him deeper into the office. Another woman at another desk explained she'd have to check with the Director of Operations, who in turn called the shift foreman.

Zep was asked to wait on the visitors' bench and was offered water, which he declined. None of the twenty-odd employees paid any attention to him as they went about their work, most of which seemed to involve typing or scribbling on papers.

After a few minutes, a side door was opened, allowing a sudden burst of machinery noise to flood the office. Nobody inside seemed to notice. Two men walked in and the door closed behind them, restoring the office to silence. The first man was dressed more nicely, and he walked toward the Operations office. The second man, much smaller and dressed for labor, walked towards Zep.

They shook hands and the worker identified himself as Vic.

"I hope this isn't bad news," he said loudly, not yet accustomed to the quiet of the office.

"Nope, not bad news."

"That's a relief. I ain't never had anyone call on me during the day before, except my wife. I was worried maybe somethin' terrible happened."

"Can we talk outside? It will only take a minute."

Vic shrugged and looked around, unsure of the protocol for receiving guests mid-shift. No one in the office paid him any attention so he stopped at the first desk Zep had visited and informed the woman of his intentions to step outside for just a moment. "Personal business," he explained. The woman listened with polite confusion, unsure why anyone would wonder about his whereabouts.

Outside on the sidewalk, they waited until a mother with a stroller had passed by before beginning their conversation.

"Thanks for talking with me, Vic. I'm here from Stout City to pick up that painting."

"What painting?"

"The one you inherited from your mother."

"I kept a few from her," Vic confirmed, "but that was a while ago. And I wasn't giving one to anybody."

"Oscar didn't contact you?"

"Who is Oscar? I think you might be talkin' to the wrong fella."

"Hmmm, maybe I am. Is one of the paintings you got an abstract? Lots of colors but no real subject?"

"Nope, don't have one like that."

"Did your mom have one like that?"

"Not that I remember. There was one that was sort of a jumble of colors but you could tell it made up a sunset on the water when you stepped back from it. She had a lot of paintings, though, so maybe it was stuck out of the way somewhere. That still doesn't explain who Oscar is. Matter of fact, I don't know who you are."

"I told you, I'm from Stout City."

"Yes, but..."

Zep held up his hand to indicate he was thinking, and this seemed to placate Vic.

Zep needed to consider his next move carefully since none of Vic's answers had led down an anticipated path. It was possible that Vic was a good liar and *Number 17* was hanging in his living room, and it was also possible that Oscar had equipped him with a line of fibs. *But why wouldn't Vic just stick to the story of the yard sale and send me on my way?* Zep wondered. *And is this fella really capable of lying so well? I can usually tell when someone has that sort of capacity or when they are being evasive. This one seems too genuine.*

"You said that your mother had lots of paintings and that you kept a few. So there are paintings you remember from visits that you didn't keep after her passing?"

"There was lots of stuff I didn't keep. Mr. Bigelow and I walked through the house and I told him what I wanted and he helped me sell the rest at an estate sale there in Dellton. It worked out well since I needed money more than I needed a lot of those things."

"And everything she owned was there when you went on this tour?"

"As far as I could tell. Mom liked to buy little things so it would be impossible to know everything."

Zep began to rub his forehead. Maybe he had misunderstood the story as Addie had related it. Did the lawyer know for sure that this painting sold at a yard sale, like he told Addie in the telegram, or was he just speculating? Or was it ever in Dellton at all? Maybe, from the start, Oscar was chasing the wrong painting based on Addie's original description in the pawnshop. After all, a painting with no specific subject can be confusing to track.

Zep noticed that Vic kept turning to look inside the office window. He was obviously nervous about being outside and missing work. With the national unemployment rate at a staggering twenty-three percent, nobody wanted to fool with their employment. Zep fully understood. He would have been devastated if he caused Vic to lose his job, so there was no choice but to let him return.

After shaking hands, Vic hustled back into the office and was nearly to the side door when Zep, who had dashed in after him, called across the office. This time everybody looked up from their work. Vic waited with his hand on the doorknob to show any watching superiors that he was dedicated to returning to work.

"I'm really sorry," Zep begged as he reached Vic. "I will tell your boss it's all my fault, I promise."

"Fine, fine, just hurry, please."

"All right, listen: how did Bigelow describe the painting when he called you yesterday? Maybe you two are talking about different paintings."

"He didn't call me yesterday. I haven't talked to him for a couple months."

"Are you sure?"

Vic rolled his eyes and went through the side door, leaving Zep standing there trying to contemplate the newest wrinkle in his hunt.

But Zep was a man of his word. He found the Director of Operations and took full responsibility for detaining his employee. Then again, Zep claimed he was a preacher who'd only wanted to thank Vic for a wonderful deed.

His visit completed, Zep stepped outside and began walking quickly toward the train station. A certain attorney in Dellton had some explaining to do.

25

Normally, Mabel McClendon had prescriptions filled at Baker's Drug Store. Her family had been loyal customers ever since she was old enough to remember. Baker himself used to give her a lollipop when she was little and he knew the family's medical conditions by memory. But for some reason, Baker's didn't have the new pill that had just been prescribed to her mother for dizzy spells.

Fortunately, Archer Heights had added a second drug store two years earlier. It was part of a chain known as Drug Qwik, and it was three times the size of Baker's. The soda fountain featured a marble counter that seemed to stretch a mile and one could order almost any combination of soda, ice cream and gooey goodness imaginable.

The pharmacy took up the entire back wall and was a split-level temple whose shelves contained every known solution to human suffering. It took four full-time employees to man this hub of salvation and the gravity of their work left no time for friendliness. Place your order on one end of the assembly line and receive it on the other end.

Mabel was fascinated by the place. Being a loyal Baker's customer, she had resisted the temptation to shop at Drug Qwik despite the rumors of greatness she'd heard from acquaintances. She was now seeing firsthand what she had been missing.

As she waited for her prescription to be filled, she wandered the aisles, surprised at the unexpected varieties of standard items. The Reputation Tooth Brush display offered not two or three toothbrush models, but nine! There were the Professional, Tufted, Dental Plate (for false teeth), Massive, Sloping, Massage, Kleanal, Junior and Handituft. They were each available in different colored handles at twenty-nine cents each or two for fifty-five cents. Mabel had no idea where one would even begin to determine which model was best.

Just to her left were four shelves stacked completely full of toothpaste options. She grabbed one that had Milk of Magnesia Dental Cream emblazoned on the box. She turned it over in her hand. There it told her it was "scientifically prepared by experts." That was a relief. And in case one wasn't trained medically, there was an explanation of its superiority: "Acts upon acids in the mouth the same as milk of magnesia acts on acids in the stomach." She paused to wonder if the two things were compatible.

"Can I help you make a choice?" asked a male employee who had silently appeared at her side.

"Oh, um, no, I was just looking around while I waited for my prescription," she explained nervously, feeling put on the spot.

"Mabel?" the man asked, craning his neck to get a better look.

Mabel looked up at him in surprise but couldn't place the face so she just smiled.

"You don't remember me, do you?" he laughed. "Well, I could never forget you. You were one of the prettiest girls at Stumpf High and you haven't changed a bit."

Now she remembered him, but what was his name?

"You're awfully nice," she conceded. "High school feels like a hundred years ago, though. How have you been doing?"

"Real swell. I landed this job when they first opened, and boy, am I glad I did. Most places around here are trying to survive but this joint really hops. How come I haven't seen you before?"

"This is my first visit."

"How do you go that long without needin' a drug store?"

Mabel giggled at his confusion.

"Actually I've been out of state since high school," she explained. "Went to a college over in Iowa and then took a job there as a bookkeeper after graduating. I've only been back a couple months."

"Whaddya think of Archer Heights these days? Changed a little, huh?"

"I guess so."

"Well, it's grown quite a bit," he informed her. "A chain store like this draws 'em in from Centon, Browner Gap, Tawnley and all over. We do big business. I've already been promoted twice and make more in this terrible economy then my dad ever did in the '20s."

"Your parents must be very proud. And your wife, too, if you're married."

"Yeah, I'm married," he admitted with a hint of disappointment. "You remember Darlene Jacobs. She was a class ahead of us and was on the school newspaper."

"Oh yeah, I knew Darlene. She was a sweetheart. Any kids?"

"Just one. A boy named Jesse. What about you?"

"Nothing on either count yet. Still single, but I have a boyfriend back in Stout City."

"Well don't rush into anything, 'cause you gotta be careful. Darlene is a real good mother but she never seems happy and we bicker a lot. Most gals would be happy to have a husband with a job like mine."

"I'm sure she's happy. Being a mother can be tiring and stressful."

"Maybe, because you don't look tired or stressed. I bet you could wear the same clothes you did at Stumpf."

169

Mabel knew she was in good shape. She had been eating carefully and exercising religiously since leaving Zep. Even though she knew there were philosophical differences that needed to be solved with Zep, she instinctually believed that her appearance was somehow part of the blame and the solution.

She was at her heaviest when she fell in love with Zep, even if it wasn't what most people would consider heavy. It was a few extra pounds, and she'd thought nothing of it when she started dating him, but when their relationship foundered, she wondered if she had slipped in his eyes compared to other women.

Marion Eliot, a coworker at the college, was tall and thin and looked like she belonged in the Ziegfeld Follies. And of course, working at a women's college meant Mabel was surrounded by little wispy things who augmented their skinniness with giggles and ribbons and coyness. Mabel was the "old" bookkeeper, nagging Zep about bills and bad investments. She was only a few years removed from being a coed, but the division felt enormous, just like she did.

At first, her only reason for returning home and living with her widowed mother had been to put Zep on notice. His actions needed to support his words. Yeah, she knew he loved her, but he loved his golf clubs too. What she needed was to be the most special thing in the world to him, to be adored above all other adorations. He could still love and enjoy other things, she just needed to know that none could top her. In exchange she would forgive his multitude of bad traits (though she was still determined she could change every one of them and would probably try despite her best intentions).

After she moved home, however, her insecurities began to erode her resolve. Yes, Zep needed to show commitment, but what if it was her appearance that was giving him pause? Wasn't that all that mattered to men? So, with time on her hands and a need to do something besides waiting like an angry damsel, she began to revitalize her body. When Zep finally came to his senses and they met face to face, he would get an eyeful of what he could be enjoying, and that would be the end of their separation. Suddenly he would find a way to address his shortcomings.

In the meantime, her improvements were a dangerous condition that attracted all sorts of unwanted attention. This Drug Qwik employee, whose name she could not remember, was just the latest to become less enchanted with the wife every second he spent near Mabel.

It was flattering, but at the same time it made her question the entire male gender. They were like some farm animal, unable to resist the simplest visual urge. That women felt compelled to vie for a man's reluctant loyalty was quite possibly the cruelest trick of nature.

"I remember some of the cute clothes Darlene wore," she responded to his hint about her nice figure. "She was really nice, too. I'm happy for you and I bet you adore your son."

"Yeah, he's a good kid. The other day in kindergarten he was the first one who was able to count backwards from twenty to one."

"He's going to be successful just like you," Mabel declared generously. "Well, I better go grab my mother's prescription. It's been fun seeing you again. Tell Darlene I said hello."

"I will," he promised with a defeated smile.

The truth was, he would not have known what to do had Mabel responded to his flirtations.

26

February 19, 1932

Dear Julia,

You have never met me but I'm hoping that will change soon. My name is Addie Sumner and I live in Stout City where I have had the pleasure of meeting your lovely daughter, Irene, and your three charming grandchildren. You have much to be proud of as a grandmother, and I am writing this letter in hopes that you will all see each other soon.

First, I need to explain who I am so that you will understand why I'm writing you. It wasn't so long ago that I was a student at Ponder Grove College in Elberton, Iowa, where some of my favorite subjects were history, art, and government. As a matter of fact, it was my interest in government that got me noticed by the school president who just happened to have an ambitious plan in mind for an unusual publicity stunt that would make our school known. He had me run for mayor to show off our school's growing expertise on the system of self-governance, and would you believe it? I won! Perhaps you've already heard this story since it was a minor fascination in national newspapers at the time. I served as the legitimate Mayor of Elberton for two years, and it was quite thrilling despite all of the troubles caused by our nation's economic plight, which still affects every town in America no matter its size.

After I was done as mayor, I moved back to my hometown of Stout City without any specific plans. If you recall earlier, I mentioned my love of art, which had been cultivated at college, and because of this love I used some of my spare time between job searches to learn more. It was during one of my learning experiences that I discovered the stunning art of a local artist from three decades ago. By now I'm pretty sure you know I'm talking about Armstrong.

Curious about him because of his previous work and our local connection, I found him and had some conversations. What I discovered was very sad, indeed. He has not only ignored his talents as a painter, but he has neglected to take proper care of himself, which was very disturbing to me. I find it almost unbearable to watch anyone ignore their problems with alcohol, but think it's even sadder when it involves a man who could be doing so much to make others happy.

This is the part of the letter where I must get personal for a moment, and I beg for your understanding since we have never met. Please trust that I am aware of what a wonderful person you are and it is only because of this that I dare proceed.

What I want to say is that in my discussions with Armstrong it has become very evident to me that he punishes himself for causing the end of his marriage to you. He has not offered any details and I have not asked, but it is quite clear, nonetheless. I've never been married so maybe I'm a naïve fool, but after all of these years it is hard to believe he could still feel so bad unless he truly cared about you and still does. I'm just wondering if a few words of forgiveness on your part might end his suffering and keep him from slowly drinking himself to death. Again, I do not know the circumstances between you and he, and I have no doubt whatsoever that he must have hurt you very badly so it would take an incredible act of sacrifice to forgive him. If this is impossible, I understand.

There is one more thing, though. In the course of meeting him I learned of Irene and sought her out because I wanted to understand him better and thought she might have answers. She has been so kind in allowing me to visit and see her adorable children. In the course of our conversations it is evident that she has the utmost love for you. Due to her age at the time she has no firm recollections about the strife that occurred between you and Armstrong but still feels very badly about how it hurt two people important to her. You can imagine how hard it is to hear her sadness regarding this situation. All of this leads me to my final point.

Because you are so respected and play such a crucial role in the emotional lives of these people I have met, and because you have never met your grandchildren, I would like to ask your permission to have them come visit. I know you have been sick and traveling is impossible so I would find the means to have them travel to you. Irene allowed me to have your address but she has no idea I'm asking this. Armstrong has no idea either, but I'm certain he would go. If that makes you uncomfortable I will arrange his lodging far from you and you would only have to see him for a few minutes or not at all if that is your wish.

I may be young but my time as mayor allowed me to be part of many difficult meetings as well as many beautiful meetings. I truly believe that this visit would be both difficult and beautiful and I beg you to trust me that I would do everything in my power to arrange things in your best interest. If you would be willing to take a small chance then maybe there could be some peace of mind and comfort for all involved. If nothing else, I know you would thrill to see your grandchildren as they are beyond precious.

I realize this is very sudden and it is a lot to consider but I thank you from the bottom of my heart for reading this entire letter. Please think about these things and let me know what you feel. Again, I promise to do what is best for you and I know you will do what is best for all of these people who need you for different reasons.

Very Sincerely,

Addie Sumner

27

Zep climbed the steps of Dellton's only professional building and located the door of Lloyd Bigelow, Attorney at Law. It was the door he'd dreamt of kicking in ever since his visit with Vic Upton in Decorah. There was just one problem: Zep wasn't entirely sure if he should actually be mad at Bigelow.

He was almost positive that Vic had been truthfully ignorant regarding *Number 17*, and if so, Vic's claim that he had never been contacted by Bigelow meant that the attorney had willfully lied to Addie. Or Addie was misunderstanding the lawyer, or Zep was misunderstanding Addie. None of the choices was more concrete than the others.

For Zep, this whole pursuit was difficult enough without taking over midstream from his partner Addie. He was dependent on her version of a story that could go many directions based on misrepresentation or forgotten facts. All signs pointed to Bigelow as the center of the story, but whether he was a crook or just a dope was the question.

Either way, Zep figured kicking a man's door open was a great way to get his attention. At the last moment, however, Zep opted to just jerk the door open without knocking.

The door flew open with a whoosh, banging into a file cabinet, and Zep stepped inside wearing his most menacing look. This would have scared Bigelow to death under normal circumstances but since Bigelow was leaning back in his chair enjoying a little snooze the fright quotient was tripled. Bigelow levitated ever so slightly before scrambling into an upright position.

Even though Zep was on the other side of the room he instinctively reached his arms out to steady the poor man.

"Geez, I'm so sorry," he pleaded.

"What's the matter with you?! You could kill a man that way."

"I'm really sorry. I had no idea you would be asleep, I promise."

Bigelow climbed to his feet and stomped around, trying to burn off the adrenaline that had just surged through him.

"If you must know," he argued, "I was actually preparing myself mentally for a court case I have after lunch, OK?"

"OK, sure, but again, I feel bad."

"Well you should. Now what is it that you need?"

"Um, I wanted to discuss a matter with you," Zep began. He was so flustered that he forgot he had planned to be outraged. Now he had to pause and regain his suspicious edge.

"Listen," he tried sternly, "I want to know what you did with that painting."

"Painting?"

"Come on, don't play with me, you know which painting I'm talking about."

"Well, there was a woman here yesterday who was asking..."

"That would be the painting in question. Now where is it?"

"Didn't Miss Sumner tell you? It was sold at a yard sale. I sent her a telegram explaining."

"And how do you know it was sold at a yard sale?"

"I contacted the owner. He received it as part of an estate and apparently he didn't need it or have room for it so he sold it along with several other items he'd inherited."

"So you're saying Vic sold it? Vic Upton of Decorah? The man I spoke with this morning?"

Bigelow cocked his head and silently studied Zep. He realized he was dealing with someone who had good information, but how much information was the question.

"Who are you, by the way?" Bigelow asked, suddenly very curious.

"Just someone looking for a painting, and you've got one chance to change your story," Zep threatened.

Bigelow sat back down in his chair and dropped his hands in his lap. He looked defeated.

"OK, so the story isn't exactly true but there is some truth involved. The painting, if it's even the same one you are looking for, was actually sold as part of a pre-estate sale."

"This sounds good already," Zep interjected.

"Just hear me out, all right? I feel bad enough about this. When Miss Sumner surprised me yesterday I sort of panicked and said some things I shouldn't have. I should have just told the truth then but she caught me off guard, and my initial reaction was..."

"...to be an attorney. I understand why you're a liar but I want to know where the painting is."

"I told you it's sold. And that is the absolute truth. Where I lied was in saying that Vic had sold it when it was really me. It was stupid on my part, I know."

"Just stop with the dramatics, OK? I only wanna hear what happened to the painting."

Despite being cautioned to stop the drama, Bigelow rubbed his brow and looked heavenward.

"It was a few days after Minnie passed away in her sleep. She and I had been friends for many years and so initially all of my thoughts and actions were regarding her funeral, with Vic's permission, of course. He couldn't get here for a couple days so I arranged things and it was only after getting that part in order that I actually took time to wander in her house. This was my right as her legal representation and my duty as a friend. I wanted to inspect the house and make sure everything was up to snuff."

"What does that mean?"

"Well, on rare occasions I've tided up houses in anticipation of relatives arriving and discovered things that perhaps the family would not like to know. There was one man who had a trove of love letters that were not from his wife, or from a woman, for that matter. In another case, I discovered that a much respected woman indulged in, um, mail order pornography."

"Wow, that's weird. I never pictured women ordering that stuff."

"Yes, well, she was actually filling orders. She was quite talented in photo and in verse. She also had a fair sized inventory that would have devastated some of her relatives. And just to prove that I am not in the habit of playing fast and loose with ethics, I destroyed all of the items which I could easily have used to blackmail certain family members."

"Ahhh. See, the blackmail angle wouldn't have even occurred to me," Zep added smugly.

"So, anyhow, I was going through Minnie's house in order to ensure her reputation remained intact, both for her and her survivors. I had found nothing unusual and was actually cleaning some things out of her refrigerator when a woman called out from the living room. She was probably in her seventies and very nicely dressed, wearing a sumptuous fur.

"She said she'd seen the car in the driveway and asked if she could have a word. That's when she shocked me with a request. There were four paintings of Minnie's which she had always admired and she wondered how they might be obtained."

"Was this woman a friend of Minnie's?" Zep asked.

"That's what has always puzzled me. I didn't recognize her and I know most everyone in Dellton, if not by name at least by face. All I can figure is that she read the obit in the paper, although that still doesn't explain how she knew exactly which four paintings she was after."

"Maybe through some area-wide social club and Minnie hosted one of their affairs?" Zep theorized aloud.

"Perhaps. That's a very good guess, which I never considered. Anyhow, I explained that all of the property had been left to Vic as prescribed by Minnie's will and that he would have discretion regarding its potential sale. But she was quite determined and this is where the story turns embarrassing. She began to make offers, each one higher than the last. I kept refusing but a voice in my head reminded me of all the work I had done for Minnie over the years as a friend that maybe another attorney would have charged for. And I had done much for Minnie. She was a single mother who sacrificed for her son and gave to the community. When she needed some small advice or simple aid—in drafting a charter for an aid society during the Great War, for example—I was always happy to oblige as a friend even though I had every right to collect on my professional work."

"So what you're trying to say with this long defense is that you buckled and sold the paintings?"

"That's it exactly. I buckled. I've regretted it ever since but the deed is done, there is nothing to do about it now."

"And I suppose after you buckled, you felt so bad you immediately took the money and added it to Minnie's estate?"

"No. No, I kept the money. I'm sure you understand that the downturn in our economy has made us all nervous and caused us to cross lines we never thought we would. But I'm glad you brought this up, actually."

Bigelow pulled a letter from his desk and handed it over to Zep.

"This is going out in the afternoon mail. It contains the check I wrote to Vic immediately after Miss Sumner left my office yesterday. Her visit was a sign that I would never escape my indiscretion until I made good on the trust Minnie had placed in me. It's for the exact amount I was given for the four paintings. Open it and see."

The letter was sealed and stamped but Zep opened it anyhow. He needed some sort of proof of something, anything. Inside was a check with the previous day's date along with a letter explaining that the amount enclosed represented residual income from the final settlement of Minnie's estate.

"Couldn't you have just told Addie this story when she was here?" Zep asked while handing the envelope back.

"Like I told you, I panicked. This sort of thing could lead to my disbarment. I had no idea who she was or what her motives were and so I acted out of selfish need. And really, the truth *is* that some unknown woman has the painting and that's what she needed to know, either way. My involvement doesn't change any of that so why open myself up to recrimination?"

"But I could get you in hot water as easy as she."

"Yes, but you have me cornered in my own lies. I have to tell you the truth. However, I should also tell you there is no proof that she owned the painting at the time of her death. It hung in her bedroom, which saw light traffic, much to her dismay, and even if someone claims to have seen it, there is no proof she possessed it the day of her death. After all, she may have given it as a gift, just before passing."

"You're quite a crook, beyond being a lawyer," Zep marveled.

"I'm the worst crook you've ever met. I tried and failed and shall not try again."

Afterwards, Zep thought about visiting the Dellton Library and trying to dig up some leads on the woman in the sumptuous fur coat. The social club angle really did make sense as a starting place since it had to be someone who wasn't local but had spent time in Minnie's house. He doubted, however, he would find his answer easily and he was too tired to follow up if he did, so he headed home for the day.

As for Bigelow, he'd watched through the blinds of his office window as Zep disappeared before making an urgent phone call.

28

Two hours into the train trip to Greeley, Colorado, and Addie's traveling party was already showing signs of social fatigue. Like any good mother, Irene felt responsible for keeping her three children halfway tame and that meant constant warnings and pleadings. She wanted them to make a favorable impression on their grandfather, Armstrong, who was spending time with them for the first time. But the normally well-behaved children were excited and they fed off of each other, twisting, jumping, saying silly things, "accidentally" burping, poking, crying, and arguing about things they would normally not argue about. The coach compartment they all shared began to feel smaller and smaller. Irene was exhausted from shepherding, and Armstrong was exhausted from everything.

He'd spent the last decade holed up in his apartment listening to the silence when there wasn't a game on the radio. The busiest thing in his life was a fan running in the corner.

He'd avoided his duty as a grandfather up until now, but that was mostly because he didn't feel worthy. He'd destroyed the bond with their mother and didn't know where to start in rebuilding it. He was also a certified drunk and felt self-conscious about the idea of being around impressionable children. He was afraid he'd say something inappropriate or stumble, or worse yet one of the kids would ask why he smelled funny, referring to the permanent scent of alcohol that he wore.

He was glad to have been invited on this trip, however, and to be "forced" to spend time with his grandkids. They really were adorable and each one had a fun little personality. He couldn't believe how quickly they accepted him and it nearly made his heart melt. Unfortunately, his brain felt like it was melting too. Compared to his silent life, this was more like being trapped inside a circus. The sensory overload was overwhelming. And making it worse—much, much worse—was his attempt to start the trip sober. Out of respect for Irene and the kids, he'd had his bottle for breakfast but nothing more. Five hours later, the combination of relative sobriety and energetic children had him feeling like he might lose his mind.

Genuinely concerned that he could snap and ruin everything, Armstrong finally asked to be excused, and then practically fled to the bathroom where he pulled out a flask and downed it with desperate flourish. The alcohol hit his bloodstream, sending shivers from head to toe. He sat on the toilet and leaned back, soaking in the calm.

That's when he remembered the purpose of the trip: to see Julia. A feeling of terror replaced his alcohol shivers. He wasn't sure he could confront his past, wasn't even sure how Addie had talked him into this trip. Thank goodness he had tucked a flask into each sock. The second one came out and he began working on its contents as he tried to picture Julia's face. No matter how he tried to age her face, though, it always wore that same expression of pain and disappointment, just as he'd left it sixteen years earlier. And he was still the cause.

***

When Armstrong left the compartment, the two women had shared a knowing look.

"He's really trying," Addie explained.

"I know," Irene agreed.

184

"It's not easy curbing one's intake so severely after all these years, and honestly I'm not sure this is the time or the place to try. It's hard enough for him to see your mom without battling withdrawal at the same time."

"And I appreciate that he's trying for the kids. I can't tell you how happy it makes me to see them get along with him. This is how I always wished it would be if it could...all work out."

With their Grandpa Armstrong gone, the children hit the wall. Hugh napped with his head in his mom's lap, and Madeline snuggled up next to Addie on the other seat, slowly losing the fight with exhaustion. Only Olga remained upright and alert, reading a Nancy Drew book she had pulled from her little bag. After every other page she would peek over the top of her book to make sure her brother and sister were OK. She also listened carefully to everything being said by the women, even if it meant re-reading the same paragraph three times.

"So, are you getting excited about seeing your mother?" Addie asked Irene. "When was the last time you saw her in person?"

Irene sighed and thought about it.

"It was just after I turned eighteen. She wanted me to go to college but I just wanted to get away without adding new restrictions. You know how it can get with moms and daughters at that age. It wasn't anything she had done, really, it's just that...well, she seemed so sad and defeated. She kept giving me depressing advice and warning me about men. It was like the shadow of Armstrong hung over us. My response was to flee and create a new life while hers was to surrender and accept that joy wasn't meant for her. And remember, this was just a few years after she had been this energetic, free-spirited artist, darting around Cambria like a hummingbird in search of nectar. It kind of angered me, really, the way she changed."

"Has she changed much in the years since you left, as far as you can tell?"

"It's hard to say, really. She doesn't write a lot about herself. I mean, she does, but not where serious things are concerned. She'll tell me what she ate or about a funny thing at work—when she was there—but not much about her feelings. Mostly I think she is OK but still not in love with life. Some of that may have to do with her being ill so much. I don't know if I told you but her doctor thinks too much stress has dangerously weakened her immune system."

"Mommy, what's a moon system?" Olga asked, forgetting to pretend she wasn't listening.

The two women smiled, trying not to laugh and embarrass the little girl.

***

Later that evening, when Irene and the kids had retired to their sleeping berths in the Pullman car, Armstrong and Addie stretched their legs and kicked off their shoes in the compartment. He asked if it was OK to bring out a bottle from his suitcase and she said she didn't care as long as the Feds didn't bust down the door and arrest them.

For a while, they just rode in silence, enjoying the calm they took for granted at home. They stared out the window into the passing darkness, wondering about the occasional lights they would see in the distance. Somewhere out there were farmers or ranchers living in a different universe from Stout City.

"Maybe I shouldn't have come on this trip," said Armstrong, breaking the silence.

"We both knew it was going to be hard," Addie reminded him.

"You don't know how hard."

"I'm sure I don't."

Addie looked back outside into the darkness. She heard a slosh as Armstrong took another big drink.

Something about that slosh sounded harder than usual and it was soon followed by the confession Armstrong could no longer keep inside.

29

"Julia and I had been married for eight years and we'd lived at this artists' colony in Cambria the whole time. All sorts of artists came and went during that time. Most of 'em showed up looking for inspiration from nature, but some of them just wanted to be part of some fanciful utopia where artists commingled in an orgy of creative thought. There were also a few of them like me who just wanted a corner of the world where they could be lazy with other clever people. Unlike me, though, they all ran out of money sooner rather than later. I was the rare bird who checked in with some dough in his pocket and success under his belt. In other words, there were lots of reasons for arriving but always the same reason for departing: money.

"What I'm getting at is that Julia and I had been there longer than almost anyone and we'd seen it all. We laughed about their dreams as they came racing in and the excuses as they went moping out. At least I was laughing, anyhow. Julia it turns out wasn't laughing at them so much as she was humoring me. The truth is she was one of them and I shoulda recognized it.

"I'd watched her from the start, after all. I'd seen her move in and claim her little cabin with Irene in tow. Within a day Julia was out trying to sketch the bluffs over the ocean. And I mean she was practically racing out to the cliffs, she was so excited. I thought it was pretty cute and after a while I kind of admired her relentless spirit. And while I was watching Julia I was getting to know Irene, who was clever as hell for a little girl—a lot like Olga today. Anyhow, that led to me to knowing Julia more and the rest is history.

"The three of us—me and the two girls—seemed to fall in love if that makes sense. We just sort of understood we were supposed to be a family, and sure enough we made a great family. The problem was me, and it was a problem that grew as time went on.

"I continued my lazy ways, content to watch with amusement as Julia darted around creating art like her life depended on it. She teased me about my apathy and I teased her about her obsession. Now don't get me wrong, we had a certain respect for each other's talent. She was impressed by my past success and I was impressed with her creative output. But she could never reconcile my waste of talent and I guess I didn't encourage hers enough. I sorta patted her on the head and congratulated her like a kid coming home from school with her little projects.

"So back to the others, the rotating colonists. They were in and then they were out. I guess she looked down on them for not sticking with their claims of artistic ambition even though she knew she was only able to continue thanks to my bucks. I just looked down on 'em for everything. Or so I thought. It's taken me many years but I now realize I was actually jealous of their dreams and restlessness. They had a passion...a....a thing in their souls that compelled them to create. I had come out hoping to magically learn good painting technique while they showed up determined to *work* at it. Ultimately, I was no great artist, just a lazy lizard looking to sun on the rocks all day."

Armstrong fell silent and looked out the window. He drank some more before glancing back at Addie.

"You must think I'm pretty pathetic the way I cling to this bottle like a calf to its momma."

Addie just shook her head. Any words would have sounded insincere and they both knew it.

"I'm telling you this story because I need to say it out loud," he explained to her.

"And I'm honored that you trust me," she answered.

He gave her a soft grin before continuing.

"So Julia and I were in love but we were starting to resent each other a little. Does that make sense?"

"It does," Addie agreed.

"Maybe we should have left that place. You can only play art camper for so long. We'd have gotten a place in the city and had bills to pay and I would have been shocked back into doing something productive. Or we would have gotten a divorce, who knows?

"Anyhow, we were on the verge of beginning to dislike each other because of my laziness. That's when a new couple arrived at the colony. They rented a cabin about a hundred yards away. A husband and wife from Moses Lake in Washington, although they never really settled..."

"What were their names?" Addie asked.

He licked his lips and then took a slow drink.

"Tom and Sadie. The Coopers. They were about my age—I was forty-eight at the time, Julia was, um, thirty-nine—and they seemed very nice. More than nice. That's a meek word. They had it together, as in they were self-assured to the point of not needing to compete or brag. Most art types would pull into the colony and immediately begin explaining their credentials or their vision—basically their insecurity. Not the Coopers. They had traveled around the world, they were tan and they knew more than others about most any subject you could bring up.

"We took an instant liking to them, spending evenings and sharing lunch on the days it worked out. They'd never had children but Irene got along great with them. Neither of them sought to be an artist, it was just another part of the life experience they wanted to explore with purity and vigor. I thought there was something wonderful about that at first but as the weeks went by they became sort of a mirror for Julia and me to look into. Julia saw what she wanted to become and I saw what I would never be. And so it began in earnest.

"She became a fan of the Coopers, trying to learn their secrets for getting the most out of life. And what she learned was that one can never compromise and that each day demanded purposeful enjoyment. Naturally, the more enamored Julia became with these types of concepts the more despair she felt towards me. I was the opposite of the Coopers. I was a charming loafer who had achieved a nice run of success and called it a day. Like I said, we'd been on the verge of disliking each other before and now, all of a sudden, we began to explore that dislike a little bit.

"Julia began spending more time with them than she did with me. And when we were together she would tell me all about the Coopers and their way of life. This was no mistake on her part, either. She knew how these things were affecting me. She smiled at me as she told me the latest story she'd heard from them or their latest nugget of wisdom, trying to get some reaction out of me.

"At first I refused to give her that satisfaction of an emotional reaction. I let her have her fun with the Coopers while I took long walks, disappearing into the landscape where I would drink in solitude as a means of denial. Looking back now, I think I was trying to counter her game, trying to elicit reaction. Maybe I thought Julia would feel bad for driving me away and repent for loving the Coopers instead of me. Instead it just validated her belief in them.

"So one day I decided I would find a weakness in the great Coopers. I would expose them for being earthly creatures like the rest of us. I went over to their cabin where Tom and Julia were working on some wood sculpture and I invited Sadie for a walk. We headed eastward and upward into this forest-like area behind our colony. There was a light rain that day and the evergreens smelled magnificent as we walked along with needles softly crunching under our feet. I was determined to be at my charming best and I was. I had her acting like a schoolgirl. We must have spent three hours together and I can honestly say she had a great time. We returned to her cabin in a great mood, which thrilled Tom and Julia. They wanted us to be the four musketeers sailing around the world and climbing mountains together.

"So Sadie and I began taking semi-regular walks during the day while Tom and Julia practiced being artistic. By now you've probably guessed what happened. I was determined to seduce Sadie, to seduce her so slowly and deeply that she had no idea the fall was coming.

"Somehow I had channeled all of my emotions into this quest—my anger at myself, my anger at Julia, my jealousy of the Coopers. I know it makes no sense to you, Addie. How can I claim that Julia is the love of my life when here I was working so hard to hurt her, right? Well, love makes people crazy especially when it's mixed with self-disgust."

"No, I understand. I might not agree, but..."

"But, you haven't heard the final, ugly ending. You see, I patiently played with Sadie's heart for days and weeks, even talking myself into loving her. I knew what I was really after, but I made myself believe it was something else, something less distasteful. Anyway, the perfect day finally presented itself. She and Tom had fought a little the night before and she spent the first part of our walk recounting his foolishness. Sensing my opportunity, I went for the kill, consoling her as I led her toward a little abandoned cabin I'd been eyeing for this purpose since the start.

"Well, I exercised all of my emotions there in that cabin. I made her my conquest and it wasn't lovemaking, it was an emotionally and physically supercharged act. We were silent as we walked back. There was simply nothing left in us. We separated when we neared the colony and that was that. I hadn't even planned out how this affair would proceed.

"A couple days later I walked into our cabin and found Julia in bed sobbing. I knew instantly that Sadie had confessed. I guess I was hoping she would. Somewhere in my convoluted, angry mind I wanted Julia to hurt for exposing *my* weaknesses by enjoying the Coopers' strengths.

"But as I stood there looking at her, all of my dislike for her suddenly vanished. It was like a fog lifted and all I saw was the most wonderful woman in the world, broken and devastated. I was supposed to cherish her heart and instead I had stomped on it because I was a selfish failure...who..."

Addie watched in stunned silence as Armstrong stopped talking to wipe away the tears in his eyes. This time the tilting of the bottle was unmistakably angry. He gulped the gin like he wanted it to skip his mouth and throat and go straight to wherever it was that made him feel things.

"Julia told me to get out and I did," he continued sullenly. "I went and lived with an old fella I knew back in the forest who eked out a living collecting and selling rocks. Six days later Irene arrived and told me Julia was in the hospital. She had not eaten the whole time I'd been gone. When I got to the hospital, I couldn't believe how frail she looked. There was no color except for the pink in her puffy eyes. I tried to tell her how sorry I was and why I had done it but she didn't react at all. Just stared at the ceiling. I finally gave up and stood there like an idiot and then she looked at me for the first time.

"That's when she told me she was pregnant with our son. I was so stunned to hear this that I just stared back at her. It took a few seconds for me to finally ask how she knew it was a boy. I will never ever forget the way she looked at me. That was the moment that my life ended, if you know what I mean.

"I had killed our child and I had destroyed the bond between me and Julia in one atrocious deed. And then there was Irene. She didn't know any details but she knew I was the cause of this destruction and so she shunned me out of loyalty to her mother. Later I found out that Tom and Sadie had also split.

"Everything was shattered in every imaginable direction. No one cared why I had done it or how sorry I was, and believe me, I got down on my knees next to that hospital bed and begged Julia to feel something for me even if it was pity. But she just looked at me with such profound sadness that I was sure I'd never be able to fix what had happened. I figured the best thing I could do for everyone involved was leave, and I did. I went down to Coronado and began my endless intoxication. You're the first person I've ever told this story to."

Armstrong took a deep breath and ran a sleeve across his face to make sure he had gotten every tear. He was done confessing and now it was time to numb his brain in earnest.

"I'm glad you shared this with me," Addie said softly. "You must have had strong feelings for Julia to still feel so badly. I just don't know what to say."

Armstrong just nodded impatiently. He didn't want Addie to say anything. He hadn't told her the story seeking consolation or advice or even admonishment. He just needed to confess out loud before he saw Julia.

Addie wanted to tell him that it was going to be all right, that Julia would forgive him and that he would live happily ever after, but she had no idea how this would all play out. She still hoped to eventually get a painting or two for all her effort, but right now she was just hoping that a sad family could find some peace.

She told him goodnight and left for her sleeping berth in the Pullman car.

Armstrong remained in the compartment alone, working on his booze and staring into the darkness as the train raced toward Colorado. He could feel himself pulled nearer to Julia every second, and he wondered whether she was hoping to see him or dreading it.

30

Addie and her gang of weary travelers arrived in Greeley late the next morning. After disembarking from the train and claiming their luggage, they stopped at an information booth and got the address for a hotel near Julia. Since Julia rented a room in a boarding house it would've been impractical, if not impossible, to meet there. Plus Addie and Irene had already agreed that Armstrong needed his own room for reasons of sanity. The hotel was yet another expense, but Addie was already committed to going broke in her pursuit of getting rich.

Outside, at the taxi stand, Addie gave the hotel address to the captain. He read it and winced before looking sorrowfully at the children. Apparently Julia didn't live in the best part of town.

As they rode toward their hotel, Irene nudged Addie in the ribs and had her look over at Armstrong. Squeezed into the corner, he had Madeline in his lap and they couldn't have been happier. She played with his beard and asked silly questions, laughing halfway through his silly answers. Irene and Addie smiled at each other.

Like most hotels with ambitious names, the Aristocrat was lacking in anything resembling class. It appeared sturdy enough, all right, but it would need a good cleaning just to attain the status of dirty. None of the traveling party cared, though, and they checked in to their rooms—Armstrong in one and the rest in the other.

As planned, Irene called her mother after they settled in. Despite the fact that mother and daughter would see each other face to face very shortly, they engaged in a lengthy telephone conversation detailing the entire train trip. All the while "Aunt" Addie did her best to keep the kids from talking loudly and jumping on the beds. Naturally, the harder she tried the more they wanted to do the opposite.

In the other room, Armstrong collapsed on the bed. He had engaged in more social activity during the taxi ride alone than he normally did in a year's time. He loved growing closer to his family, but the sudden influx of babble was causing his brain to shut down. It was so bad he didn't even have the strength to pull out a bottle. He just lay on the bed, moaning ever so slightly.

Then there was a knock on his door. For just a moment he considered ignoring it but realized that was fruitless.

"Enter," he commanded while reluctantly sitting up.

"Hey Armstrong, how you feelin'?" Addie asked as she entered.

"Just a bit weary, that's all. At home, traveling to the bathroom and the kitchen consecutively has been known to tire me."

"Listen," she began with a slightly serious tone. "Irene just talked to Julia and she'll be over to the hotel in about an hour. What they decided was that maybe she should initially meet with just Irene and the kids. I don't really need to explain why that would be best, do I?"

"I'm actually quite relieved. Our meeting will be tough enough without the awkwardness of so many witnesses. Wait a minute, she did say she was willing to see me at some point, didn't she? Maybe I'm assuming."

"No, you're not," Addie assured him with a benevolent smile. "She wants to see you after. Just remember she is very weak from an illness so it might have to be a short first meeting."

Armstrong nodded before collapsing back on the mattress.

"Just give me a minute's warning before she sees me," he added.

"OK. And, um, it's really your decision, but maybe..."

"...don't get drunk. I will drink for the safety of my nervous system but I will not get drunk."

"Thanks," said Addie softly before pulling the door shut behind her as she exited.

After Addie left, Armstrong waited as long as he could—seven minutes—before removing a bottle from his suitcase. Wanting to keep his promise to Addie, he took just a few swigs before lying back on the bed and promptly falling asleep.

***

Two hours later he awoke to a knock on the door. Before he even had a chance to properly awaken, the door opened and Irene entered. She sat down on the edge of bed and spoke quietly to her stepfather.

"Hey, Armstrong," she said soothingly. "In a few minutes Mom is going to come visit you. She is very nervous after all these years so please be nice, OK?"

"Of course I'll be nice. I'm more nervous than she is."

"You'll be pleased to know the kids and I have had the most wonderful time with her. It's been like a dream come true for all of us."

He smiled and squeezed her forearm.

"I'm glad," he said with deep sincerity.

"I don't think she will visit you long. She is really weak and being with the kids has just about wiped her out, but she insisted that she wanted to see you. Are you OK to see her?"

He nodded.

Irene left and Armstrong found his bottle and knocked off one hellacious gulp to replace any buzz lost to nap time. It gave him a jolt of excitement. He looked in the mirror—something he rarely did at home—and frowned at the beard. *I should have cut that beard off like Addie suggested*, he thought.

There was a small knock on the door. Was this really happening? He had been imagining this moment for sixteen years.

31

Armstrong opened the door and there stood Julia, his ex-wife, the only woman he had ever truly loved.

She was older with shorter hair and looked frailer than he remembered, but there was no doubt it was his Julia. The shape of the eyes and those perfect freckles on her cheeks had not changed one bit. But as she smiled at him there was also no mistaking the tiredness deep in her eyes.

"Hello, Armstrong," she said coyly.

"Hello, Julia."

They studied each other a moment, each trying to reconcile the face frozen in time with the new, older face.

"You want to come inside?" he finally asked.

"Thank you."

She took two steps inside and then stopped, unsure what to do next. Her arms hung in front of her, hands clutching the strap of her dangling purse.

"Let me pull out this chair for you," he offered as he grabbed it. She smiled politely and sat down while he took a seat on the edge of the bed. Two feet and sixteen years separated them.

"Irene told me she had the best time with you. You must have been very excited to see your grandkids."

"My heart is full right now. They were so precious that I just wanted to eat them up and of course I've missed seeing Irene for so long. They told me they had fun with you on the train trip."

"Yeah, they're good kids."

"This feels bizarre after all these years," she admitted, saying what was on both of their minds.

"I guess we're the same people, though. There's just been a giant pause."

They smiled in agreement before falling silent. The tension was so thick that each thought the other could probably hear their heart beating. Armstrong had been building up to this moment for so many years and now that it was here, he could hardly trust himself to speak. And then with a wavering voice it tumbled out of him.

"I know it's been a long time, Julia, and...I'm...just so sorry. I'm so, so sorry..."

Before he knew what was happening he began to sob. He just hung his head and cried, covering his face with his hand.

Julia was caught by surprise. She had feared he would act like nothing happened or maybe even give her a bit of the cold shoulder. She never expected that he would fall apart like this. His emotion seemed genuine and part of her wanted to comfort him but it was too soon, she didn't know this man well enough anymore. And deep down, she wanted to see him feel bad over the thing she had mourned about for all these years.

The wait was painful and awkward and when he finally looked up again there was much sniffling and wiping of eyes before he was ready to proceed. Julia couldn't help but feel somewhat sorry for the sad little boy in front of her.

"Sorry about that," he whispered without looking her in the eye. "It's been a long trip and I guess I've been working myself up for this meeting. You can't imagine how bad I've felt all these years."

"You'd be surprised," she said with a sardonic smile.

He dared to look directly at her and caught her hint of smile. There was some bitterness in it but it was still a smile, the thing he needed more than anything in the world. He smiled back like the little boy forgiven, told he could return to the dinner table.

"I don't want to talk about those...events," he confessed.

"Neither do I," she whispered.

"But I gotta tell you some things, Julia. OK?"

"OK," she said, shocked at how she felt herself melt just a little bit when he said her name.

"Those things...what happened to us...it was all my fault. You deserved better than me and I know it now, and I should never have punished you for being better than I deserved."

"Maybe," she admitted with a benevolent smile, "but you are all I wanted and I wanted all of you, including the parts you gave up on."

"But why me?" he begged so sincerely.

"How does anyone know how that works? You stole my heart and everyone else ceased to matter. I had no choice. It was like I woke up one day and you were my purpose. What I never understood was how you didn't see the same priceless man that I had fallen in love with."

"That's how I felt about you, the priceless part. I just didn't know how to grasp it."

"There was nothing to grasp. All you had to do was look at me with wonder and lust in your eyes and you did that for the first years of our marriage. I didn't even need you to rediscover your passion for art; I just wanted you to be as happy as I felt. But as you floundered and drank more and more, it made me feel like I was killing your passion when I only wanted to stoke it."

"But that had nothing to do with you, Julia. That was my problem. I was confused and my confidence was gone and I just hid from what I was afraid I could never become."

"Don't you understand? That's exactly what a woman in love wants more than anything—to inspire her man and make him feel like he has so much support he can't fail. Your surrender was an indictment of my power as a wife in love."

Then, just like that, there was nothing more to say. They had poured out their long held grievances and it had only run them in circles. The blinding emotion had receded over the last sixteen years but the misunderstanding had not.

"All I know," Armstrong finally said, "is that I have hated myself ever since I did those things. So many people were hurt and...our son..."

He trailed off, unable to say the words, unable to admit he'd killed their boy. He wasn't surprised when Julia's lips quivered and her eyes flooded with tears. He knew he had touched the rawest spot in her heart.

But he didn't know the truth behind that raw spot.

32

Julia covered her mouth and stared at the floor as her eyes filled with tears.

Already feeling horrible for causing her pain, Armstrong wanted to say something, but no words came to him, so he just watched in shame.

When Julia finally caught her breath and she looked back at Armstrong, he could instantly see by the look in her eyes that something was different.

"What happened at the end hurt me so badly," she whispered. "It felt like everything in the world had been taken from me—my love for you, my passion for life, for art—it felt like I had died in a flash and I wanted you to hurt as much as me. When you visited me in the hospital and looked at me with pity after destroying everything, I said something terrible, Armstrong."

"What do you mean?"

"I told you I lost our son, but...there was no son, there was no baby. I made it up to hurt you and I have been living with my guilt just like you. I'm so sorry, I swear I am."

Her voice trailed off as she stared at him, waiting for his reaction, but he just looked toward the window and rubbed his chin.

"Say something, please," she finally implored.

"What do you want me to say? That I hate you? That I deserved it?"

"I don't know," she admitted.

He stood up and walked to the window and looked some more. Then he turned and walked past her to his suitcase.

"I guess it's been explained to you that I'm a hopeless drunk," he said while extracting his bottle from a jumble of clothes.

"I've known for a long time. Irene told me."

Satisfied with the answer, Armstrong grinned and knocked off a Paul Bunyan-sized swig before walking back to the bed and sitting on the edge where he had started. He grabbed another quick gulp and set the bottle on the floor.

"You know a good part of this drinkin' has to do with my guilt for killing our son, don't you?"

She nodded while looking down at her lap. There was a long silence before Armstrong leaned over and gently lifted her hands and held them in his. He waited until their eyes were locked.

"I deserved that lie, Julia. Because of me we never had a child and we should have had half a dozen. You should have had a husband who tried harder. I am fully responsible for everything bad that happened to us including that lie. I don't deserve it, but...would you ever forgive me, Julia?"

"I forgave you a long time ago," she whispered through a sad smile. "You broke my heart but it was yours to break, and that kind of love doesn't just disappear. I know you better than anyone ever will and I know why you did what you did."

"I did it because I was an ass."

"An ass that didn't know how to love himself and because of that he didn't know how to let his wife love him."

Armstrong nodded slowly with a grim, sorrowful expression. She did know him better than anyone ever would.

"Have we forgiven each other?" Julia asked softly, hopefully.

It was the question he had dared not to dream, and even after sixteen years of trying to numb his heart, it still responded to her in an instant.

He slid off the bed onto his knees. He looked up at her sweet smile and smiled back before laying his head in her lap.

The room was completely silent as she rubbed his head and played with his hair. His arms clung to her as he savored peace for the first time he could remember.

33

A couple days after returning from Dellton, Zep lucked into some extra work. The freight company called him in to cover a few loads, replacing a regular who had sprained his ankle. The good news ended there.

As a relief driver he was assigned the oldest, worst truck in the company's fleet. It was a 1920 chain drive Mack, which had been nicknamed "The Pig" by the other drivers. It was slow, cumbersome and steered like a pouting mule. The driver was practically required to lift out of his seat and tug on the steering wheel with all his weight when turning hard.

Within the laws of nature there exists a subset of drudgery laws, one of which states: by pure chance a substitute worker will always end up covering a regular worker's worst day. This law immediately applied to Zep. When he arrived at the site of his first load, he was greeted by three large piles of bricks, salvaged from the rubble of a demolished building. Attached to the first pile was a note telling him where to deliver the bricks. There were no further instructions and no one on the premises to assist him. So, after a couple phrases unsuitable for even a pirate, Zep accepted his fate, put on his gloves and got to work.

Three hours later, The Pig was loaded and on its way to deliver the bricks—until it reached Morwell Street, anyhow. That was where it decided to quit running while sitting at a stoplight. Still sweating from heavy labor, Zep stumbled from the cab and glanced at the angry drivers behind him. An old man laid on his horn while staring Zep in the eye, urban conversation at its finest. And it didn't stop there. As Zep stood on The Pig's bumper, leaning into the engine compartment, he received occasional comments from drivers stopped at the light next to him. They pointed out what a jackass he was for holding them up and that he should have known better than to drive an iron dinosaur in regular traffic.

By the time he fixed the engine and delivered the bricks he was so behind schedule he had to skip lunch in order to get to his next load on time. This was unfortunate because Zep struggled with patience when he went too long without food, and his next load involved an older lady shipping a cast iron sewing machine to her niece. It seems she neglected to mention the machine being on the second floor when placing her order with the dispatcher. Maybe she forgot and maybe she knew they would charge her extra for a second man, but either way, Zep was on his own. Hungry and cranky, he tackled the job with enough ruthlessness to worry the old lady.

When he'd finally yanked the machine to the stairs and begun the descent, the iron beast was so heavy it was moving Zep more than Zep was moving it. The older woman was too frail to physically assist, but she was generous in giving needless advice and warnings about carpet damage as Zep risked his life one stair at a time. When he had finally wrestled the machine onto The Pig, she was even thoughtful enough to remind Zep that the day was slipping away. So are you, he wanted to say, but smiled instead and waved goodbye.

The joy of this delivery was solidified when he arrived at the niece's house where she informed him that she really had no use for the cast iron sewing machine and was only appeasing her aunt.

"It'll make a nice little side table," Zep offered, determined to get rid of his load. "You can set drinks on it or some flowers in a pretty vase."

The niece brightened upon hearing the idea.

"Next to the bed in the guest room. That would be kinda cute."

"Just point the way."

"You'll have to take it through the back door and up the back staircase, then down the hall to the last room on the right."

"Say, could I trouble you for something to eat? Anything. Like an apple maybe?"

***

The day's wages had come at a good time, as his money was running low, but the work itself reminded Zep of why he had wanted to find that painting so badly. Yes, he wanted to help Addie, and yes, she would profit the most, but he would still make enough to avoid days like this one.

That night he thought some more about the elusive *Number 17*. Although he had taken no further action since returning from Dellton, the painting had continued to intrigue him. Of particular interest were Bigelow's two stories regarding its sale to an unknown lady wearing a sumptuous fur.

There was something about Bigelow that made Zep feel uncertain. It was just hard to believe a second story after the first one was an admitted fib. But every time Zep started to seriously doubt the attorney, he remembered that check that Bigelow had written to Vic. There was no way that Bigelow could've known Zep would be paying a surprise visit and thus he had no reason to write it except for genuine restitution. But wouldn't he be admitting wrongdoing by sending that check? No, Zep admitted, the slippery lawyer would have a story for that, too. Something about discovering an old savings account of Minnie's, probably.

And even if Bigelow were lying to everyone involved, proving any wrongdoing would be difficult. It would require circumstantial evidence, which would be tedious and time-consuming to gather, if it even existed. The best witness was dead and the painting's location was unknown.

As Zep paced in the living room of his apartment, he boiled it down to a pair of scenarios. Either Bigelow knew the true whereabouts of the painting and wasn't saying, or his second story had been a true confession after he'd been caught in a lie on the first story. Neither scenario could be proven, but the second one offered the most hope. If he was going to pursue *Number 17*, then it made more sense to focus on the mystery lady with the sumptuous fur.

Zep stopped in his tracks. What about the other three paintings she had acquired from Bigelow? Being so specific about the ones she wanted—including an unsigned Perzie—she must have a strong knowledge of art value. If he could track her down and put some fear into her about being an accessory to a questionable transaction, maybe he could get *four* great pieces on the cheap.

He had work as a relief driver lined up for the next day, but after that, he was headed back to Dellton to poke around a bit.

34

Based on his original thought that the lady in the sumptuous fur had a social relationship with Minnie Upton, Zep's plan was to start at the Dellton Library. It was his experience that most of these small towns had newspapers that recorded every little social event, including tea parties and visits from out-of-town relatives. Surely a woman with such refined taste in art would stand out in a place like this and be duly recorded.

Zep went from the train station directly to the library only to find a sign on the door explaining that they were closed for lunch. He shouldn't have been surprised but he was anyhow. He looked around to see if he was being watched as part of a prank but the only one looking back was a squirrel at the base of a nearby tree.

Surrendering to local custom, Zep walked down Front Street and entered the first eatery he encountered. It was a small café run by a weary looking Swede and his wearier looking wife. A lack of riches always seemed to affect the wife worst. It wasn't the lack of things, per se, as much as other women noting the lack of things.

Zep stood inside the door looking for an empty table, but it was difficult to see through the haze of cigarette smoke. As he waited for his eyes to acclimate, a temporary break in the cloud occurred as a customer walked past, stirring up the smoke.

He spied an empty booth and slid into it, grabbing the menu propped against the wall. Having been printed a decade ago and subjected to harsh conditions since, the menu had a slight limpness to it—as used and weary as the owners. And where each item's price had changed over the years, the proprietors had scribbled out old costs with a fountain pen and written in new ones. The writing wasn't as careful as warranted, though, and Zep was unsure whether the meatloaf plate was forty cents or ninety cents.

He looked up and squinted through the smoke, catching sight of the kitchen. An enormous man with a filthy cap and a shiny face whistled as he constructed lunches. If the cook was happy, then the food couldn't be too bad, Zep reasoned. Then again, one of the happiest people he ever met ran a garbage dump. Maybe it was just the peace that came with not having to meet any standards whatsoever.

Before Zep could decide if he wanted to go through with this, he sensed somebody standing above him. It was the wife, waiting to take his order.

"Any recommendations?" Zep asked.

"The hot dog won't kill you...and nobody has sent the chili back today."

"Truthfully, it seems like everything in here would taste like cigarette smoke."

"It does. Probably the only thing that saves us."

"You're a funny gal, and nice lookin', too. What keeps you here?"

"I'm married to the owner."

"Yeah, I noticed him when I walked in. So, what really keeps you here?"

"I'm too old to do anything else. You should have seen me when I was young, there was a time when boys got jealous over me, but that was about a hundred years ago."

"Don't get me wrong, I have a girlfriend and all, but I think you're selling yourself short. Not that I want you leaving your husband, but you should know for a fact that you could still make a man jealous. Matter of fact, your husband has looked over here three times with a frown."

"Because I'm not movin' fast enough. Whaddya wanna try?"

"Gotta be a chili dog."

"Your stomach will thank you. And I thank you, too...for the pep talk. It's harder when a woman gets old; too much of our self is tied up in our looks. When they fade, so does our value."

Zep shook his head and gave her a polite smile, but he didn't say anything. He couldn't. She'd said it the way the world saw it, right or wrong. And *that* was what kept her here.

***

Zep was relieved to find the library open upon returning. Relative to the size of this small town, the library was no broom closet, and it had the most modern interior of any building he had entered in Dellton. Government money works in mysterious ways, he decided.

He moved to the back where the reference materials were contained and found the librarian in charge of the section at her desk

"Good afternoon, madam," said Zep, using the goofy charm he saved for when he needed something.

"Good afternoon. How may I help you?"

"Um, well, is there any way I could look over some local newspapers from about a year ago? I'd be most grateful."

"Certainly. The *Dellton Blade* is our local paper and it is published weekly except in May and September when the editor visits his parents in Alta."

"The *Blade* would be fabulous, thank you."

"If you want to choose a chair I'll be back in a few minutes with issues from last February and March."

"Perfect, thanks."

Forty-five minutes and eight issues later, Zep had caught up on current events in Dellton but hadn't gained any particular insight into Minnie Upton's social life. The

213

only mention of her was in regards to a dinner party she had hosted for her cousin and husband who were visiting from Topeka. A good time was had by all, but none of the other guests was listed by name.

Zep had also failed to come across anything resembling an art club or even a visiting artist, save for the man who swallowed fire as part of Dellton Days.

Zep considered his next move for a few minutes before approaching the same librarian.

"Here are your papers back. They're very impressive," he exaggerated, "and I think I found what I needed."

"Oh, I'm so pleased."

"Yes, thank you. Now, there is one other thing I'm working on that maybe you can help me with."

The librarian smiled with professional anticipation.

"I'm helping a friend with some art stuff, turn-of-the-century American paintings mainly, and I was curious if there was some sort of local expert that people around here go to for assistance."

"I hate to say it," she confessed, "but we don't get much call for such services in our fair town. I'm sure there are residents with an interest in art but my guess is they would go to Stout City if they needed important information."

"Makes sense."

"Now, we do have a handful of books here in the library that might be of assistance to you."

"You don't need to..."

"Oh, it's no problem at all," she insisted as she began walking to another section.

Zep followed behind her and noted that she had great posture. There was something to be said for the way a woman carried herself. It gave the suggestion of physical confidence, which men found subconsciously intriguing. *It's the unappreciated trait,* Zep thought.

The librarian turned between two towering rows of books and stopped at the desired destination, where she tilted her head to read the classification numbers. Her eyes zigged down one shelf, then zagged back down another before finding the precise spot. She removed four books in quick fashion and handed them to Zep.

"Now, to check them out you'll have to apply for a card," she explained. "If you just wish to peruse them or look for a specific piece of information you are more than welcome to enjoy them here in the library."

"Thanks," said Zep passively, not really wanting the books in the first place.

Feeling obligated to give them a quick viewing, he found a seat and soon discovered a section in one of the books devoted to Perzie. Zep was impressed. Not only were the examples of his work stunning, but the little biography made Perzie sound like he'd been quite the playboy in his heyday. The vision of Perzie cutting a swath through the city hardly jibed with the old drunk he'd met in a sad apartment.

Zep was about to close the book when he noticed for the first time that the page had been bookmarked with a tiny scrap of paper. He removed the scrap and examined it more closely. It appeared to be the torn-off corner of a paper and it contained just two words: "next week." The words meant nothing but the style of the writing was definitely masculine.

An idea clicked in his mind and he tracked his librarian down at her desk.

"Could you tell me who the last person was that checked this book out?" he asked her.

"I'm not really at liberty to share that information with other patrons. It wouldn't be fair to them just as you wouldn't want me to share your reading habits with others."

"I completely agree," he said with his top-of-the-line smile. "But in this case I found a dollar bill being used as a bookmark. It seems like it should be reunited with its owner."

He held up a tired dollar, which had been in his wallet a moment before.

"I'm sorry," she said. "All I can do is return it to them on your behalf."

"OK, but could you at least look them up before I leave? I hate to sound greedy but if no one has checked this baby out then this sawbuck is fair game."

The librarian gave him a slightly disappointed look, but he had a point, and so she motored toward the front of the library with Zep in tow.

At the front desk the librarian searched through some boxes under the counter before extracting one and flipping through some cards. She finally stopped and studied a particular card before informing Zep of the result.

"It shows here that a patron did indeed borrow this book a few months ago. I would assume that the dollar bill you found belongs to him."

"I'd be glad to save you the trouble and return it to him."

"Its no trouble," she countered. "He is a regular patron and I will make sure his property is returned."

"It's Lloyd Bigelow, isn't it?" he blurted out.

Zep studied her face and noted a hint of anger in her eyes.

"I really can't say," she apologized sternly.

But she already had.

35

For their second day together it was decided that Irene and the children would meet Julia at a nearby park. The kids could run and be silly and the fresh air would do everyone some good. Irene had initially been hesitant about her ill mother sitting in the February cold, but Julia insisted that she could bundle up and be happy. Addie would tag along and act as a nanny while Perzie remained in his room loading up on solitude and bootleg gin.

When the gang first met at the park, Julia took advantage of her morning energy to play with her grandkids. She stood at the bottom of the slide as they took turns laughing and squealing on their way down toward her happy embrace. Later, she complimented Olga on her castle built in the sand box, listened intently to Madeline's wild, vaguely true stories, and fretted as Hugh ran around narrowly avoiding injury at every turn. Julia had dreamed about these precious children for so long she hugged them continually, to the point of being a loving nuisance.

All of this activity was far more than normal for Julia, so after the greatest hour she could remember, she plopped onto a bench, exhausted. Irene turned the kids over to Addie and joined her mom.

"Having fun with them?" she asked while cozying up to her mom.

"How could I not? They are absolutely wonderful, Irene. You should be so proud of them."

"I am. They are the greatest thing I've ever done."

"Which is just how I feel about you."

They smiled sweetly at each other, and Irene slipped her arm inside of her mother's. There is something about mother-daughter relationships that teeters on the extreme. When they are bad they are the worst, and when they are good there is nothing stronger. Julia and Irene had overcome sixteen years of separation in less than a day. Whatever that thing was that they shared—love, understanding, need—it required no words and no explanation. It was simply joined in progress at any time, no matter the argument or the space that had temporarily halted it.

"I hope they didn't tire you too much," Irene worried.

"Oh no, I'm fine. I've been saving my energy for them. I just have to be sure and rest."

"So what does your doctor say about this?"

"He doesn't think there is much to do, really. It's just a matter of eating right, getting sleep, avoiding stress—that kind of thing. Apparently my immune system is more fragile than most, which requires me to be a little more careful with my lifestyle. Mr. Trener at the jewelry store has been a life saver, letting me work when I can, even letting me take some bookkeeping work home."

"Is that enough to support you? Don and I don't make a lot but we could..."

"No, honey, I make what I need."

"But maybe with a little more you could see another doctor. I'm not saying yours is bad, but it makes sense to get a different medical perspective."

"You're sweet, but really, I'm fine. I have actually been to a few doctors and it's the same. Plus every dime you two make needs to go to those children. I bet Don adores them."

"He does when he can. Work takes a lot of his time and he's usually tired when he gets home. I understand his need to relax, but the kids and I are excited to see him, so it's a bit of a balancing act. He does good, though. And the kids love their daddy."

"Your dad loved you, too. He thought you were sent straight from Heaven. It's probably a good thing he passed or you'd have been spoiled rotten. I'm not kidding in the least."

"How did he die, by the way? You never would tell me the whole time I was growing up."

Julia smiled sheepishly.

"I just wanted you to remember him in the best light," she admitted. "Not that there was any dark secret I was trying to hide. It's just that...well, he drowned after sleepwalking over the side of his ship."

Irene gasped and looked at her mother incredulously.

"Are you telling the truth?" she demanded.

"You think I'd lie about that? Of course I'm telling the truth, and now you know why I didn't want to give you specifics. It was better just to say he died at sea and leave your imagination to fill in the details with heroic drama. He loved you so much and I...I couldn't bear to have your primary memory of him being his, well, silly death."

Irene just shook her head.

"I can't believe it," she muttered. "How sad. And he was really sleepwalking?"

"He did it all the time at home. Or at least that's how he explained ending up in bed with the neighbor."

"Mom! That's terrible."

"I know, I'm sorry," Julia pleaded while trying to stifle a laugh. "That was actually a joke of his that he always teased me with. It never happened. You would have enjoyed his humor. It was very irresponsible humor and I guarantee you he'd have laughed harder than anyone at the nature of his passing."

There was silence as Julia remembered her first love, while Irene smiled at knowing more about him.

"That must explain your attraction to Armstrong," Irene finally said. "The dark humor."

"Actually, there is some truth to that. I've always been a sucker for funny men. Not clowns, mind you, but men who could find humor where others don't. Your father and Armstrong would have gotten along well with their cleverness and sarcasm."

"I'm glad you two made up last night. It feels like such a weight off of everyone's shoulders. And truthfully, I don't want to know what happened way back when, I'm just glad you two found some peace. You're both important to me even if we all have these odd relationships."

"Well, we both think you're special," Julia shared while patting the arm intertwined in hers.

"Maybe, but it hasn't felt special with him for a long time—ever since we reunited in Stout City," Irene confessed.

"I'm sure some of that is the drinking, honey. His whole purpose for two decades has been to dull his thinking and you can imagine how that doesn't help a relationship one bit. It certainly didn't help ours when we were married. Maybe after this trip and all the good things that come from it, he'll open his heart back up to you. I know he really cares, Irene."

"So why does he drink, why does he want to dull his thinking so badly?"

Julia considered the answer, wearing a vexed expression. She had debated this question a million times since the divorce.

"Only Armstrong knows for sure," she finally decided. "I never got a chance to help him fix it, but I have always suspected it was a combination of several things. Most of them have to do with himself, though, and you should always remember that."

"Listen to you. You think you're pretty clever trying to soften me up so that I will forgive him the way you have."

They both giggled softly at their mutual understanding.

"You don't need to forgive him in the same way I did," Julia added. "Just be the stronger one where it comes to love. Keep giving it to him and I think he will surprise you. There is a sweet little boy in there that just doesn't know how to understand the world in which he's been placed. He's gone to a corner to pout about it."

Irene leaned her head on her mother's shoulder and snuggled in tighter. They smiled and watched Addie trying to keep up with three happy little kids.

"You think Addie will ever have any children after this trip?" Irene joked.

"If she could be guaranteed that they'd be as wonderful as yours, she will."

"There are days I'd give one or two of them to her."

"Don't you dare," Julia mocked threateningly. "You'll have to answer to Grandma."

They both liked the sound of that last word and silently enjoyed it while they sat on the bench they'd always remember.

36

Spending several hours at the park with her family had been a dream come true for Julia, but it had taken its toll. She couldn't remember the last time she had felt so physically drained. When they'd dropped her off at the boardinghouse, she had barely had the strength to get to her room before plopping onto the bed, spent. Irene and Addie had offered to help but their offer had been declined. She'd be all right, Julia assured them, but she was done for the day. However, maybe they could have Armstrong stop in. She needed to talk to him for a few minutes.

Armstrong was pleased but anxious upon receiving the news. The women suggested he wait a couple of hours so that Julia could recover. They reminded him not to stay too long as there were still two days left in the visit and they wanted Julia to pace herself so she could fully enjoy the time. Also, maybe he ought to skip the alcohol before visiting, they warned before leaving.

Armstrong agreed with all their advice and told them so with sober conviction. But as soon as they left he was hitting the bottle. The upcoming visit was just too much for his strained psyche, not to mention Julia would never know whether he was slightly sober (which he wasn't) or slightly drunk (which he was aiming for).

What was bothering him the most was the unknown. They had forgiven each other the night before and seemingly made amends. So, why had she summoned him? Did she change her mind? Was she going to try and talk him out of boozing? His emotions were already so edgy where she was concerned that every scenario seemed fraught with peril.

***

Later that afternoon, a taxi deposited Armstrong at Willson's Boarding Home. He was wearing a brand new suit he had purchased in preparation for the trip. He may have been shameless on his own, but he was not about to make Julia feel ashamed in her own place. It was one of the few things he had left to give her.

The landlady greeted Armstrong in the lobby and directed him to Julia's room. She issued a reminder that guests of the opposite sex were not permitted in rooms after 7 p.m. Speaking in the most dignified manner he could conjure, Armstrong assured her that his meeting would be brief and businesslike. The landlady was a little leery about his meaning but was certain Julia would not engage in anything illicit for money.

When Armstrong knocked and entered Julia's room she was sitting at her dressing table having just checked her hair for the third time. She smiled and started to rise but Armstrong quickly threw out his hands to signal that she should stay seated. She was glad to accept his courtesy and watched as he took a seat in her reading chair nearby.

"You look nice," Julia said.

"Oh, well, it's just a suit I picked up for the trip."

She smiled at his discomfort over being discovered. Men hated being caught while trying too hard. It exposed their deep insecurity, born from a lifetime of being the designated pursuer. Men were more afraid of rejection than of snakes, spiders, and bullets combined.

"So did you buy it to impress me?" she asked, enjoying his discomfort.

"Well...I didn't want you to think I was a complete disaster. Not sure a new suit can help that much but I'm glad you like it."

223

He shrugged, knowing full well she was playing him but finding it impossible to stop himself from defending the effort.

"The thought is even better than the suit," she admitted as reward. "Thanks for coming over. I was so tired after this morning that I didn't think I would last another minute even though I needed to talk to you. I really preferred to see you here, anyhow, away from the others."

"Sure."

"Now don't be nervous. I'm not going to ask you for money or anything."

Julia laughed at her joke and Armstrong joined her.

"I'm not nervous, really," he lied. "It's just that I have been carrying a lot of guilt for a long time and it's sort of got me on my heels, if you know what I mean. Like you're the victim and I'm the cur."

"I did lie about the baby. That makes us even, doesn't it?"

"No. You never would have lied had I not started the chain of events."

"It doesn't matter, Armstrong. Didn't we agree to that last night? What's done is done and now it's time we helped each other."

Armstrong looked at her curiously.

"I need you to help me," she confirmed seriously.

"With what?"

"With something I'm about to tell you."

"What is it?"

"I'm dying," she said matter-of-factly.

"What?"

"I'm dying, Armstrong. I have cancer and there is nothing they can do about it."

"What are you talking about?" he asked while standing up. "Irene already explained the whole immune system thing. Why are you talking about cancer?"

"Because it's the truth," she said softly but sternly, "and I haven't told anyone else. Yes, I've suffered from immunity issues for years, but this time it's cancer. Cancer all through my insides. It's why I tried to get Irene and the kids out here for the last few months. I was taking medication and receiving treatments..."

"What do you mean 'was'?"

"I mean I stopped as soon as I heard you all were coming. They were only prolonging what is inevitable but I'm done. I'm tired."

"But maybe those things they were doing will help, or maybe you just need different things," he pleaded. "We should really explore all the options, Julia."

She smiled sweetly at his concern. It was all that she'd hoped it would be, even if she knew it would be hard for him to comprehend.

"I know you want to fix me but it's no use," she explained calmly. "I've already had an operation and what they found was...not good. Please don't argue, just help me. I'm really going to die—they've told me—and I'm sad and scared."

Armstrong walked over to where she sat and caressed her head while she leaned into his stomach. Then he leaned down and kissed her curly hair before beginning to pace around the room.

"When are you going to tell Irene?" he asked.

"I'm not. I want her to leave with beautiful memories of me. And those children will pick up on her sorrow if I say something. I want our only time together to be happy."

Armstrong rubbed his chin as he listened to her explanation. It made sense but hiding such a catastrophic piece of news from their daughter troubled him. Would Irene eventually understand or would she always be angry with them for deciding for her?

"So what are you going to do when she leaves?" he asked. "Just wave goodbye like there is nothing happening?"

Julia nodded, afraid to think about it lest she cry.

"And you're really dying? This isn't the final revenge to make me feel even worse?"

"Are you kidding me, Armstrong?" she asked with a flash of anger. "You must really think I'm a monster after what we shared last night."

"No, no, no," he begged, waving his hands for her to stop. "I didn't mean it that way. I'm sorry, OK? Please?"

Julia nodded but her feelings were hurt.

"Listen, Julia. I have always loved you and I know you don't believe it, but that's what made me act like such a fool back then. It doesn't make sense but it's true. I've never had feelings for another woman since you."

"Only because you sit alone in your room and drink all day. How would you ever meet another woman?"

"Believe me, I wanted to, but I just couldn't. You ruined me for other women."

This made Julia smile just as he'd hoped. She didn't really want to be mad at him and she desperately wanted to believe what he was saying.

"OK. You're forgiven...again," she conceded.

"Good," he declared with sudden happiness. "Because I'm not going back with them on the train. I'm staying here and taking care of you."

Julia looked at him dubiously even though her heart was thrilled.

"That's ridiculous, Armstrong. I'm just going to waste away and you'll end up hating me when I can't walk to the bathroom anymore."

Like any woman worth her salt, she had to test a kindly offer to make sure it was true. Sometimes a woman had to test it twice, or three times, or until the person was sorry they'd offered.

"I don't care about those things, Julia. You're not going to scare me off and I'm not leaving you this time."

"Even if I'm in pain and there is nothing you can do?"

"Who knows, maybe I'll nurse you back to health. Ever thought of that?"

She tried to smile but the emotion nearing the surface made it impossible.

37

Four days didn't seem long enough for a reunion that mother and daughter had wanted for years. But Irene needed to get back home and put her girls back in school, and she felt guilty for leaving Don too long. Julia understood, and though she wouldn't admit it, her illness could only support so much activity. So it was with sadness that they traveled to the train station in one taxi with Addie and Perzie in another behind them.

"Grandma, what's your favorite kind of animal?" Olga asked. "I'll draw you a good one and mail it to you."

"That would make me so happy," Julia cooed. "I'd like any animal you drew for me."

"I'm serious," the little girl pleaded, wanting to cut through the patronization and get down to business. "What's your favorite animal?"

"I really enjoy birds."

"Like a turkey?" Madeline interjected with a silly laugh. Her brother, Hugh, joined in the mirth, even though he had no idea what was funny.

"A turkey isn't really a bird," Olga argued. "It can't even fly."

"It is too a bird, isn't it, Mommy?" Madeline protested.

"Well, I think you're both right," Irene decreed, "but let's not argue about turkeys right now."

Hearing the word "turkey" caused Hugh to laugh again, but his sisters ignored him while they stewed, dissatisfied with their mother's answer.

"Are you going to be all right?" Irene asked her mother. "I'm worried about you."

"It's only because you're seeing me sick like this for the first time. I've been weak off and on like this for several years; it's just hard to relate it through letters. I'll be fine. I always am."

"I can't believe we waited so long to see each other. It's rather stupid in hindsight."

"We're not supposed to say 'stupid'," Olga reminded her mother.

"Yes, you're right, honey. But in this case it wasn't being used to put anyone down."

"It was putting you and Grandma down."

Irene started to protest, but her kid was right. She beamed inside at having such a clever girl.

***

In the trailing taxi, Addie was laying the groundwork for her confession.

"Now that you've made up with Julia, I was hoping I could tell you something and you'd be understanding," she said hopefully.

"Are you going to tell me that you really are a prostitute?"

"Well, if I am, I'm not very good, spending all my time trying to improve your relationship with other women."

"Excellent point. So what is it I need to understand?"

Addie started to talk but hesitated. She knew her next words might compromise their relationship and make her look like a scoundrel. She smiled at Armstrong sheepishly before taking the plunge.

"I told you when we first met that I was a big fan of your paintings, and it's true. I saw *Number 16* and thought it was so beautiful that I forgot to breathe. But it's also true that I'd only seen it a couple days before I met you, not in college like I claimed."

"Uh huh."

"And, well, the reason I tracked you down was because I had an idea that maybe I could, um, see about getting you to paint again, and if I could do it maybe I'd be able to get one of your paintings and maybe sell it for a profit. Gosh, that sounds so terrible out loud."

Armstrong studied her with a trace of a smile on his face.

"What made you think you could make money off one of my paintings?" he queried.

"An art gallery owner told me she had customers who still requested your work."

"Which owner?"

"Marry Yo."

"Ah, my old conduit to the wealthy. I've thought about visiting her a hundred times. Did she come up with the plan to fleece me?"

"I wasn't exactly looking to fleece you," she said with a hurt expression. "My intention was that you would resurrect your career and we'd all make some money."

"So it was your idea, then? And you initially visited Irene in search of the painting I gave her as a wedding gift so you could buy it and sell it?"

"You make it sound like I'm a bad person, but really I'm not. Didn't I just help bring you happiness?"

Armstrong looked away and pondered all that he'd heard.

"I guess I never really thought too deeply about your motives," he finally admitted. "I've lost my touch where it comes to understanding the human condition. My initial feeling is to be hurt, but that's not entirely fair because I was allowing myself to believe what I wished. And really, when I think about it, your plan has a certain cleverness to it, and I can't deny that all involved would benefit. But there's one big problem: I'm not sure I want to paint again."

Addie tried not to look crestfallen because she still felt bad about lying, but Armstrong could see it nonetheless.

"I know it's not what you want to hear," he confessed, "and I know you've done a good thing healing my family, but business is business, and in this case business depends on a tired old drunk who isn't inspired anymore."

"I understand," she said with soft surrender.

"But listen, I still want us to be friends. No matter how this started it's evolved into a relationship that is special to me. And, well...like you said, you really did like my painting."

"I loved it, I swear. Ask Marry. I was dumbfounded by its colors. That's the reason I even started this scheme, because I believed your art was worthy of riches."

"Well, I'm sorry. It's unlikely that I'll paint again and thus your plan will have a sad ending. But there is one bit of good news for you. I know you've spent a lot on this trip and, well, I had already wanted you to have this."

From his pocket Armstrong pulled out an envelope embossed with the logo of the Aristocrat Hotel. He handed it to Addie and told her to open it, which she did, untucking the flap and peering inside at a small collection of cash. Embarrassed, she looked up at him, unsure what to do.

"Its two hundred dollars," he explained. "I brought most of my money with me in case Julia needed it, which she still insists she doesn't, but we'll see about that. Anyway, that's yours to keep since I'm sure you've accumulated many expenses in connection with me. And even though you were a little devious, I'm grateful that you have entered my life."

"I have to admit I was running pretty low on money, so...thank you. And even if you didn't give me this we would still be friends. You did mean that, didn't you?"

Armstrong smiled and nodded.

***

As the lead taxi neared the train station, Julia felt sick to her stomach with the knowledge she was about to say goodbye to her girl forever.

"I guess I haven't been much of a mother," she said sadly to Irene.

"What do you mean?! You're a great mother. You've written me almost every single day for years, what other mother does that? I have always felt completely loved and before that you were the best mother ever when I was growing up."

"Until I got derailed and let my sadness affect you."

"That was years, ago, mother. Every mom and daughter have that odd period in life. You have no reason to apologize."

"But it's led to our being apart, and that's my greatest regret."

"That's no one's fault, it just happened. There was always money or illness or newborns squashing our plans. All that matters is that we finally did it, and we'll do it again soon."

Julia responded with a brave smile that couldn't hide the tears that began to fill her eyes. She knew they would never be able to do it again.

"Oh, Mother, please don't cry."

"Why is Grandma crying?" Madeline wanted to know loudly.

"Because she is going to miss us when we leave."

"I'm gonna miss her, too," Madeline declared proudly.

Still unable to talk, Julia pulled Madeline tight and squeezed a lifetime worth of love into her tiny little body. She prayed for the taxi ride to never end, but the car finally stopped in front of the train station.

Julia tried so hard for the children, but she could not stop the tears and the sniffling. Not that it mattered. They were excited about the train trip and they hugged her sloppily and quickly. She tried to hold them but they slipped away, not understanding how precious love is to a grandma.

"Write me when you get home," Irene said. "So I can have my next letter."

"I will, honey. You have fun on your trip and kiss those little children's cheeks for me."

The kids were laughing and running around, distracting Irene, who was afraid one of them would dart into the street.

"This has been better than I imagined," she said to her mother. "I love you."

"I love you, too. Please don't ever forget how much."

"I won't."

They hugged one more time and Julia was sure her heart would break. They smiled sweetly at each other and then Irene was gone, taking Hugh and Madeline by the hands and marching toward the station with Olga, a porter, and luggage in tow.

Addie, who had just arrived, raced after them, pausing to turn and wave at Julia, who waved back.

The taxi door opened and Armstrong slid inside next to Julia. He gave instructions to the driver and as the cab pulled away, Julia buried her head in his arm and let forth all of the sobbing she had bravely held back. He put his arm around her and that was how they rode back to her place, without a word ever being spoken.

38

After surmising that Bigelow had checked out several books on American paintings from the local library, Zep was almost certain the attorney was lying. Now it was just a matter of determining how much and whether Bigelow could be frightened into telling the whole truth.

Ready for confrontation, Zep went to Bigelow's office, but the door was locked and knocks went unanswered. So Zep returned to the library, borrowed a Dellton phone directory and looked up the lawyer's home address. He was done playing with this guy.

It wasn't Zep's nature to be confrontational unless circumstances required it. He preferred flattery, psychological tricks, and logic, in that order. When those failed, he resorted to controlled anger. There were, however, certain things that caused him to skip all of these measures and jump straight to wrath. Being made a fool through a series of lies and trickery was near the top of that list.

When he arrived at the attorney's house, Zep was ready to unload. He rapped on the front door with measured fury, then stepped back to see if the front blinds shifted, proof that the coward was actually home but choosing to hide.

Much to his surprise, though, the front door opened almost immediately. And even more unexpectedly, he was greeted by a pleasant, smiling woman.

"Good evening," she said.

"Good evening," he responded with hesitation. He was taken aback by the friendly face, and he wasn't sure what to do with all the ruthlessness he'd built up on the way over.

"I need to speak with Lloyd Bigelow," he said stoically, trying to recapture the upper hand. "It's very important and if he's home..."

"Well, actually, he isn't home," she interjected sweetly. "He left town a little earlier on a business matter. I'm his wife, though, and maybe I can help you. My name is Delores."

"Nice to meet you, Delores. Do you know when he will be back?"

"All I know is that it will be tomorrow sometime. He didn't say when. Come inside if you'd like and you can write a message for him."

"Um, sure, that would be great. Thank you."

Zep politely stepped past her as she held the screen door open. He hadn't planned on being invited inside but it did allow for an unexpected opportunity. Part of his hunch was that Bigelow not only knew the whereabouts of *Number 17*, he might actually have possession of the painting. The possession part was rather farfetched, he admitted, but entry into the house would allow him that slim chance of catching sight of the painting.

"Just have a seat anywhere you'd like," Delores offered while shutting the door. "I was just warming up some leftover casserole for supper if you'd like a plate."

"Thank you for offering, but no," he answered while taking a seat on the couch.

"Let me pull this out of the oven and I'll be right with you," she called from the kitchen.

As he waited, Zep carefully scanned the walls but there was nothing resembling *Number 17*. This wasn't really surprising. If Bigelow had it he probably kept it hidden, especially after having surprise visitors inquire about it lately.

Done with the walls, Zep's gaze rested on Delores as she moved about the kitchen. He hadn't previously considered the idea of Bigelow even having a wife. It just hadn't occurred to him. Had he envisioned it, he'd have probably pictured a somewhat bitter wife, emotionally defeated by bad choices and bad luck. She'd have circles under her eyes from sleeplessness, haunted by her role in bearing the weasel's offspring.

In reality, she appeared to be pleasant and upbeat. Her smile seemed natural and the way she moved indicated an industrious connection with life. She wasn't thin and dull like he'd have predicted, but rather she was largeish and colorful. Everything about her was full-sized, but it was proportional and she moved well on her feet, as though her size were meant to be. She also seemed infused with confidence, which created the effect of her size being purposeful and thus more desirable than one would normally assume.

When she had finished her kitchen work, she rubbed her hands to rid them of any debris then reached behind her and untied her apron with the greatest of ease. She flipped it on the counter and moved over to the chair across from Zep.

"I'll just let that cool for a minute, and by then the smell may tempt you," she explained with a giggle. "Now who did you say you are?"

"My name is Zep. I guess you'd say I'm an acquaintance of your husband's. We've been, uh, working on a project together. Maybe he has discussed it with you, something about a painting."

"Don't recall any mention," she said with empathetic sorrow. "But believe me, attorneys get involved in all sorts of strange projects and it's better that I don't know half of what goes on. So, where are you from, Zep?"

"Stout City."

"That's what I figured. Most visitors are from there which makes sense given its size and proximity," she rambled. "Matter of fact, that's where Lloyd is now. Are you an attorney as well, Zep?"

"No, I'm not. I do special work for a wealthy client. This painting business is directly related to that, and I was prepared to get some answers from your husband."

"The way you said that sounded a touch hostile. I take it you two are not agreeing on something?"

"You could say that."

"Then your visit was not intended to be sociable? Were you thinkin' about punching him?"

Zep started to answer but she continued.

"You wouldn't be the first, you know? A fella last year—his wife was Lloyd's client in a divorce case—he punched Lloyd right in the gut when Lloyd answered the door. No words or nothin', just boom, and then he walked away satisfied, I guess."

"Sometimes that's all that's needed," Zep confirmed.

"Hold that thought," she requested while jumping up and returning to the kitchen.

Zep scooted down the couch a few inches so he could look deeper down the hallway, but there was still no *Number 17* to be seen, so he scooted back. Frustrated, he even looked up at the ceiling before wondering what he'd been thinking.

"Would you like something to drink?" Delores called out while leaning over her casserole, poking it for signs of readiness. "We've got water, milk, orange juice, beer and maybe a little a gin, but I won't confirm or deny that in case you're actually a federal agent."

"Actually, a beer wouldn't hurt."

Zep needed to figure a way to get one decent look around the place. He wasn't sure yet how to make that happen, and he still admitted it was a long shot that the painting was even on the premises, but as long as he was here it made sense to cross possibilities off the list. Maybe he'd get a chance while she went to the bathroom, or maybe he could make up some harebrained story.

Then again, maybe this was going to be trickier than he thought. Delores had returned from the kitchen with two glasses of beer and this time she had chosen to sit on the couch just inches from Zep.

"Thanks for the suds," he said with all the nonchalance he could muster.

"I figured you'd worked up a thirst walking over here to slug Lloyd in the jaw," she answered with a giggle.

So that's how it was. A woman with a lotta drive who also harbored a little hatred for her old man. Or maybe it was a little drive and a lotta hatred. Either way, she was looking to release something and Zep was the handsome fly who had just landed in the spiderweb.

In one respect this was helpful. Give her what she wanted and she'd probably lead the search for the painting. On the other hand, he still loved Mabel and he knew how she'd feel about this. Then again, Delores's proximity didn't prove her intentions.

He glanced over at Delores and her eyes confirmed his hunch. She was interested, all right. And if the eyes didn't give it away her blouse sure did. It was open two buttons further down than when she last got up. This was bad and delightful all at once.

For men there is something magical about cleavage. In any other instance, the squeezing together of generous amounts of fatty tissue would generate little interest. But stuff the fat in a brassiere and declare it off limits and a man will steal glances like he is discovering the secret to life

"That casserole does smell good. Maybe I will stay for a bite," he offered.

"You won't be disappointed," she confirmed with a knowing look.

"Um, while we're waiting for it to cool, maybe you could give me a quick tour of the place. I like to know my escape routes ahead of time."

"I told you, he is gone until tomorrow."

"Yeah, well, many a man has believed such facts only to end up catching a bullet or two when the husband changed his itinerary."

"Suit yourself," she said while standing up. "We'll start with the guest bedroom."

Zep stood up and followed her down the hall.

At each room they visited she would stand inside the doorway and tell a couple stories or point out particularly noteworthy possessions. All the while, she would wait for Zep to make a move, but he only stood in the doorways, looking for the painting while pretending to admire the room's charm. Delores was feeling a little impatient as she finished showing all of the rooms, having put none of them to use.

"I suppose you wanna look in the basement, too?" she asked with weary sarcasm.

"Actually, yeah. I like to know a woman's house before I know the woman," he flirted, hoping to buoy her enthusiasm.

It worked. She led him downstairs, albeit with a bit of trepidation, worrying what constituted fun for a man who found basements a desirable spot for action.

Once down there, however, Zep seemed more interested in the useless junk than in her.

Delores found it odd that he could be so fascinated by the clutter. As opposed to the crowing she'd done upstairs, Delores now felt compelled to explain why a broken tricycle was being saved or why a pile of mismatched wood took up an entire corner. But he didn't even seem to be listening as he intently poked around through things. She only hoped he would show that much curiosity about her when they got back upstairs.

It didn't quite work out that way, but she ended up happy, nonetheless.

Upon returning upstairs, Zep admitted that he was stalling, that he was too attracted to her and that he feared he couldn't contain his ardor to just one magnificent episode. She was a voluptuous work of art who aroused an appetite so intense that it frightened him. Turning red with desire, she tried to explain that one magnificent episode was perfectly acceptable to her. She had even heard there were healthful benefits to such trysts. But Zep insisted he would fall in love with her and he couldn't do that. So instead he kissed her on the cheek and departed before she could plead any more.

She was left standing confused and flattered, cursing the misfortune of being too desirable. The game had ended a few more blouse buttons too soon.

In reality, the game had changed in the basement while they were making small talk. While explaining how she would love to get rid of some of their unused possessions, she mentioned that one reason for Lloyd's visit to Stout City was to meet with a man named Oscar, the owner of a pawn brokerage.

39

Zep made the last train out of Dellton and arrived in Stout City as darkness descended. He caught a cab from the train station and had the driver stop a block from the Top Dollar Pawn Shop. He wasn't sure what he would find at the shop, or if he'd find anything at all, but now was not the time to get sloppy and rush into something headlong.

He stopped when he arrived at the corner of Broadway and 3rd Avenue. On the opposite side of the street sat a coffee shop and next to it was the pawnshop. From where he stood could see the lights were still on inside the Top Dollar, but he couldn't decipher much more than that. To get a good look inside, he needed to get closer, so he began crossing the street. A car honked and braked. He'd forgotten to wait for a green light. So much for keeping a low profile.

When Zep finally arrived at the other corner he had to make a decision. The entire front of the pawnshop was made up of large plate glass windows, meaning Zep had two choices: gently poke his head past the first window and spy inside or do a quick walk past the entire front and hope for a good look without being spotted.

Peeking around the corner seemed the safest route but it would certainly make him look conspicuous to anyone watching. Knowing his luck, some wannabe hero would alert a cop that Zep was casing the shop as a theft target.

Walking past the entire front would offer a better view but this was riskier. Although he and the store's owners had never seen each other, there was the risk that

Bigelow would be inside *and* looking toward the street. The gig would be up in a flash.

He decided a quick peek wouldn't look too suspicious if he leaned his back against the wall next to the window and casually twisted around and glanced inside like he was impatiently waiting for his wife. But when he snatched a look inside he discovered he was at the wrong side of the storefront. The counters and office area were what he wanted to see, and it turned out they could only be studied from the other side. He was at the wrong angle, so it was back to Plan B.

He walked briskly past the windows, turning his head toward the street to avoid possibly being identified. When he arrived on the other side he paused as though he was looking for something, then he casually whirled around and grabbed a full look toward the back office. What he saw was exactly what he'd hoped for. There in the office with two other men was Lloyd Bigelow. The attorney was sipping coffee and listening as the bigger of the two other men spoke. He remembered Addie's descriptions of the owners and guessed that the talker was Lazy and the other fella was Oscar.

What he didn't see, however, was any sort of painting. This was a big problem. He couldn't just burst through the front door and begin making accusations about a scheme without the star of the scheme. *Then again*, he thought, *don't I have enough circumstantial evidence to ruin their plan? If I surprised them right now they wouldn't exactly scramble like cockroaches when a kitchen light comes on, but it would be clear that I'm onto their setup and will do all I can to muck it up. Maybe they'd just give in and sell me the painting at a reasonable price and be done with the whole thing.*

Or would they just smile at me and shrug their shoulders? There is no proof they have actually broken any laws. Bigelow could change his story again and claim he bought Number 17 *directly from Minnie Upton, fair and square. Maybe Oscar would say it was never actually sold from the pawn store; that it had been in the backroom all along. The last proven transaction involving the painting occurred when Irene sold it to them, and that was a legitimate sale.*

Zep decided he had one big card left to play but he needed to use it for maximum effect, and surprising them right now was not the right play.

How would he ambush them anyhow? He wasn't sure what time the shop closed and he wasn't about to study the sign on the front door, but if the store was already closed, that would mean the door was probably locked. That kind of made an ambush a moot point.

It was settled; he would bide his time and keep an eye on them until he saw something indicating it was time to act. The hardest part would be spying on them without attracting attention. A lone man standing on a sidewalk without any purpose just looked suspicious. Zep needed to be doing something.

Two doors down was a little drugstore, and it gave Zep an idea. He would pop in there quickly and return to his surveillance with a clever little purchase. After one more glance inside, which confirmed the three men were still talking, he made a dash to the drugstore.

Luckily, when he stepped inside there was no other customer at the counter, just a bored young clerk waiting to serve him. Behind the clerk was the object of his plan: cigarettes. He figured it would look more natural for a man to be standing around on a sidewalk smoking. No one would think anything of it.

Even though he had an extensive alcoholic past, Zep was the rare drunk who had never taken up smoking. He'd thought about it a few times, but ultimately it just seemed like too much work, not to mention that he'd never liked the way it smelled on others. Tonight, however, called for him to dip his toe into the final pool of vice.

243

"Evening," he greeted the clerk.

"Can I help you?" the clerk responded with boredom.

"Yeah, uh, I need a pack of smokes, please."

The clerk stared at Zep waiting for more.

"Cigarettes," Zep clarified. "Like those stacked behind you."

"Most customers ask for a particular brand," the clerk explained with mock kindness.

"Oh, yes, a brand," Zep laughed. "How about those right beside you? I enjoy those."

"You smoke Vogues?"

"Sometimes. One pack please."

The clerk shrugged, grabbed a pack and laid it on the counter.

"That'll be ten cents."

Zep handed him a dime, snatched the pack and headed for the door before stopping. He retraced his steps.

"How about some matches?" he asked.

With an expression of mild curiosity, the clerk reached under the counter and snagged a few matchsticks, which he handed over.

Once outside, Zep scooted over to the edge of the pawnshop and looked inside again. The three men were still talking. Relieved he hadn't missed anything, Zep began to settle into his surveillance mode.

He pulled the pack of Vogues from his coat pocket and extracted a cigarette. Instantly he recognized why the clerk had looked at him funny. The cigarette was long and skinny, a ladies' cigarette. He stepped toward a streetlight and examined the box closer. The word "Vogue" was written with a feminine flourish and bracketed by bouquets of flowers. He frowned and stepped back into the darkness.

It pained him to go through with this, but he figured nobody would be paying close attention, if they could even tell in the dark. Reluctantly he stuck the dainty smoke between his lips and struck a match against the wall. As he began lighting the cigarette he heard a door close and looked up hoping it was Bigelow leaving, but it had been a random car door at the curb. He returned his gaze to the cigarette just in time to realize he'd held the match to it for too long. The end of his Vogue was ablaze. A small flame danced straight up, casting a glow on him that made him recognizable from across the street.

Zep pulled the Vogue from his lips and threw it on the ground, stomping on it until it was a battered mess of paper and tobacco emitting a sad, final wisp of surrender. He quickly looked around to see if the small inferno had attracted any attention, but everything seemed normal. Inside the shop, the three men continued to talk. He had not blown his cover, or so he thought.

A woman sidled up to him.

"Listen, brother, if you're not gonna smoke 'em any better than that maybe you wouldn't mind if I put one to better use."

"Oh yeah, sure. Here you go."

He held the pack toward her and she gingerly selected a Vogue. She studied it for a moment and then studied Zep. Both of them wanted to say something but didn't know where to start, so they each let it go.

"Here, let me light that for you," he offered.

She extended her hand and leaned back a tad in case the last lighting was no fluke. This time, though, he gave the action his full attention and the Vogue began to glow properly. She smiled and stuck it in the corner of her mouth, taking a big drag before removing it and exhaling a cloud of smoke.

They both pretended to be interested in the happenings of the street as they waited for the other to talk. Finally, it was the woman who spoke.

"So, you always stand around downtown smoking ladies' cigarettes?"

"Not always. Sometimes I dress up as a woman and smoke men's cigarettes."

She giggled and took another drag, studying him out of the corner of her eye.

"You're funny. And cute," she declared.

Zep smirked and gave her a shrug as if to say she was correct but there was nothing he could do about it.

"Now it's your turn to say something nice. What about me?" she asked. "Most fellas find my looks agreeable."

"And they're right. You are a nice lookin' gal."

"Maybe we could go on a date tonight," she suggested with a knowing smile.

Something clicked in Zep's mind and he realized he was talking to a prostitute.

"Not tonight," he smiled politely. "But I appreciate the offer."

"That was no offer," she immediately argued, her face snarling. "Are you a cop or something? Because I made no offer at all, OK?"

"Easy, lady. I'm no cop, just a man minding his own business. And for your information, you have a nice figure but I wouldn't pay to see more of it."

"Yeah, sure you wouldn't. Too many men have already done it for me to believe that."

"You know, you might make more money getting' hitched to one of them instead of getting rented by 'em."

"Now you sound like a preacher," she said. "But you're not far from the truth. If a girl works it just right she makes the most of her beauty per hour when she is young, and then latches on to a rich one just before her looks start to go."

Zep nodded. She might be right. This was the second time today he'd heard a woman explain her life in two parts. There was young, smooth and hopeful, followed by old, tired and resigned. Both parts revolved around the appearance. Zep understood but wished it wasn't the case. What could he do about it, though? It had been this way forever. It was nature's way or something. Attraction, fertility and all that business. Still, he'd always found a woman with class to possess the best of all aspects, and class got better with age.

He squinted at his prostitute as she stood and smoked. Yeah, even she had a chance at class. It just required her to have a little confidence in the face of obstacles. Maybe her plan would come true and some rich dude with a keen understanding would see that she had some undeveloped class to offer. She'd definitely have a certain amount of experience to offer, that was for sure.

Just then the door to the pawnshop swung open, causing the little bells above it to tinkle. Zep's eyes darted to the source. It was a man entering. He was dressed nicely and carrying a briefcase. Oscar had let the visitor in and now he locked the door behind him.

"Sorry, I need to concentrate on what's going on in there," he explained to his prostitute, figuring she had little moral footing from which judge him for spying.

"That's OK," she shrugged. "I'm getting older by the minute. I better soak a few more toads while I can."

"Thanks for thinking I was a toad," he answered sarcastically.

"Are you rich?"

"Nope."

"Then you're a toad. But a cute, funny one. Thanks for the Vogue."

She moved on and he returned his attention to the innards of the pawnshop.

He was just in time. The four men appeared to be studying a colorful painting that had no discernable subject.

40

Julia was done. Even before the doctors had peeked inside and told her the gig was up, she'd felt it in the very depths of her being. Fighting was useless. Before her visitors had arrived she'd already stopped visiting the doctor and had ceased taking any more pills.

But, after being estranged from Julia for sixteen years and then reuniting in a flurry of forgiveness, Armstrong had no desire to help her die. His instincts screamed for him to save her, to seek better medical care or to force her to try any possible medication that might help.

Armstrong understood that he'd volunteered to comfort and care for Julia during her final weeks, but he told himself he was helping to heal her instead. If he could remove the stress and effort from her life, then her body would get stronger and fight the cancer. She didn't know it yet, but he was staying to save her.

The first thing he did was find a place where they could be together. Her boarding house was too constrictive and his hotel was too impersonal, so using the classified ads, he found a small bungalow for rent. It was in a nicer part of town than her boarding house—which wasn't saying much—and more importantly it was quiet with a nice little view of the city from one of the windows. The drawbacks were the small size of the place and the lack of upkeep, but the ex-spouses didn't care. They were together, and it felt like they had space to breathe.

For the first couple of days Armstrong was kept busy getting things up to speed. The bungalow needed many little repairs and lots of cleaning. He worked harder than he had in the last two decades combined, determined that Julia be at ease in her little home.

They also needed food and the nearest market was a mile away and down the hill. He wanted to save money where he could so he chose to walk to and from the market rather than use a taxi. It was exhausting for a man who was so out of shape that a long burp had recently left him winded. But because he didn't know how long it would take to save her, conserving money was crucial, and he had to do what was needed.

Ironically, at the end of the second day he was so tired upon returning from the market that he collapsed in a chair, requiring Julia to comfort him. The deathly sick woman brought him water to drink and hand towels soaked in cold water for his forehead and neck. She took his shoes off and then put the groceries away. Armstrong wanted to protest but just needed a minute to recover. Then he needed another and another. Before he could properly nix her exertion she was done and sitting in a chair near him. Soon she was asleep, taking one of her daily naps.

He sat up and removed the cloth from his forehead and really studied her for the first time. Until now, he had looked closely at her but with eyes that sought forgiveness and then with eyes that appreciated her graciousness. Now he was looking closely at a very sick woman, taking stock of her appearance.

How had he not grasped just how terribly thin she was? There was not an ounce of fat left on her. Her collarbones protruded and her cheeks were hollow. Her eyes were sunken and dark. A stranger would have guessed that she hadn't eaten in two weeks. And there was the hair. It was gray and getting a little unkempt, which only emphasized her forlorn condition. Needing to conserve every bit of energy, Julia simply couldn't afford to waste any effort on making herself up each morning.

Not that she had ever gone overboard with her beauty rituals.

It was one of the things that had attracted Armstrong to her way back when. He loved her simplicity, the way she trusted her face without slopping lipstick and rouge on it. She didn't even wear earrings or jewelry. She didn't need to. Julia had the cutest freckles along her cheeks, and those lips were genuine and soft. To crave her was to crave the real woman, not some cartoon version wearing a costume of insecurity.

Even now with her face so gaunt and ashen, she was still recognizable as that woman he had fallen in love with twenty-four years ago. Sickness couldn't touch those little freckles.

Armstrong felt pity as he stared, and he felt sick about her plight, but he still admired her bravery. She continued to trust her face as her own even as she was dictating the terms of her ending. Why had he alienated such a marvelous woman? It was hard to believe there was a time when they had nearly hated each other.

No, he told himself, he would not dwell on the anger and the years of pain. He would instead remember the happy woman with the insatiable zest for creativity.

He closed his eyes and thought about the sunny days and the happy marriage that had once existed at an artists' colony one thousand years ago. Soon, he too was asleep.

41

That evening, Armstrong cooked some tacos, rice and refried beans while Julia sat and directed him. It was a funny exercise in teamwork. She was too weak to cook but she knew the procedures by heart. He was inept in the kitchen but managed progress with her coaching. Along the way they laughed continually over miscommunications and Armstrong's naïve questions.

"Am I stirring too fast?" he asked.

"No, your stirring is good. It's just that you are stirring the wrong thing. Try the rice."

The meal turned out wonderfully and they ate until they were stuffed, which didn't take much in Julia's case. Her appetite was declining in concert with her body's fight.

When it was dark, Armstrong suggested they sit outside and enjoy some fresh air, but Julia was soon chilled and they retreated inside. He pulled up two chairs to the window, which viewed the city, then after helping her sit, he put a blanket on her legs.

Finally settled in, they silently enjoyed the majestic view of lights twinkling by the thousands. The power of the image was difficult to describe but neither was trying.

"Did you at least have some steady girlfriends after me?" Julia wondered aloud with no warning.

Armstrong started to chuckle but when he looked at her she was serious.

"No steadies," he answered. "There have been many, um, disposable trysts, so to speak."

"You mean prostitutes?"

"A few of them were, but that was just doing my part for the economy," he smirked. "The rest were lonely women who needed human touch just like I did. Maybe a couple of 'em thought that more would come of it, but they figured things out quick enough. I never wanted to love again after us. I'm glad you did, though."

"It's not in my nature to stop loving. Paul might not have been my dream husband but he was kind and strong and I loved him. We were a good match in many ways, but we both entered into it hurting a little. His fiancé had dumped him for his best friend, and I was still jaded over our surprise ending. So even though we might have been fabulous together in normal circumstances, we began our marriage in love but also leery of each other."

"Sorry about that."

"And you should be. But that's life. It's not like our marriage was bad or anything. Paul and I were both happy even if we never could fully relax and trust each other. I think we'd have settled in and made it, but my illnesses wore us down. You think you mean it when you're in love and giving your vow about sickness and health, but reality is too much sometimes. He tried, he really did, but he wasn't cut out to be a nurse. And of course I felt guilty and projected my frustration on him. Subconsciously I practically dared him to leave me, and he did."

"I'm sorry about that, too."

"Oh, stop being sorry for everything, Armstrong. What's done is done. He probably saw my sickliness as another woman retreating from his love. People don't always use logic, especially where the heart is involved. Besides, like I said, I didn't want to give up on being loved. I would never want to be a martyr like you."

"What do you mean a martyr?"

"Actually I don't even think you are a true martyr. In truth, you've used losing me as justification for your laziness. And actually," she added with a laugh, "I don't even think it was just laziness that you were covering. It's insecurity. You told me early on that you had come to the colony to learn how to paint like a real painter. But then you never had the guts to try and learn because you knew you'd fail. So you pretended to be lazy—which didn't require too much pretending—and justified it by living off your past success even though you felt guilty about the success."

There was silence for a moment as he processed her condemnation and she internally berated herself for sounding so cruel.

"You might be right about everything," he finally proclaimed. "I've always been a bit of a mess. I guess what happened to us was inevitable."

"Maybe. Then again, maybe I should have pushed you harder. I think you were silently begging to be pushed. But I didn't have enough knowledge at the time. Remember I had never seen a single painting that you had done. I only knew you were successful enough to seemingly live off the profits forever, and I figured that your desire to learn how to *really* paint was just a gimmick to look humble and stave off boredom."

"No, I really wanted to know how to paint well. But like you said, I didn't ever truly believe I was capable of learning. It's harder being a master than you think, though."

"But you were already a master," she cried out. "A couple of years after you were gone I decided I ought to see your work. So I sent away for a limited edition book. It was very expensive but I had always been curious as to who my ex-husband really was. Well, believe me, I was stunned when I finally received the book and looked inside. I can honestly say I had no earthly idea that you were such a talented artist. You can call your work whatever you want—'pedestrian,' you used to say—but I melted while staring at your work. I sighed out loud like a love-struck teenage girl. Had I seen these when we were married I would have begged you to paint more, and then I'd have whined, and then I'd have nagged, and then I'd have threatened you with a revolver."

"Maybe my stuff was good and I was just a fool, but I'd trade it all to go back in time and be with you..."

"But you already traded it all, you dope," she declared with a smile that faded into seriousness. "You could have had it all: me, the painting career, Irene, maybe even a child of our own. Armstrong, you could still have it all. Those things are still attainable. You've already got me...at least for a while."

"But I just found you again," he complained. "And I never dreamed we'd be sitting here talking on peaceful terms. You can't leave me again, Julia, you really can't. I need you."

"So enjoy what's left of me. Stop worrying about the past and the future. I'm here with you tonight, and there is nowhere else I'd rather be. And then, after me, you can do those other things. The world needs beautiful art, and Irene needs a father, and my grandbabies need someone to spoil them..."

Julia could not go on as tears began to arrive and her throat burned.

In awe of her words and the power of her emotion, Armstrong could only stare straight ahead and wait.

In the silence he felt her hand reach out and clutch his. It was so thin it felt like he was holding hands with a skeleton, but he'd dreamed of this particular touch for years and his heart leapt. It felt like the final act of forgiveness and restoration.

He was afraid to ruin the moment by looking at Julia, but he couldn't quell the impulse. She felt his eyes and looked back. They smiled sadly at each other, a summation of their years together and apart.

"I love you, Armstrong," she said with glistening eyes.

"I'll always love you," he answered softly.

There was another moment of silence before Julia said what was on both their minds.

"We've wasted so much time," she whispered with a shake of her head. "So much time."

42

The next morning Julia slept in late. When she finally got up at 10:30 she explained to Armstrong that she hadn't slept well during the night and didn't really snooze well until daybreak.

Armstrong wasn't sure if this was connected to her illness, but he figured a good breakfast was the proper response. He made eggs and bacon while Julia sat in her chair watching. Besides answering a couple of simple cooking questions, she didn't readily talk. Armstrong could tell something was troubling her. After all the years of separation, he could still read her.

After eating, she asked him to bring her a bottle of "pep" pills the doctor had given her. She thought that might pull her out of her funk. Armstrong was only too glad to help. He'd been prodding her to get back on medication and was pleased to see that maybe she was ready to begin fighting for her life.

He went to her room and found the bottle in her suitcase just as she'd described it. Knowing she was weak he opened the bottle for her and discovered the cotton plug was still inside. This usually meant a bottle was unused. He was surprised she hadn't needed any pep during all of the activity of the past week but remained hopeful this was a start toward recovery.

Later, as he made the long walk for groceries, he began thinking that maybe he should find some other pills which might also help Julia. They were making scientific advances all the time in this crazy modern world. So, before hitting the market, he made a detour into a drugstore and asked the pharmacist if there was anything available that he might recommend. The pharmacist apologized, but said there were no magic cures for the condition Armstrong was describing. The pharmacist was curious, though, as to why her doctor would even prescribe a pep pill, and he asked Armstrong the name of the drug.

When Armstrong answered, the pharmacist nodded and smiled sadly.

"You misunderstood her," he explained. "That's a form of morphine. It's an analgesic, intended to relieve severe pain. It's a standard drug prescribed to patients with metastasized cancer, although usually it's given in intravenous form."

All the way home Armstrong battled to keep his emotions in check. If those pills were really for severe pain and she was just now using them, then it must mean her condition was worsening. He wasn't a medical whiz but he was well read and he knew that the pain was worst near the end. He began to panic at the thought of Julia sitting in their house dying and alone. Even though his arms were loaded with two grocery bags he began to run.

He arrived home by bursting through the front door and practically stumbling into the kitchen. His red face was soaked with sweat and he was breathing heavily. Julia, who had been dozing, awoke with alarm. Her body instinctively scrambled to its feet, forgetting how sick it was.

"What's wrong, Armstrong? Are you having a heart attack? I begged you to take a taxi."

He kept trying to interrupt, but he was out of breath, and she wouldn't stop making concerned proclamations. He finally held his hand up and she waited with large, frightened eyes.

"I was running, that's all. I just need to rest."

"Running?!" she asked incredulously. "Was a dog chasing you?"

"No, I would not run from a dog," he scowled, disgusted at the insinuation against his manliness. "I just needed to make sure you were still alive. The pharmacist told me your pills are for pain and it scared me that maybe...Why did you lie to me?"

"Because you'd end up worrying and doing something stupid like running up a hill with bags of groceries. Now just sit right there and I'll get you some water."

"I'm fine," he protested. "You are the one who needs to sit down."

They stared at each other for a moment before breaking out in laughter.

"I guess it's better that we are fighting to comfort each other rather than sitting hundreds of miles apart," she concluded.

After lunch they lay on the bed to recover from their morning. Side by side they lay on their backs with eyes closed. The room was completely still except for a lace curtain gently moved by the breeze. But soon Armstrong thought he felt some shaking. He looked over at Julia and caught her trying to suppress laughter.

"What's so funny?" he asked with curiosity.

"I was gonna ask you if you wanted to fool around but remembered you already had your exercise for the day."

"Oh yeah, well, I'm sure I could still knock your socks off if you wanna try."

"I have no doubt you could," she said patronizingly while patting his arm.

"Listen, woman, if you weren't so sick..."

His voice trailed off at the mention of her sickness and they returned to silence. Julia was practically asleep when Armstrong said something she didn't catch.

"What did you say, dear?" she inquired through her drowsiness.

"I asked you if you wanted to get married."

Now she was wide awake. She rolled onto her side and studied him.

"You must really wanna fool around."

"I'm serious, Julia. Tell me you have ever loved a man more than me."

"I haven't."

"And I have never loved a woman more. It's almost our duty to get married."

"Our duty? Is that really your proposal?"

He started to argue that she wasn't taking his idea seriously enough, but when he saw her mischievous grin he couldn't help but grin back.

"I'll tell you what," said Julia. "If you agree to resume your painting career I will marry you. My parents would insist on a man with prospects."

Armstrong looked at her while he considered his answer. He wanted desperately to say no, but those damned freckles defeated him one more time.

"OK, but not until after, when you're...healthy again, OK?"

"OK."

Armstrong leaned over and kissed her on the lips while she ran her hand along his upper arm.

He pulled away from her and shook his head.

"No heavy petting until we're married," he admonished her.

She gave him a pouting expression then brightened.

"You realize you agreed to paint again, don't you?"

"Yes, I realize that. I also realize that man is forever mesmerized by feminine beauty. There is just something maddening and wonderful about it that can't be denied. Should we celebrate it or curse it? Both, I reckon, but mostly celebrate."

Her smile grew bigger.

"You just called this bag of bones beautiful," she beamed, ignoring the rest of his little speech. "I couldn't ask for a better wedding present than that."

He kissed her hand and then grinned at her lasciviously before rolling onto his back. It was silent again as they faded into their naps.

43

All things considered, Lloyd Bigelow thought he'd played his hand quite nicely. There had been some surprises along the way, but he'd been smart enough to have measures waiting in place. Now it was reward time. Like a proud father, he admired the painting lying on the desk in front of him inside the Top Dollar Pawn Shop. An art expert from Chicago had just arrived and was now studying the work with a magnifying glass.

From the first time Minnie Upton had introduced him to the painting, he'd been fascinated by its unique beauty. It was during a casual visit to her home that she had taken him back to her bedroom and shown him her latest prize. She was beyond thrilled about her purchase from a pawnshop in Stout City. She explained that it wasn't signed by the artist, but everything about it screamed Armstrong Perzie, a legendary Stout City artist who was presumed dead.

When she had passed away suddenly and he had granted himself a private tour of her house, it was that exquisite painting that had beckoned him. It was not only hypnotizing with its brilliant colors but it also held potential value on a scale none of her other collected pieces did.

He was sure that her son, Vic, the sole inheritor, had not visited his mother since the painting had entered the home. And even if a couple of Minnie's friends had seen it, they were unlikely to question its fate. This certainty was the final straw in his struggle with temptation. That night he had told his wife that he had to bail a drunken client out of jail, and instead he had returned to Minnie's house, removed the painting, and took it to his office where he hid it behind a bank of file cabinets.

But, just in case somebody did try to connect the dots, he'd decided to leave the painting behind the file cabinets for a few months. That would be enough time for any curious friends to show their faces, and if they did, he'd simply claim he was holding it per her instructions, to be sold at a later date, with the proceeds given to charity.

Minnie's latest will and testament had been drawn years before and therefore no mention of the painting even existed, nor was it mentioned when the estate had been handed over to Vic.

Bigelow had consulted some art books at the Dellton Library and had come to the same conclusion that Minnie had: the painting was eerily Perzie-like. So it sat behind the file cabinets like a treasure in a safety deposit box, waiting to be cashed in at the right time. And boy, was he glad he'd been patient.

Addie had come calling on him out of the blue, and he'd been forced to recite the cover story he'd kept in the back of his mind for an emergency. What had spooked him and forced him to use the tale was that he had no idea how she had traced the painting to Minnie and then to him. But being that she was a young woman and her desire for the painting was seemingly symbolic, he'd felt confident that she'd drop her pursuit when he ultimately explained it had been sold. First he'd set her up with the part about the painting going to Vic, and then he'd placed the phony call in front of her, which went unanswered (mostly because it had been placed to a local Lutheran church with an office that closed at 1 p.m.). Then he telegrammed her later with the unfortunate news that Vic had sold it to an unknown buyer.

In the meantime, a fella named Oscar had visited his office mere minutes after Addie's departure, also inquiring about the painting. That was when he'd gotten the scoop on the sudden interest in the piece. At first he'd denied knowing anything about it, but when Oscar mentioned he had underworld connections that would fetch big cash, Bigelow had formed a quick partnership. They would get a greedy evaluator to declare it a Perzie, and then another shadowy figure would simply forge a signature before it was sold to some collector who wasn't particular about the source of his good fortune. There would be no legitimate trail leading back to them, but there would be a neat pile of cash in their dirty hands.

Fortunately for Bigelow, he had remained cleverly cautious the whole way. On the miniscule chance that Addie found Vic and discovered that he knew nothing, Bigelow had prepared another story—a confession in which he was tricked into selling it by a woman in a sumptuous fur.

In a final twist, the confession ended up being needed, not for Addie, but for some friend of hers who never gave his name. This snooper seemed a little more suspicious than Addie, so it was a good thing that a final, brilliant prop had been waiting.

Bigelow had written a check to Vic in case he had to use the confession angle. The check—already sealed in an envelope and stamped for mailing—seemingly proved his remorse because it had already been executed and prepared for mailing when Addie's friend burst onto the scene.

Thankfully, that fella seemed resigned to the painting being sold to the woman in a sumptuous fur, but Bigelow decided he'd better move the painting before its presence became a liability. He'd called Oscar and told him it was time to sell the piece. The quicker they got it into another person's hands and the quicker they got their money, the better. So far, no malfeasance could be proved against Bigelow, and as a practicing attorney, he needed to keep it that way or risk facing disbarment.

Now, Bigelow and the pawnshop owners watched the art expert, enraptured by his meticulous study of the painting. Occasionally the expert would make a sound or crinkle his face and the boys would all exchange looks of nervous curiosity.

Finally the evaluator sat his magnifying glass on the desk and removed his white gloves. He had come to a conclusion. This was undoubtedly the work of Armstrong Perzie. It was impossible to rule out the possibility of an art forger, he cautioned, but the elements of the piece were so unmistakably Perzie that even a forgery this fine would be worthy of applause. Either way, once the signature was added by a handwriting scoundrel, nobody would be able to prove it *wasn't* a Perzie.

Upon hearing the evaluation, the boys smiled greedily. Oscar had been informed by one of his dubious connections that a genuine Perzie would be worth several thousand dollars. And being that it was a previously unknown Perzie, well, the bandied number might be doubled. Had they been able to sell it through a legitimate auction it might even have fetched triple that number, and the pawnshop boys were about to broach that subject when an unexpected visitor wandered in from the back warehouse.

"Good evening, dolts," Zep greeted them with aplomb.

"Who the hell are you?" Lazy asked with a hint of threat.

"Get out of here," Oscar added. "This is private business."

Bigelow said nothing at first. He was the only one of them who had met Zep and knew he was connected to the painting. The attorney's mind spun furiously to create a new angle.

"Maybe this private business is something I should be a part of," Zep answered his accusers.

"He's right," Bigelow interjected. "This is something he should be part of. I'd have called you if I knew your name or address," he said to Zep.

"To tell me that you were the one who had been holding this painting all along? I already figured that one out. That's why I'm here."

"And I'm glad you are," Bigelow said confidently. "We were just talking about you earlier and how you had a foot in the door on this painting. I told them you were a clever hustler and you'd show up sooner or later wanting in the game."

"Wait a minute," Oscar growled. "We don't need a fourth and this deal is just about wrapped up without him, anyway. Bigelow may need to protect his reputation but we don't care about ours. Folks already figure that pawnbrokers are heartless slobs, and it's true. But only because they make us that way, like we made 'em broke."

"I don't know," Bigelow warned them. "This fella knows something and he could cause trouble for all of us if we don't cut him in for..."

"I'm not asking to be cut in," Zep corrected. "I'm here to claim this painting and deliver it back where it belongs. It would be best for all concerned."

"Listen, son, you got no more claim to this thing than any of us," Oscar replied. "Matter of fact, we are the last known owners of record. You might want to give up on your mission before you get in over your head."

The art expert had retreated to a chair in the corner, where he watched the conversation with alarm. Working with lowlifes was just a side job. He was a reputable expert and the last thing he needed was to be connected to a scandal. He was already calculating a way to distance himself if things took a turn for the worse.

"So what exactly do you plan to do with this painting?" Zep asked, changing his tactic. "You gonna try and sell it? I doubt you'll get whatever amount you're dreaming of, considering that it's unsigned."

"That could change," Lazy said with a proud grin.

"Oh, I get it. You'll find some schmuck to add his signature," Zep grinned knowingly.

"A signature could suddenly appear if it had previously been covered by grime," Oscar theorized with a smirk.

"I don't understand why you two are playing it this way," Bigelow declared to the pawn boys. "There is enough profit to give our friend a bit. Considering he's joining the party late and hasn't shouldered any risk during this venture, I'm sure a tiny slice would be satisfactory to him and beneficial to us."

"Again, you're not listening," Zep reprimanded them. "I'm here to retrieve this painting and return it where it belongs. And if you're smart you'll play it my way before you three end up in jail for trying to sell a painting with a fake signature."

"And we are trying to tell you that your moral objections are meaningless," Oscar responded wearily. "Nobody can prove we're not the rightful owners and nobody will be able to prove the signature is fake. And even if they do, an expert will still declare it's a Perzie. End of story."

"What if Perzie says the whole painting is a fake, that he's never seen it?" Zep countered triumphantly. "How much will it be worth then?"

There it was. Zep had played his trump card. And the way he said it left the others concerned that Zep knew something. There was silence as they looked at each other and then at the art expert.

"Perzie is dead, right?" Oscar asked the expert. "We know this for a fact?"

"We do not know. That is only the assumption of the art community. However, no one has seen or heard from him for more than twenty years, nor has any more of his work surfaced anywhere in the world during that time."

They looked back at Zep differently now—like poker players who had almost fallen for a huge bluff only to recalculate their odds and realize they were safer than originally assumed. They waited smugly for Zep's next desperate play.

He was waiting too. His plan had a couple moving parts to it and he wasn't able to synch everything like he'd hoped. He decided to kill a little time by telling the truth about Perzie. He launched into a description of Perzie's time at the artists' colony and of the morphine trouble on Coronado Island.

The resolve of his listeners began to waver. If Zep was doubling down on his bluff he was doing a very good job. The details flowed easily, without pause, and Zep seemed so earnest in his delivery. They began to wonder if Perzie really was alive. *But*, until they had proof, this was just another big bluff from a brave man.

A loud knock on the front window caused Zep to stop talking. Everyone else spun around wide-eyed.

It was a man and a woman.

Oscar, Lazy and Zep recognized the woman as Irene.

"What's she doing here?" Lazy drawled. "I can't believe the bad luck we're having tonight."

"She's here because I called and asked her to meet us," Zep explained. "Let her in, Lazy. You'll want to meet Perzie's stepdaughter. And that's her husband. I won't tell you what he and his friends do for a living but it's not in your favor and one more reason you should just let him in."

Now, Zep was bluffing. Whether they assumed the husband was a cop or a hit man didn't matter. Too many people were involved and there might be others waiting.

Lazy let Irene and Don inside and they returned to the increasingly crowded office. During the next fifteen minutes there were no angry words and nobody pulled a gun like they always did in the gangster movies. Bigelow and the pawnshop boys were reduced to sullen observers as Irene overwhelmed them with proof of Perzie being alive through letters, pictures and information. The art expert came in handy as he was able to verify facts as well as confirm Perzie's face in photos— including one with Perzie standing next to *Number 17* during his only visit to Irene's house.

Everyone knew the full story now and Perzie had the best hand of them all. He was not only alive but he could choose whether to acknowledge the painting as his or not. Bigelow and the pawn boys were pretty sure the old artist would not be taking their side in any scenario.

A bargain was struck. Irene and Don would leave with the painting and a bill of sale for two dollars. The pawn boys would have two dollars to replace the lock Zep had busted on the back door. They would also destroy any paperwork involving the sale to Minnie Upton. As for Bigelow, he was instructed to mail the check to Vic. If he did, there was a good chance his indiscretions would never reach the wrong desks. The ringing of the bells over the front door was the last they ever heard of him.

***

When Zep, Irene and Don departed with *Number 17*, they walked a couple blocks until the pawnshop was out of sight before stopping for a moment. They ducked inside the entrance to a Chinese restaurant, where they finally smiled and hugged. The painting was back where it belonged, and Irene couldn't thank Zep enough. They talked rapidly, while gleefully recounting the emasculation of the enemy. Irene laughed about her desperate attempt to find a babysitter in time to make it to the pawnshop. Don was surprised and heartened to find out he had been portrayed as a tough guy. He'd have put a little extra fear in them if he'd known, he joked.

Finally, spent from the emotion, they sighed heavily and gave weary goodbyes, promising to talk by phone in the morning.

Zep stopped on the way to the trolley and handed his pack of Vogues to a vagrant.

44

Julia was sitting in her chair near the front window, enjoying a sunny afternoon when she was surprised by the sight of an unknown automobile parking in the driveway. Armstrong and two strangers—a man and a woman—exited the car. Seeing as how Armstrong had left on foot for his usual market visit, his return was puzzling. Julia's first thought was that he'd had a medical issue, requiring a ride back from town, but he seemed to be moving toward the house with long, easy strides.

The front door swung open and the three stepped inside. The man removed his hat and they all stopped and stood side by side facing Julia.

"Julia, this is the Reverend Dunford and his wife, Sally. They're here to marry us."

The pastor and his wife smiled sweetly in an attempt to disarm any awkwardness.

"Oh my. I had no idea today was the day or I might have dressed better," she said politely while giving Armstrong a loving but slightly evil eye.

"That's my fault," Armstrong admitted. "I wanted it to be a surprise."

"It's definitely that," she agreed.

"Don't worry about a thing," Sally chimed in, trying to sway the conversation toward the happy marriage part. "Mr. Perzie explained that you haven't been feeling well and I am here to be your lady in waiting. We can go to your room and get you all fixed up, if you'd like."

Julia hated being pitied but she sensed Sally meant well, so she just smiled and struggled to her feet. They moved slowly into the bedroom.

"I think you may have surprised her more than you should have," the Reverend Dunford joked with Perzie after the women had left.

"I'm sure of it. But I didn't want to give warning and get her stressed, or for her to overexert herself in preparation. You know how women are. They have such high standards for celebrations and I knew she'd practically kill herself trying to make everything perfect."

"You did the right thing. You can already hear them chatting away excitedly back there."

Armstrong listened and heard Julia's laugh. It was a beautiful sound that he had once given up on ever hearing again. To bring her unexpected joy after ruining a stretch of their lives with unexpected malice was a feeling he couldn't put into words.

He slipped into the other bedroom to change and it was all he could do not to indulge in gin, but he held fast, determined to respect Julia's day. He emerged twenty minutes later looking dapper in his suit, but the biggest improvement to his appearance was the shaving of his beard. He looked twenty years younger and his firm chin added a sense of physicality.

The two men chatted about baseball as they awaited the bride, but the wait was worthwhile.

Julia exited their bedroom looking radiant in her best dress, a light lavender piece made from chiffon that moved gingerly at her ankles. In addition, Sally had worked on her hair, giving her some light curls which added another layer of sophistication to her beauty. But it was her face that had everyone entranced. A glow of happiness had transformed her from sickly to heavenly.

Armstrong and Julia met in the hallway, and they looked at each other in wonder. He rested his hands on her little waist, and she ran her hand across his smooth chin. They then moved toward the living room before stopping and having a whispered debate. He thought they should sit during the ceremony out of concern for her minimal stamina, while she thought they should stand, otherwise it would look like he was corralling a helpless woman. Armstrong laughed at her silly notion but he also knew they would be standing. And they did.

The Reverend Dunford recited the traditional words of the marriage ceremony while Sally stood behind the couple, eyeing the bride in case she really did need a chair at a moment's notice.

When it was time for vows, the pastor asked them if they had prepared any, and they looked at each other and laughed. They had not prepared anything, they confessed, but Armstrong decided he wanted to offer some impromptu words to his bride.

"Well, um, I can't really offer you as much as I did the first time, and as it turned out I didn't fulfill my promises like I should've, and for that I apologize in front of these witnesses. And, well, I didn't appreciate it then, but I know now that you are more fantastic than any woman I'll ever meet. If I could live my life over a hundred times I'd always find you and love you until you couldn't stand it because you were so happy. Thank you for marrying me again, even if I never did deserve a wife as clever and beautiful as you."

He finished by giving her a humble grin. Julia then told the pastor she, too, would like to speak.

"Thank you for never forgetting about me like I never forgot about you. That love we had the first time never died, Armstrong, it just got hurt a little. I'm proud to be the wife of such a brilliant, silly artist and I pray that you will continue your creative work knowing how important it is to me. I want nothing more than to be your inspiration when I'm gone. I would also like to add, for the record, that you look very handsome without the beard."

The pastor began to finish his duty when another conference was required. He'd forgotten to ask the couple about rings. Armstrong's pained expression answered that question, but Julia had a surprise. She reached inside her bodice and withdrew a ring.

"Sorry, this dress doesn't have pockets," she explained, in answer to their alarmed expressions.

"It's the ring from our first marriage," Armstrong exclaimed. "I can't believe you hung on to it."

"I guess it was the symbol for my dream. And now it's coming true."

She gently handed the ring to Armstrong, who then slipped it onto her finger. The beauty of the moment was compromised as they both noted how the ring hung loosely on her thin finger. It was supposed to represent hope and future, but instead it reminded them that he was joining her in time to lose her.

"It will fit better when you get well," he whispered.

"I'll wear it close to my heart until then, just like I was a minute ago," she said with a wink.

They kissed to the amusement of the pastor, who admonished them for jumping the gun. He then finished the ceremony by pronouncing them married, and they kissed again.

After the Reverend Dunford and Sally had departed, the newlyweds sat on the couch, intertwined and content. After a while, Julia had regained enough strength to change out of her wedding dress and into her pajamas. Then she lay down on the bed for a nap.

Standing next to the bed, Armstrong held out her pain pills in one hand and a glass of water in the other. She had been taking them every eight hours for the last two days, but this time she declined, insisting she just needed a nap. He reluctantly accepted her decision and lay down next to her, and they soon fell asleep.

When they awoke it was late afternoon and the bedroom was covered in shadow. He awoke first and lay quietly, imagining himself trying to paint again. He would attempt it one day, just as he had promised, but right now, the feeling of excitement did not exist.

Lying on her side facing him, Julia awoke without stirring. Her eyes just popped open. It was the pain inside of her that had ended the nap. She studied her groom as he looked toward the ceiling unaware. Without the beard he looked so much like the first Armstrong she had married—the confident, irreverent, humorous man who had stolen her affection.

She could tell he was thinking by the tiny expression changes on his face. Even with some wrinkles and a little less hair, he actually looked better than ever in an unexplainable way. *Why is it men seem to age well and women just seem to age,* she wondered. It was hardly fair considering how much stock was put into a woman's appearance and how men barely tried.

She remembered her mother telling her that for every loss there was a gain. Lose your shoes and enjoy the feel of grass between your toes. Lose your direction and enjoy the new sights you'd never have seen otherwise. Lose your youthful looks and enjoy the freedom of surprising yourself.

Maybe I can surprise myself *and* my husband, she thought.

"Hey," she whispered.

"Hey," he whispered back, rolling over so that they were face to face.

"You promised that when we were married there would be some heavy petting," she reminded him.

"There has not been a second since we moved in here that I haven't wanted to."

"But?"

"But, you're not well, honey. I'd be a jerk if I..."

"That never stopped you before. I recall you having a way of always making me enjoy what you had in mind."

He grinned and ran his hand along her stomach where her shirt had ridden up during sleep. She looked into his eyes suggestively until he could not resist kissing her, which he did lustily. His hand wandered higher where it remained happily even as he pulled his face from hers.

"I don't want to hurt you in any way," he said quietly.

"It's not a real marriage unless..." she teased. "And it's important to me," she added with pleading eyes.

***

The shadows were darker in the room when they were finished, making it harder to see each other in detail.

"Are you OK?" he asked with concern.

"Wonderful," she cooed. "That was the first time I'd forgotten I was in pain. I don't think I can move, though. Wow."

"You are so beautiful, Julia. I just want to chew you up."

She giggled. The desire she caused was almost as satisfying as the act.

"There is one more thing we have to do on our wedding day," she declared with sudden spunk.

"Which is what?"

"Make a wedding cake."

"Make a cake? Are you kidding? Let's have traditional wedding waffles instead."

"I'm sure you just made that up, but we need a wedding cake first. You need to learn so you can surprise one of my grandbabies on their birthday."

"Julia..."

"You can't say 'no' to a bride on her wedding day. Plus, you had your way with me so it's only fair I get my way with you now."

275

Her seductive grin was the final selling point, and he reluctantly climbed out of bed before gently helping her up.

In the kitchen, Julia took her seat and Armstrong reprised his role as the reluctant cook. They were missing a couple of standard cake ingredients, but Julia assured Armstrong that her suggested substitutes were perfectly acceptable. He wasn't so sure and wondered aloud if this cake was actually going to be edible or whether she just needed the wedding symbol.

Julia wanted both, she admitted to herself, but what she really wanted was to watch Armstrong persevere toward what she needed. That he wasn't thrilled and kept getting flustered made his perseverance an act of love, which perfectly complimented the one just finished. It made her feel satisfied, body and soul. His being unaware of the flour on his eyebrow only served to make it perfect for her.

In the end, the cake turned out to be marginal, but the Perzies didn't seem to mind. They finished their wedding night looking through the window at the lights and sharing memories from twenty years ago, including the one where she'd accidentally cut his hair too short.

45

The five days following her marriage were some of the happiest Julia had ever enjoyed. She and Armstrong felt like young newlyweds once more as they engaged in spirited, clever conversations like they'd had the first time. The weather had also turned spring-like, allowing them to sit outside and soak in the smells while watching lizards and butterflies go about their business in the yard.

Things were so nice that the only time she really thought about her dire health was when Armstrong made his daily trip to the market. This was when she would write letters to Irene and the children, including some final letters she was working on for each of them to be delivered when they were...final. It was while penning these that her mortality returned to center stage and she began to find herself angry about death.

It was cruel irony that her life was arcing skyward just as her body was plummeting. Two weeks ago she was surrendering a life that was already dead in many ways, and part of her was almost relieved. There would be no more electric bills to pay, no indigestion, noisy neighbors, or leaking faucets.

But now there was Armstrong, and he made life worth living even if he hadn't improved so greatly from the man who had troubled her years before. After all, he still wasn't painting and his drinking had only grown worse. She was quite aware that he was using part of his daily market trip to stop in somewhere and plow through a few shots, but she never mentioned it because she understood his need.

Plus, it didn't really matter. It never had. When he directed his full attention at her she had always been helpless. So smitten was she these days that she actually believed that perhaps his love was curing her cancer. He was helping her eat well and avoid stress, but even more than that, she felt his presence had changed something. She hadn't shown any particular improvement since their wedding day, but she hadn't declined either. She still had pain and she was still tired all of the time, but none of it had worsened. If anything, it seemed like her appetite had increased a tad.

But on the sixth day she felt terrible. Her stomach hurt all day. Everything made her feel warm and restless. It scared her. Was she suddenly getting worse or were these signs that her body was fighting to heal itself?

That night as they lay in bed, she decided to have the conversation she had been saving. It was probably premature, but she couldn't risk not saying what was on her heart.

"Armstrong?"

"Yes?"

"I know you promised to continue your painting someday soon, but I need you to promise me something else."

"I can't promise to quit drinking," he declared. "I really can't."

"I know," she said with a sad smile. "And I'm grateful that you've cut back while we're together, but that's not what I need you to promise."

"Oh."

"When I'm gone, sweetheart, I need you to be a good father and grandfather. If you really love me—and I know you do—then you know without a doubt that nothing is more important to me than their happiness."

"I understand."

"No you don't. Sending birthday cards is not enough. You have to make an effort to leave your dungeon and spend real time with them at their house. Take the kids out for ice cream. Babysit while Irene and Don go to dinner. Tell Irene that you love her and that you are proud of her. She is a marvelous mother and those babies are mine too, in a way. When you look at them, please see me. OK?"

Armstrong was silent as he considered all that she asked. He wanted to do all those things but felt like such a fraud after doing so little for so long. *Maybe they'll have nothing to do with me,* he thought.

"What are you thinking?" she asked after waiting.

"Nothing really," he lied.

"Do you not want to be part of their lives?"

"I'm afraid to be part of anyone's life," he admitted to his own surprise.

"Because of what happened to us before."

"Yeah."

"But you loved me once and look at us now. I've never been happier. And didn't you love Irene? She was like a daughter to you."

"She's still my daughter, but I'm not so sure she feels the same way. Too much time has passed..."

"Yes, we've wasted so much time. All of us. But I know my daughter's heart and I know it would mean the world to her if you took a chance just like you did with me."

It was silent again except for an automobile horn that could barely be heard honking far away down in the city.

"Please, Armstrong. For your wife, the only one crazy enough to say 'I do' to you twice."

She could feel him grin in the dark. She always knew how to love him the way he needed to be loved.

"OK," he said softly. "I will make a fool of myself for you. Does that make you happy?"

"Very," she whispered while rubbing his arm.

"Not that it matters anyway," he added, "You're going to get better and then you can buy ice cream and babysit to your heart's content."

She squeezed his arm.

"I love you, Mr. Perzie."

"And I love you. Now go to sleep so you can feel even better tomorrow."

The faraway car honked again, and Armstrong imagined it was a getaway driver warning his accomplices that they needed to hurry. Julia pictured a young man urgently trying to elope with a girl who always had trouble being on time.

46

When Armstrong awoke the next morning he knew without looking. Somehow he felt it as soon as his eyes opened. He was afraid to look, but knowing he must, he peeked over at Julia and saw a face that was too pale and a body with no life in it. His beautiful Julia was gone.

He'd known this was how it was to be but had been living in denial the past two weeks thinking that enough happiness would somehow revive her body. He hadn't truly prepared himself for this moment and at first he felt nothing but numbness and disbelief.

He got out of bed and sat on a chair and stared at her, not knowing what to do. He wanted desperately to crawl up next to her and hold that little body in his arms but he also didn't want that to be their last embrace.

His mind went back to bedtime the night before. Oh, how he wished he'd squeezed her one more time. What were her last words? He couldn't remember but he had to know—he had to—so he tried to replay their conversation. He recalled promising to love Irene and the kids as strongly as he could, which had pleased her, and then...what? Wait, she had said she loved him. She had said it like she was *in* love with him, right before she went to sleep.

Emotion hit him like a freight train. He dropped to his knees and buried his head on the end of the bed and sobbed so hard that it hurt. Only when there was nothing left did he lift his head back up, hoping he'd been wrong and that she was looking at him with pity in her eyes, but she remained still.

She was on her back, with her head leaning toward where Armstrong had slept. He wondered if she woke up and tried to say something to him. What if she was in pain and needed help, he wondered, cursing himself for the nightly ritual of gin consumption that caused him to sleep so heavily. But her face looked peaceful, so maybe she just passed from sleep to death without ever knowing it.

He walked over to her side and sat on the edge of the bed.

"I love you so much, Julia," he whispered. "I'm so sorry."

Armstrong rubbed the back of her hand but it felt too cold. He pictured the young version of the body next to him, the one from when they'd first met. She had been so vibrant and restless for things she didn't even understand. Her humor was sharp and her legs were taut and perfect. He would watch in awe as she practically skipped away from their cabin each morning in search of some new sight, which she would then try to capture through art.

But some things just can't be captured. They're fleeting, imbued with a special essence that simply defies exact words or brush strokes. And that's exactly what Julia was—too wonderful to capture. Despite his foolishness he had been given the gift of her love twice and now that was just a memory.

He leaned over to get a closer look at her face. Even in death the little freckles on her cheeks and nose made him grin. They were so delicate yet so strong. Somehow, he decided, those freckles *were* her, and so he tried to memorize them.

"I will keep my promises," he reminded her aloud. "I will begin painting again and I will love our daughter and our grandbabies, as you call 'em. You are the greatest thing that ever happened to me and you were right, we wasted so much time."

He rubbed her arm and it felt too stiff to be hers, but he couldn't help himself, and he tried to memorize her freckles again but his eyes kept getting blurry.

"Oh, I love you, Julia," he begged while fighting back more emotion.

But it was no use and he began to cry again, this time softly. He got up and walked around the room, unsure what to do next.

It occurred to him that he should call the police or a hospital but he knew that would end their time together, so he walked to his corner of the bedroom and grabbed his bottle of gin and took a long drink. It felt disrespectful, drinking in front of her, but he knew she would understand. She always had. He took another long drink and his nerves began to calm.

Before he called the hospital he needed to call Irene. She had left her number, which he found in his wallet, and after a deep breath, he dialed.

It didn't even feel like him talking as he delivered the shocking news to their daughter. There were long stretches when he could only wait as she cried. He tried to explain that it had been peaceful and how much Julia had loved her and the children, but nothing could soothe the unexpected pain.

"I need to go," Irene finally declared with a choked voice. "Thank you for calling and telling me."

"I'm bringing her to Stout City," he added. "Do you think that's good?"

"Yes, I want her close to us even if it's too late."

"Irene?"

"Yes?"

"I know this is a strange time to tell you this but I love you."

There was a pause and Armstrong regretted saying it.

"I love you, too," she said.

283

It sounded sincere and Armstrong exhaled, not even aware that he'd been holding his breath.

"See you in a couple days," he said.

"OK. Bye."

"Bye."

He took another exceptionally big gulp of gin and telephoned the hospital.

While he waited for someone to come, Armstrong lay back down on the bed next to his wife.

"I talked to Irene and it's going to be all right," he quietly informed her. "No more wasted time. I may even keep the beard off just for you."

He felt her smile and for a moment he was happy.

47

Two days later, Armstrong left the rental house that he and Julia had shared, never to return. He was leaving on a train to Stout City in a couple of hours.

All of Julia's possessions had been boxed by a freight company and would accompany Julia's casket back to Stout City. He had simply been too overwhelmed with sadness to even consider going through her belongings, and he'd felt it best that Irene help him at a later date when they could do it right.

Rather than take a taxi to the train station, Armstrong decided to walk using the same route he had on his daily market runs. He wanted to feel the melancholy of leaving their honeymoon house without some taxi driver blabbing about the weather.

He'd also decided to wear his wedding suit. Even though he and Julia wouldn't be side by side on the train, they would be "together," and he wanted to honor his bride. With his suitcase in tow he shut the door behind him and walked away without looking back.

When he got to town his first stop was at Tippy's speakeasy, much to the delight of the regulars. Most of them were old retired folks who used the place as a low-key social club while they sipped beers during daytime. For two weeks they had been fascinated and entertained by the quiet visitor who stopped in daily and knocked back twelve shots of gin like it was water. Noting his suitcase and figuring this might be his last visit, their cheering today was a little more raucous than usual. A couple of the old fellas patted him on the back as he left.

His next stop was the market where he'd daily bought food for the honeymoon nest. He picked out a couple of apples and a jar of peanuts to snack on during the train trip.

Finally he stopped into the telegraph office two doors down from the market and filled out a telegram form. He paid the thirty-five cents and asked the clerk to call him a taxi to take him the rest of the way to the station.

It was time to take Julia home.

***

Less than an hour later, Zep received a knock on the door of his Stout City apartment. It was a delivery boy, who handed him a telegram. Zep gave the kid a nickel and shut the door. He opened the envelope and unfolded the telegram, reading it where he stood.

Greeley, CO
Western #378

Zep—
Returning to Stout City. Will resume painting when settled making sure you and Addie share profit of first piece. However one condition must be met. It is not negotiable. You must marry Mabel immediately. Too much time has been wasted. Call her this minute.
Love, Perzie

Zep could hardly believe what he'd read and he scanned it again slowly. When he was done, the hand holding the telegram dropped to his side as he looked quizzically at the floor.

"*Love*, Perzie?" he repeated aloud. "How drunk is he?"

Zep read it one more time. After pausing for a moment he made up his mind and walked to the phone. The old man was right. Too much time had been wasted.

48

Olga could hardly contain herself, she was so excited. Ever since Irene had told her that Granddad Perzie was coming over to give her a painting lesson, she had been a jabber box, nearly driving the family crazy. He'd been over a few times since Grandma's funeral, but Olga had never imagined that he would want to spend time with just her, painting and talking.

When Armstrong arrived, Irene explained that dinner was still cooking but it wouldn't be long. She told him to sit down and rest, which he did—only it wasn't too restful having three kids and a dog descend on him with lots of stories, questions and wagging tongues.

While listening he took a moment to look at *Number 17,* which hung in Irene's living room. Part of him wanted to find fault with the painting, probably because it represented a dark time in his life, but each time he studied it during a visit he had to admit it was a nice piece. Nice enough that he had finally signed it. And on the back he had written, "For my daughter, who is more beautiful than any painting could ever be. Love, Armstrong."

He didn't have much opportunity to study his work this time, though, as the little natives vied for his attention. But as he tried his best to satisfy their need for interaction he couldn't help but notice Olga off to the side, pacing and swinging her arms. Usually she was the leader of the chatty pack.

"Whatcha doin' over there?" he asked her.

"Just waiting until we paint," she admitted with no shame or tact.

He smiled at her childish exuberance and imagined Julia elbowing him to go on and paint with her grandbaby. *You can paint some now and some after dinner,* she would have implored. So he got up from the couch, found the bag he'd brought with him containing painting supplies, and led her into the garage where Irene had set up a table and easel for them.

They sat down at the kid-sized table and Armstrong tried to make his knees fit underneath but it was no use. So, he scooted his little chair back from the table. He smiled at his eager little student who sat waiting with her hands folded.

"Your mom tells me you're a whiz at drawing things," he told her.

"Sometimes," she answered with a shrug and an embarrassed grin. She felt she was a good drawer indeed, but feared her granddad the famous painter would not think so.

"Well, I'm a terrible drawer," he declared.

"You are?" she asked with a confused expression.

"Yep. I'm a whiz at making good colors but I've never been so good at drawing things. That's why we are going to be such a good team. You can teach me how to draw and I'll show you how to make colors you've never seen before."

Olga grinned at the prospect of helping her granddad.

"Do you want me to show you how I draw an elephant?" she asked. "It's not too hard and I've done a lot of them."

"An elephant would be great," he agreed.

Dinner interrupted their collaboration, but as soon as they were finished eating and had been excused by Irene they rushed back to their little studio.

"This time we should put the elephant at a circus," she offered. "Sometimes it's better when there are more things to look at in a picture."

Armstrong knew he was being patronized but how could he complain about having such a smart granddaughter? He watched with pride as she went to work, the tip of her tongue poking out from between her lips as she concentrated on her work.

And as she added circus details, he told her stories and explained things about life that Julia would have wanted him to share.

It was a small art colony—just two artists—but an unusually happy one.

49

Addie retrieved her morning paper from the hall, stopping on the way back to the kitchen to check the clock on the wall. It said 7:12, although she couldn't remember if the clock was three minutes too fast or too slow. Either way, there was plenty of time, she crowed to herself.

After dropping bread into the toaster she moved into the living room and reached behind a bookcase, pulling out a small painting, which she then hung on the kitchen wall. It was the newest addition to her morning ritual.

The painting was done on a two-foot-by-two-foot canvas and it had no subject, just a fantastic array of colors "carelessly" arranged in perfect proportions. It was Armstrong's first work in over a decade. He had done it as a test piece while he regained his feel for the brush. Had an expert examined it closely they'd have noted that the strokes were a tad heavier than those in earlier Perzie works, but his instincts were truer than ever. And that was the secret to his style: the planned lack of planning. He would envision a hazy fundamental goal and then turn his instincts loose, transposing one experimental color with another, setting off a chain reaction that resulted in a gift—a thunderbolt—sent from the gods of art.

After all these years, his skill with the brush may have needed refreshing but his skill with colors remained unparalleled. During the long period of inactivity, Armstrong had still played with color ideas in his mind. That was the part that had always fascinated him, and its grip was never fully relinquished. Thus, the test piece which Addie now owned was a spellbinding experiment in color manipulation using many of the ideas stored in his head for over a decade.

It was so beautiful that she had become paranoid it would be stolen by anybody who might see it. She was sure a normal, upright citizen would be overwhelmed with thoughts of larceny, given one look. So she kept it hidden, bringing it out for meals only, when she would stare and relish not only the beauty on the canvas, but the story behind it.

Her simple idea of finding Armstrong and profiting off him, however, had not reached fruition yet. He wanted his first saleable piece to be flawless and so it was taking weeks instead of days. Once it was finished and unloaded on a surprised and thrilled art world, she would finally reap some of the profits along with Zep and Irene, just as promised.

Armstrong understood that his imminent reemergence on the scene was fully attributable to these young people who had pushed and loved him even when he was doing neither for himself. Without them he'd have never married Julia again, and his art would just be paint on a canvas. But, because of them, his passion was reborn and the resulting art would always be tangible proof of his love for Julia.

After biting into her second slice of peanut butter toast, Addie glanced at the clock again. It said 7:31 now. Plenty of time, she crowed to herself, but with less conviction than the first time.

Not surprisingly, though the scenario had been played out this way too many times, she finished getting ready later than needed. She barely had time to leave, return for her sunglasses, and then still make the trolley on time.

Barely catching the trolley as it started to leave, she plopped into the first empty seat, out of breath and hot from scrambling. Well, the seat was sort of empty, anyhow. The woman next to her had allowed her purse to stray and it was now wedged under the left side of Addie's freshly dressed rear. The woman tugged while giving a polite but reprimanding expression. Startled by the movement below and quickly assessing the situation, Addie moved her rear and freed the purse. With the crisis averted, Addie smiled sheepishly at the woman but received only raised eyebrows in return. *You don't have to be so mean about it,* she complained in her mind.

***

Irene was not surprised that Addie was running late, nor was she worried. When a mother is knee-deep in raising three young children her previous standards are no longer applicable. Reasonable health and safety were the only goals, and if fighting among the children could be avoided that was a fine bonus.

Today's health issue involved Hugh. From her years of experience, Irene was sure that he had an ear infection. It had started the night before, prompting her to call Aunt Addie and ask if she could take Olga to school for her special show and tell day. Irene hated to miss it but Hugh was in such pain that there could be no debate. A trip to the doctor's came first.

Standing and waiting, Irene couldn't help but smile at Olga, who was also dressed and waiting. Irene's oldest daughter had picked out her favorite dress for this occasion and hanging from her hand was a small leather portfolio that Granddad Perzie had given to her on her eighth birthday.

Inside the portfolio was the masterpiece they had jointly created in their garage studio. It was a painting of animals going to a zoo where people were in cages. The idea was hers and it still made her giggle. One of the cages had a dad in his chair reading the newspaper while a cheetah—inexplicably standing upright—pointed and laughed. Granddad had helped her with the colors, which were the best part of all. He'd encouraged her to mix in funny items like toothpaste and cracker crumbs. Then he'd showed her how to take a color and make it into dozens of variations that the naked eye could scarcely separate. All in all, it was the "funnest" time she'd ever had, and she was confident that their creation would make her classmates ache with envy.

Addie arrived five minutes past the time Olga needed to leave to be at school on time. With no time for social graces, Irene rapidly dispensed instructions to Addie before bolting out the door for the doctor's office.

Addie, unsure that she'd heard everything correctly, consulted with Olga who knew the instructions better than her mother. Olga advised that it would be best to pick up Madeline from school later than Mom had instructed. That way Madeline would already have finished her homework while waiting in the classroom under the watchful eye of Miss Ewing.

"And where is Madeline now?" Addie asked.

"At school. She spent the night with Janet and her mom is taking her," Olga explained while shaking her head. "Mom just told you."

"Yes she did, and I was just, um, making sure. So, got everything you need?"

Frazzled, but optimistic that she could pull it all off, Addie then turned her focus to the first task: getting Olga to school for her big moment. Addie looked at her watch and determined they had plenty of time as long as they walked at a steady pace, but Olga knew they would be late.

As they moved along the sidewalk, Addie asked Olga lots of questions. Addie got a kick out of the little girl's thoughts, even finding some of them adorably similar to those she'd once had as a little girl. She also found it to be a great way for getting insight into grown-up matters.

"So, your Granddad Perzie visits a lot now, huh?" probed Addie.

"Yep, he comes to eat because Mom says he isn't very good at cooking. He also comes to draw and paint with me."

"Oh, I bet that's exciting."

"Uh huh. We do a lot of silly things. He made me put crumbs in yellow paint last time," she giggled.

"Yes, your grandfather is quite clever when it comes to paint."

"He's also smart about other things, too," Olga confided.

"Really? Like what?"

"Well, he tells me different things while I work. They're sorta lessons but he makes them sound like stories."

"I see. What was the last story lesson?"

"It was a good one. He told me that every girl who is born has something specially pretty about them and that they should love that special thing. He said Grandma had the best freckles he ever saw. They were on her nose and cheeks. Then he said Grandma knew how pretty her freckles were and she loved them because she felt like everyone else loved 'em too."

"That's an interesting idea," Addie mused, half to herself.

"It's not just an idea," Olga corrected. "It really works. Granddad said that because Grandma loved her freckles it made her feel good about how the rest of her looked just by concentrating on the freckles. I know it works because I tried it."

"You did? How?"

"Well, I don't have freckles," laughed Olga at the absurdity of the obvious, "so before bed I looked really close in the mirror and tried to find my specially pretty part. It was hard to decide between my nose and my ears."

"That's a nice problem to have," Addie commented with a smile.

"Well, when I looked again in the morning I kinda decided my nose was specialest. I really like the shape of it."

"It is a gorgeous nose."

"See, that's why it works," Olga declared triumphantly. "You see how special it is just like me."

"And it makes you feel pretty because you know others think the same thing and no matter what you'll always have that special nose?" said Addie, working through the idea out loud.

"Just like Grandma's freckles," Olga concluded.

"I like it," decided Addie.

"And you know what else?" asked Olga with happy anticipation.

"What?"

"My dress even feels prettier this morning. It was already pretty but now it gets to be with my nose and they both get to be with me while I show my picture at show and tell."

Addie nodded and began to consider what made her feel beautiful. She liked the way she walked, upright and light. She also thought her hair curled nicely in the back.

She looked down at the little girl who was so pleased with her picture and her nose and it occurred to Addie that she'd set it into motion and nothing felt more beautiful than that.